THE WRATH OF ELI

THE SEVEN SINS, #1

LILY ZANTE

AUTHOR'S NOTE

The Wrath of Eli is the first book in **The Seven Sins,** a contemporary romance series of steamy, angsty and emotional stories featuring characters who are loosely connected.

All books are STANDALONE.

Other books in The Seven Sins:

Underdog
The Wrath of Eli
The Problem with Lust
The Lies of Pride
The Price of Inertia
The Other Side of Greed

Sign up for my newsletter and get a FREE book:
https://www.lilyzante.com/news

CHAPTER ONE

ELI

It's not often that Lou calls me into his office in the middle of a sparring session. I figure it must be important, something to do with the fight.

"What is it?" I say, still wearing my boxing gloves.

"There'll be a journalist hanging around here for a few weeks. They want to do an interest story on you."

"A what?" My guard is already up. A journalist? What the hell for?

Lou stares back at me, his saggy, wrinkly skin hanging from his face. At times, he reminds me of a turkey. "This is publicity. You don't have Garrison's pulling power. We need this."

The hell we do. I shift uneasily from foot to foot. "I don't need it."

"You do need it. It's the Chicago Daily Herald, kid. You should be honored."

"So?" I say, with a careless shrug. "So what?"

"So shut the hell up and pretend nobody's around."

I stare at Lou in disbelief. I'm training for a shot at the World Heavyweight Championship title next month against Trent "The Tank" Garrison, the current champion. Nobody expects me to win; I'm the underdog, and a long shot, and I got this chance by pure luck.

But Garrison has everything to lose.

I have nothing.

The last thing I need is a journalist hanging around here watching me and asking stupid questions.

"How long?" I ask.

"Up until the fight."

"A month?" I shake my head. "What the fuck are they hoping to do here for that long?"

"Calm down, Eli. Quit getting so riled up."

"But, *a month?*"

"They're writing an interest piece spread over a few days of the fight. Be grateful."

My face twists. This is bullshit.

"They want to write about your training regimen, see what you're made of. You should be thankful, kid."

Thankful is the last thing I feel when my manager's telling me that some busybody is going to shadow me for an entire month during the run up to the fight.

Hell no.

"I don't need a distraction."

"Ignore him. Pretend the guy, whoever he is, isn't around. You do that to most people most of the time anyway."

I ignore the snide comment. "He better not come to the training camp." It's the week before the fight. Lou's taking me to Dwayne Banks' house for my most intensive training yet. I spar and fight and hone my technique here in the boxing gym where I've been coming for the last six years, but Lou says the final weeks we're going to build my strength and stamina at Dwayne's place. Apparently it's in the middle of nowhere, and a four-hour drive from Chicago.

"Okay. Done. Don't let this get in your way. You're Chicago's New Hope, Eli," he reminds me, "You have other things to think about."

That's exactly my fucking point.

Chicago's New Hope.

I grit my teeth. They're calling me that because Garrison is from the Bronx. Whoever coined this phrase is being nice, but I'm not stupid. Behind my back I know what everyone thinks.

I'm a poor bastard who doesn't stand a chance.

I tap my gloves together, because I'm itching to get back to the ring. Santos is waiting. "Is that it?"

"Can I count on you to be nice?" Lou asks.

I take a deep inhale because his request still pisses me off. "This isn't school, Lou. I don't have to be nice to anyone." Not that I was nice to anyone aside from Nina, much. Even my foster parents, and there were many over the years, struggled to cope with me.

He wants me to say 'yes'. The hell I will. I need to focus. I need to keep my wits about me and my eyes on the prize, and the prize is the title of the world heavyweight champion. It doesn't matter how I got this chance—sheer luck many have said, even directly to my face. *You won't last more than two rounds,* others have told me. But I have a chance at this, and I'm going to prove everyone wrong.

I remember one of the janitors at Grampton House. Dennis Swain was his name. I used to shiver when he walked past us. Nina would tug at my hand and keep me close by her side.

I grind down on my teeth and shake my head. This fucking random and unwanted thought has sliced into my brain when I least expect it. Sweat drips down my neck and back. "I'll try."

Lou nods, more in relief than anything else. "Now get back to the training. We need you ready for the big night."

"I am ready," I mutter under my breath, as I turn to leave. I was born ready. Born to good-for-nothing, sack-of-shit parents. My sister and I deserved better. When I win, when I get the money, things *will* be better.

I climb back into the ring, bristling with rage, and a few seconds later, my clean left hook sends Santos flying to the mat.

CHAPTER TWO

HARPER

"Elias Cardoza?" I frown, because the name is vague enough that I've heard it, but I can't put a face to it. "Is he a pop star?" I ask Merv.

My boss huffs out an irritated breath. "He's a boxer, right here from Chicago. How can you not know that?"

"Because I don't watch boxing."

Gerry tries to hide his laugh, but I catch it.

"You need to start watching this guy. Everyone's got an eye on him, and he hasn't lost a fight this year." Merv pauses for effect, but I stare at my nails, noticing that the color has chipped and I'm going to have to run into one of the nail salons during my lunch hour to get it fixed. Or maybe not. I have an article that needs to be finished in the next hour.

"Are you paying attention?" His tone is harsh. It's like he's still pissed that I got this job instead of his nephew.

"I always pay attention." I force a smile because I know this annoys him even more. I swear to God, I don't know why I'm still in this job two months down the line. This guy is looking for any excuse to fire me so that he can tell everyone how useless I am. Only, I haven't given him the chance because, despite my designer suits, and matching bags and shoes, I can still deliver nitty-gritty news when I need to. I never miss a deadline and it surprises many people. They think I'm an airhead, and I'm so not. This is what Merv thinks. I feel as if he's constantly trying to test me, but my father's on the board—which is probably another reason for Merv hating me—and he can't really fire me.

"That's your next assignment. Think you can handle it?"

I have a million reasons why I don't want to handle it. I don't know the first thing about boxing, and I hate the idea of it; two grown men knocking one another to pieces. It's barbaric and shouldn't be allowed. But I smile sweetly, because this asshole of a man finds things he knows will test me.

"Of course I can handle it." Then I wonder what Gerry's doing in here, and why Merv is only addressing me about it. "What about Gerry?" I ask, nodding in his direction. Gerry's a senior editor here, and sort of like my mentor.

"Gerry suggested it would be an interesting story for you to do. You can shadow Cardoza for a month in the run-up to his fight."

"A month?"

"You can get up to speed with boxing, while writing an in-depth piece on him," Gerry explains. "It will be a good experience for you, especially since this fight is going to be huge. Cardoza's not going to win, obviously, but we'll get a lot of interest because he's a local guy. Garrison is the clear favorite, and the bigger draw, no question about it."

"But a month?" I ask, thinking back to the *Rocky* movies and images of a dirty and dingy little gym rush to my mind. I don't particularly want to shadow a boxer in a place that smells like a boys' locker room all day long. Why couldn't I cover a gala fundraiser event or something more interesting?

"I want you to immerse yourself in this guy's daily routine. Our angle of interest is that Cardoza's a local boy. They call him Chicago's New Hope and, trust me, we wouldn't be doing this if he wasn't from here. This kid has come from nowhere, and if he goes on to win the fight, it's going be a huge upset."

Gerry interrupts with a smirk. "He's not going to win," he says smugly. "Cardoza got this fight because the other guys got disqualified."

Merv frowns. "He might surprise us." Gerry shakes his head again, as if this is ridiculous.

Merv laughs. It's the usual part-condescending, part-being-polite laugh he usually reserves for me, the one where I can't tell if he's being a dick, or if he's suddenly remembered that my dad sits on the board and it's because of him that Merv has to be nice to me.

"You start tomorrow. It's all been arranged with his manager, Lou McNeilly. He's the trainer manager, and he owns McNeilly's Gym."

"Tomorrow?" I ask, feeling slightly anxious. They've definitely thrown me in at the deep end. I have a lot to research, especially since I have no clue who this guy is.

"You'll do," Merv says, resting his head in his hands, arms wide open as he rocks back in his chair. "You'll be fine."

I don't bother to question what he means by that, and I

especially don't like the way he looks me up and down; as if he thinks I don't know that he's checking me out again. He's a sick and dirty old man. So many of them are. I shudder, and thank my lucky stars that unlike most people, I don't have to work if I don't want to.

At least I show up to work and do the work. Truth is, I don't want to rely on my father all my life. I want to make it on my own. He helped fund my Ivy League education and, yes, he bought my apartment in one of the most affluent parts of the city, but that's what all parents do. I can't help it if my parents helped me.

"What does he look like?" I ask. Merv throws a folded paper across the desk. I stare back at a guy who looks angry. But then my heart skips a beat as I rake my eyes over his chest. I skim over the article headline and see that this is a shot of him in the ring after he's won a fight. He's wearing a don't-fuck-with-me glare, and his hands are down by his side, his eyes a riot of fury. My heart skips a beat because this guy has abs that are so beautifully sculpted that I'm tempted to trace my finger over the paper.

I would have probably done that had Merv the Perv not been watching me.

"I think she likes him," Gerry says, grinning.

"He looks familiar," I say, trying to cover my embarrassment. He doesn't look familiar at all, and I can't believe I've almost drooled over the paper.

"Get to know him, Harper. Make him trust you." These are Merv's parting words to me.

"Looking forward to it?" Gerry asks when we leave the office. He's always checking to see if I'm okay. At first I thought it was because of my dad, but the more I get to know him, the more I realize that Gerry's making sure I settle in okay. Maybe he's trying to make up for Merv's thinly veiled hatred of me. In any case, Gerry reminds me of a kid who always wants to please his mom, or his schoolteacher, except that he's in his late forties, I'm guessing, and he's been here longer. Yet, for some reason, he seems slightly in awe around me, and I don't know why.

"It's a bit sudden," I say. "Telling me the day before I start."

"That's because we had someone else in mind."

"Then why am I running with this?" There are others here with so much more experience than me.

"This will be good for you. Merv reckons you might be better in getting more information out of Cardoza." He coughs and looks embarrassed. "As opposed to a guy, but I have no idea why he'd think that, especially in this day and age."

Merv the Perv. I wince. "I know nothing about boxing," I say.

"You're not on your own, Harper. Maybe we can get together for lunch or something once you've settled in? You can let me know how you get along."

"Sounds good."

I go back to my desk and prepare to get better acquainted online with Elias Cardoza.

CHAPTER THREE

HARPER

I left the Louboutins at home even though the black Chanel suit looked better with four-inch heels. I wasn't sure what to wear, and was almost tempted to wear my old casual clothes. I didn't relish the idea of all that sweat and dirt from the gym being all over my business suits. But, I eventually decided on a pantsuit that looked chic, and didn't look too bad with my Converse sneakers.

I arrive at McNeilly's Gym in a part of Chicago I'm not too familiar with. When I walk in, a musty, damp-ish smell assaults my nostrils. I count four boxing rings, two of them occupied. There are a handful of people scattered around, mostly young guys.

I can see an office in the corner, diagonally across the open-plan floor. The door is closed, but I can see from the half-windows around it that there's a guy inside. He's on the phone, walking around. The guys in the gym glance at me, and then get back to what they were doing.

I'm insignificant, even though, or perhaps because, I'm the only woman in here.

"Can I help you?"

I turn at the sound of a soft voice. It's another guy, old enough to be my grandpa, from the looks of it, and he has the same soft manner about him.

"I'm from the Chicago Daily Herald," I tell him, and hold out my hand.

"Ahh," he says, his eyes lighting as if this now makes sense. "I'm Ernesto," he shakes my hand.

"Harper," I say, smiling, because he's made me feel welcome. "Harper Lindstrom."

"Lou said we'd be expecting someone, but I wasn't expecting a woman," he says. There is nothing untoward in that sentence. Nothing sexist or slimy. It's just a fact that he points out. "I'm pleased to meet you, Harper."

"This is kind of a new experience for me," I say, finding myself immediately drawn to him.

"I don't suppose boxing is a sport you have much interest in? My granddaughters don't like it much either." His smile puts me at ease.

"It seemed like a good opportunity, interviewing Elias Cardoza," I say, hoping to get an insight into the man.

He nods. "Eli will take some getting used to," he says, and it doesn't seem like a warning because his eyes are soft.

I want to ask him what he means by that but he says, "Let me take you to meet Lou." Before I can say anything, he motions for me to follow him, so I do.

Nobody bats an eyelid as we walk past. The guys fighting in the ring carry on. I sense that nothing, not even a hurricane, would shift their focus.

Ernesto knocks on the office door, then opens it without waiting for a response. The other guy is still on the phone, and he hasn't even looked up as Ernesto and I hover around the open door.

"He's always on the phone," Ernesto whispers.

I smile, because there's not a lot I can say to that. Instead I look behind me at the gym area, and see if the boy wonder is here.

"Those are some of the regulars," Ernesto explains, lowering his voice. "There's Santos and Jake," he points to two guys stepping into the ring. "They're Eli's sparring partners. The rest," he gesticulates at the other guys, "are regulars. Some come with their trainers. Lou only trains and manages Eli, and he's always busy, because he owns the gym. I try to help out, but he's busier than ever now that Eli's got this fight."

"Is he ready?" I ask, because I'm not sure what to say until I've met the man, and then I can gauge how I'm going to get through my month here.

"I believe he will be more than ready by the time he steps into that ring."

"What can I do for you?" I turn around. Phone guy is off the phone and fixes me with a questioning look.

"This is Harper," says Ernesto. "She's from the paper."

"*You're* from the paper?" This new guy isn't repeating it, he's asking it as if it's a question, as if he's shocked.

"Yes." Suddenly I feel self-conscious, as if I'm not properly qualified for this assignment. I'm used to it, but I feel slightly out of place.

"Lou," he says, "I'm Eli's manager." He eyes me as if there's a problem. I'm relieved I had the sense to wear my dark pantsuit instead of my pencil skirt, and that I swapped out the heels for my sneakers. I wish I'd gone easy on the makeup, too. It's probably not a good thing that I've come in looking all dolled up, because I feel way too overdressed for this place already.

I bet Merv knew this. It wouldn't surprise me to learn that he was probably even cheering for it.

"I'm Harper Lindstrom." We shake hands, and I shake harder than usual.

"She works for the Chicago Daily Herald."

"I'm aware of who she works for, Ernie, I was the one involved in the discussions." He gives me a smile, but still looks at me as if he doesn't know what to make of me.

"Go get Eli, will you?" Lou asks.

"No, don't," I say quickly. The reception from Lou hasn't been so great, and I'm worried about meeting Elias. I've read that boxers are focused, and train like crazy. "I don't want to disturb him."

The two men grin at each other, and I have no idea what's so funny.

"You should meet him. It's better you get this over and done with now," Lou insists, and nods at Ernesto to go bring him.

"What do you know about boxing?" Lou asks as soon as Ernesto leaves. I'm beginning to think that he and Merv must have been separated at birth, because they both seem to regard me with the same level of condescension.

"Well... I don't know much," I say, deciding that it's better to confess. "But this isn't so much about the techniques of boxing, as it is about the man who'll be fighting the current heavyweight champion of the world. This story is inspirational to say the least, especially knowing about Elias's past and how he came from a broken home."

"You did your research, eh?" Lou asks, walking back to his desk and sitting down. Then he turns to some paperwork which is lying on his desk and diverts his attention there. I'm left feeling as if I'm not important since he can't even spare me a few minutes of his time. I consider that rude given that I'm going to be here for a while.

I glance at my fingernail and wonder if it was worth getting my nails painted again yesterday given where I am today. Would it really matter in this place?

Lou's still engrossed in his paperwork and doesn't even look up at me, but I'm not left hanging for long because the door flies open and Elias Cardoza walks in.

His face is dotted with sweat, and he's still wearing his boxing gloves. The room seems to shrink because it feels as if this guy takes up so much space. He's not huge. There are no bulky, football-shaped muscles on him, but there are tattoos. Beautiful tattoos all over his chest. I can't stop staring.

He's lean, and toned, and a sheen of sweat coats his naked torso. He's not a beast, but his presence is overwhelming in that suddenly small office.

I forget to talk. I forget to breathe.

He ignores me, even though I'm standing directly in front of him, and instead, he stares at his manager.

"Eli, meet Harper Lindster," says Lou.

"Lindstrom," I correct.

"That's right," says Lou, making no effort to get my name right. "Harper, meet Eli, the next heavyweight champion of the world."

With this glowing break-the-tension introduction, I expect Elias's face to soften, but the guy throws me a look of pure loathing. I hold my breath because I'm not relaxed enough to breathe. It takes me a few seconds before I inch forward. "Nice to meet you," I say, but I stop myself from lifting my hand. Even if he wasn't wearing those boxing gloves, something tells me this guy wouldn't want to shake my hand.

He observes me with suspicion. If he's surprised that I'm a woman, I can't tell. In fact, I don't think that face of his is capable of expressing surprise. He's hard, and impassive, and he looks pissed even though, as far as I'm aware, I haven't said or done anything offensive.

"Don't worry, I don't intend to get in your way," I say, to fill the awkward silence that slithers around me. I feel uneasy and I can't tell if it's because my body is on high-alert due to his blatant dislike of me being here, or if it's because I'm reacting to this man's overt sexuality.

I have to admit, he has an aura about him, something physical, and sexual, that rolls easily off his bare skin. I don't think he's aware of it, because he's not looking at me as an object of any remote interest whatsoever.

He's looking at me as if I just messed up his day.

"Remember what we talked about, Eli?" Lou says. Ernesto coughs lightly. The moment stretches out painfully.

"Yeah," Eli says. How he manages to make that word sound offensive is beyond me.

I try to smile, then look at Lou for instruction. Actually, I look at Lou because I can't look at Elias. I don't have these types of reactions to people. Not even when I've had a few drinks. I'm always in control of my emotions. I always keep it together, no matter what, but I don't understand why my heartrate just sped up.

"Harper will be here for a month, Eli. Be nice."

"You already told me."

Elias's voice is richer than I would expect for someone so young; he's twenty-four, if I remember correctly. His voice, coupled with his bare-chested torso, turns my brain to pulp.

"She's not going to be in your way," Lou tells him.

I take the cue. "I'm not," I tell him in a rushed voice that I barely recognize as my own. "I'll be so discreet that I'll be invisible," I say, and volunteer a smile. But he scowls at me. Nothing moves on his face. No upturn of lips, or the blink of an eye, and yet he's scowling at me. I can feel it.

"Good," he growls, then exits the room.

Ernesto gives a laugh, and the tension in the room breaks. "Don't mind him," says Ernesto, tapping me on the shoulder from behind. He's been standing near the door the entire time. "He's not the friendliest of guys."

"You can say that again." Friendly isn't a word I'd put within a ten-mile radius of Elias Cardoza.

"You'll get used to it," Lou adds. "Just give him his space."

I want to ask them both how they expect me to find out about him, and his motivations, and his routine, how they expect me to get information about his fighting methods and his mindset if the guy doesn't want me anywhere near him?

"You need anything?" Lou asks, clearly eager for me to leave so that he can carry on with his work.

Even if I did, I wouldn't be asking him. "No," I reply.

"Come on," says Ernesto. "Lou's another one that doesn't like people much." He raises his eyebrow at the man. "The apple doesn't fall far from the tree."

As we leave the office, I notice that Eli has stepped into the ring with a guy.

"Let's find you a place to sit, and get you settled in," offers Ernesto, and I feel a sense of relief.

CHAPTER FOUR

ELI

A woman? You have to be kidding me. What the hell was Lou thinking? I hated this stupid idea before, and now I hate it a million times over.

She looks as if she belongs behind the perfume counter at one of those fancy department stores.

I don't want her here, and I sure as hell don't want her following me around for a month.

After my sparring session with Santos, I climb out of the ring and see that she's got a desk over by the wall.

That's all I need.

I walk over to one of the benches and start taking off my headgear and gloves. I see Ernesto coming towards me, and instinctively I can tell he's not amused.

"That wasn't nice."

I put my gloves down and say nothing.

"Can't you try to be civil?" he asks, leaning against the

wall with his hands behind his back. I glance over to the side. Princess is tapping away on her laptop.

"She doesn't belong here."

"It's publicity for you."

I grunt. "I don't need her to get me publicity."

"Garrison's got the media and the people on his side. Who have you got?"

My head jerks towards him and I'm too taken aback to give him an answer. Ernesto never has anything bad to say. "I don't even know who the fuck this Harper Lindshit is."

"Lindstrom."

"She's a woman. What does she know about boxing?"

"That's her problem, not yours, Eli."

"She's my problem."

"How? I don't see her doing anything to you," Ernesto answers so easily that I'm starting to question his loyalty.

Then I remember his two teenage granddaughters, and I reckon Ernesto is getting all protective over the princess because she reminds him of them. He brought them to the gym once because they wanted a picture with me, and autographs, and a million selfies. Come to think of it, the eighteen year-old wanted my number, when Grandpa wasn't looking, but I lied and told her my girlfriend wouldn't be too happy about that.

"Try to be civil, that's all Lou's asking, He's not expecting you to take her out on a date. Who knows, she might have something nice to say about you." He walks away before I get the chance to make a comment.

Just then she looks up and catches me staring, I turn my back since it wasn't her I was specifically looking at.

I need to take a shower before I go to Frankie's Kitchen, a diner a few blocks from here, to have lunch. But before I head over to the locker room, I knock on Lou's door and walk in. I have things I need to say.

"You never said it was going to be a woman."

"I'm as surprised as you, kid."

"Are you sure she's in the right place?"

He laughs. "She's going to be a real test of your mettle."

"She's not supposed to be anything," I spit back. "She's only going to be a pain in my butt. A distraction. Can't you see that?"

"It's exposure for the gym. It will help us attract more talent to this place."

"You need more new blood?"

"A gym always needs new blood."

Unbelievable. I've given this guy more exposure than he's ever had, and now that I have the biggest fight of my life before me, he's going to get the biggest exposure yet. He should be grateful for me, instead of trying to find more fighters.

I sulk silently because it's better than exploding with all the anger that's been building inside me ever since he introduced me to her.

"She's good for business, Eli."

"She looks out of place."

"Then don't look at her," Lou growls.

I can block her out, because that's how I survived. I blocked out the stuff that didn't matter, and held onto the stuff that did.

But even so, the idea of Harper watching my every move for an entire month makes my blood boil.

CHAPTER FIVE

HARPER

It's the end of my first week here. I've only been here for four days but it feels like two weeks. And I haven't managed to speak to Eli yet.

I've tried. Meaning I've tried to get his attention. Each time I've tried to catch his eye, he avoids looking at me. It's plain to see that he hates me being around, and I'm giving him time to get used to me. I haven't yet been able to summon up the courage to walk over to him and talk to him, but I can't leave it too long. I don't even want to begin to imagine what Merv and Gerry would make of this situation.

"You don't look too happy." It's not that Ernesto is a master of observation, it's just that I don't hide my feelings or wear my mask well.

"I'm not getting anywhere," I confess. "I'm supposed to be writing an information piece on Elias Cardoza, Chicago's New Hope, and I have nothing."

"Mind if I sit down?" Ernesto asks, his hands resting on the wooden slat of the empty chair opposite me.

"Please," I say, grateful for the company. He's been good to me, so I can't complain. After all, he's the one who got me this small table from his own office. I didn't even know Ernesto had his own office. I suppose office is too fancy a word for this small room with a tiny window. It's next to the utility room. He's given me his desk because he claims he hardly ever uses it. He says he's got no time to sit down and do nothing because the gym is falling to pieces and there's something to fix every day.

He set me up with this tiny working space not long after I arrived here. My desk is next to a power socket, so that I can recharge my phone or plug in my laptop when the battery's about to die.

Ernesto sighs heavily. "So, Eli's not giving you anything, huh?" It so happens that Eli saunters past us at that very moment. He's in jeans and a sweatshirt, and he's late today, I notice. I usually get here first thing in the morning and then pop back to my office during the day if I need to, and then I pop back here in the late afternoon.

"Not even a 'hello'," I complain. Still, I'm up to speed on this guy's training regimen and his diet, but I got none of that from him. I got it by talking to everyone around him; Lou, Ernesto, Santos and Jake, who are part of his training team. I also discover more information online.

None of this is from the man himself. And he still avoids looking my way or acknowledging my presence. "He doesn't open up."

"He doesn't talk much," agrees Ernesto. His eyes are soft, and brown, and offer me a glimpse of kindness that I'm not used to here. Lou hides away in his office, and Eli still looks at me as if he wants to gouge my eyes out. I might have been a novelty the first week I was here, but now the rest of the boxers are used to me, and I'm as good as being part of the furniture. I've even dressed so that I fit in. Jeans, shirts, and sneakers.

"What's he hiding?" I ask, then smile to add a touch of softness.

"You'll have to ask him."

The way he says it puts me on high alert. "He won't give me an inch. I can't reach him."

Ernesto tilts his head, as if agreeing. "It's a boxer's instinct."

"I'm a journalist. I'm here for a reason. He's the interest and he's not giving me anything." I think back to a few days ago when I tried to make conversation with him, and he ignored me completely. I don't think I've ever met anyone so rude before.

"Tell me about you," Ernesto asks, and because I know since I've worked around enough creeps, I can see his request is genuine. He's being polite, making me feel at home, or trying to, at least.

He wants to know about my job, and how long I've been here, and about college and whether I liked it. He tells me he has two granddaughters and that's why he's asking, on their behalf. I can tell he dotes on them by the way his face lights up when he talks about them. So I tell him, and he asks me if I enjoy my work.

"I'm never bored," I reply, and I truly mean that. I can't see myself sitting in an office doing admin work, or crunching numbers, but doing investigative work is exciting. At least I think it is, in this early stage of my career.

"This must be strange for you?" Ernesto throws a glance around the room. "Maybe you'd prefer to cover more glamorous stories?"

"Elias Cardoza's story is interesting," I say, because it is. It could never be glamorous, in the way most celebrity stories are, but it is definitely interesting. "He's Chicago's New Hope, after all."

"He's going places, that's for sure," Ernesto replies, his voice full of conviction. "And he's really not so bad, once you get to know him."

"He's not giving me a chance." I glance over at the punching bag that Eli is hammering hard right now.

"Give him time."

"We'll be into the second week soon." At this rate I won't have much to do, and my being *here*, in order to have access to Eli, seems pointless.

"Gimme a minute," he says, then gets up and strides over to Eli. He has his back to us and it's wet. Sweat rolls off it. He hits the punching bag so hard that I can hear the sound even though I'm at the other end of the room.

He stops when Ernesto says something to him. I'm so glad that Eli's back is to me. If he could see me now, he'd give me a withering look even from where he is, and I'd feel the hate in it.

But then Eli turns around. I want to sink into my chair, and become part of the ugly, uncomfortable plastic. I instinctively sink lower, my shoulders slumping as I pretend to stare at my laptop screen. My phone beeps, signaling an incoming text and I check. It's Gerry and he's asking if I want to meet up with him for lunch one day next week.

Yes. I text back.

While I'm at it, I check my emails as well. "Go talk to him now," Ernesto says, interrupting me with his return.

I swallow, and look up to see the beast beating the punching bag like someone deranged. I'm not so sure I want to go over to him right now.

"Now?" I ask, my voice a whisper. "He looks busy."

"He's annoyed that you're going to take up his time."

I'm not convinced listening to Ernesto is a good thing. "Go on," he urges. "He's finishing off on the punching bag. You can grab him now."

I don't want to grab him now or later, but it's what I'm here for, and I don't have a choice.

Ernesto leaves, and I waste a few minutes trying to still my heart. I don't understand this, why I'm feeling nervous, or why my heart is behaving like I've run a marathon. Nothing fazes me, and I hate that this does. That *he* does. So on the count of three, I raise myself, and then walk over to Eli, feeling a complete phony as I try to look confident. He moves from the punching bag to the speedball.

I wait, like a dutiful butler, and watch from behind as he punches the speedball. My eyes take in the wide span of his shoulders and my gaze rolls over the dips and curves of his muscles. Each time he moves, the muscles flex. It's easy to see because his skin is taut; there are no layers of fat. I hug my arms, feeling self-conscious.

He lifts his hand and effortlessly tap, tap, taps the ball. His left hand slightly raised, his right going at it with a gentle rhythm. I'm mesmerized because he makes it look so easy.

Then he stops and turns around abruptly, as if he's sensed my presence. It has to be that, because I haven't said a word, or made a noise. I've been too enthralled checking him out and trying not to hyperventilate.

This is not me. I am not that pathetic whimpering little woman whose heart goes to pieces when she sees a man who is to be admired. Eli isn't drop-dead movie-star gorgeous, and I'm not one to be fixated on a man's body, and yet, with this man, this feral, raging beast before me, something happens to me that is beyond my control.

His eyes widen and he fixes me with that what-the-fuck-do-you-want look.

I was going to smile but in the face of such resentment, a smile seems weak. "I wanted to ask you a few questions, if I could," I say, and then realize that he hasn't said a word; he's asked no question. He hasn't even moved a muscle as he faces me. This, I now understand, is his silent threat. It's how he deals with predators, nosy people, intruders, opponents. Anyone. Or maybe just me. It's as if he sees me as an opponent. That's not the way for me to gain his trust.

Then I smile.

And he doesn't.

It is impossible to remain optimistic, and hopeful, in the face of such adversity.

But I'm a pro.

"Five minutes," he says, and before I can stumble from the shock, and before it dawns on me that five minutes isn't enough time, he's walked away. He heads towards the locker room.

"I can't go in there," I mutter to myself, then look over my shoulder. It's a relatively quiet day, and I don't care if there's anyone else inside. Elias Cardoza just gave me five minutes, and I'm going to make the most of them.

CHAPTER SIX

ELI

She watches my every move and I hate this. How does
Lou not see how pointless it is having this journalist
snooping around?

I've given her five minutes. I wasn't sure she'd follow me
into the locker room, but she has. It's a sign of how
desperate she is.

Somewhere over my shoulder, I can hear the sound of
the shower running. I glance at her and she looks at me with
those doe-shaped eyes. She already looked out of place in
the gym, but in here, she's full-on like a fish out of water.

I start to take my gloves off, using my mouth on the first
glove.

"Do you want me to help you with that?" She stares at
me, and then the gloves. I hold back a snort. How does she
think I usually manage?

"*That's* your first question?" I ask, managing to release
my hand. I take the other glove off. I notice she doesn't have

anything on her, no notebook, no pen. Not even a phone. Guess I must have caught her by surprise. "What made you go into boxing?" she asks, folding her arms as she sits down on the bench.

Yawn. Yawn. Yawn. The same old boring question. Boring is good, though. It could be worse. "I like to fight."

"Why?"

"I'm not an office guy."

If she's annoyed by this, she doesn't let on. Instead, she stares up at me.

Her hands are splayed on the wooden slats on either side of her. I'm itching to strip down and dive into the shower. I'm sweating like a pig, but by the way this woman is staring at me, she doesn't seem to care. I take a step towards her so that if she looks up at me, her face will be level with my groin. I can see this causes her some unease. It's not that I'm close. Nowhere near. But I'm close enough. I try not to smile too much, but seeing her squirm turns this into a game. And then she pisses me off with her next question. "Tell me about your early years."

"Which part?"

"When you were taken away by child protective services at age two, I believe."

I swallow. She's done her homework and I hate that she's bringing this up. I don't want to talk about that stuff.

I don't want this out there. I'm trying to forget that part of my life. My story is compelling, I get that, but people don't know the half of it.

"Things weren't so great at home," I reply, poker-faced.

"What happened?"

Before I can answer, I hear a noise behind me. I turn around and Callum's out of the shower and standing there buck naked except for a towel he's using to dry the rest of himself with as he's walking. He stops dead when he sees the journalist in front of me.

"Oh," he says, but doesn't bat an eyelid or make any attempt to cover himself up. He simply turns around and heads towards his side of the locker room.

I turn around and find myself looking at the princess. Her face has turned red.

"So, uh... your... uh... your home life?" She struggles to stay calm. I watch her, finding it amusing, and, given that this isn't a topic I want to talk about, I tell her, "Your time's up."

"But we've barely had—"

"I told you, five minutes."

"How am I supposed to get any information out of you if you won't cooperate?"

I raise an eyebrow. "Cooperate?" She's talking like a cop. I walk over to the locker on her right and open it.

"What can you tell me about growing up?" she asks, sounding indignant. She was calm, chilled and mellow a few moments ago, but seeing Callum naked has thrown her off course. This suits me perfectly because I have zero interest in telling her my life story. I owe her nothing, and whatever deal she and Lou had, I don't give a shit. "How else am I going to write anything about you?" she asks, when I don't answer.

I don't care, seeing that it's not my problem.

"I need to take a shower," I tell her, throwing her a glance over my shoulder. She's furious. Her cheeks are still red, and I wonder if it's because I'm being a real dick to her, or because she had a chance to look at Callum's dick. I snicker inwardly at my own joke.

"What's so funny?" she asks, not losing it, not raising

her voice, but I can detect her internal struggle because her voice is shaky.

"Lady, I gotta shower, and if you don't leave, I'm gonna strip in front of you. It doesn't bother me."

She's fuming now. "You were in a children's home from a young age," she says, ignoring me.

"I was." And if that's how she's going to play, I can do the same. I peel off my boxing shorts, then my training pants and groin protector. I have my back to her as I do this, so I imagine she's staring at my butt cheeks right about now.

She won't follow me into the shower, because I'm certain she can't be that desperate for a story. Still, I'm well aware of what women can be like. There's something about a boxer, and a winner at that, that gets their panties wet.

"Tell me about that time?"

The hell I will.

There is only one way to shut her up. I turn around and face her, in my full naked glory.

Her gaze dips.

Then she blushes, and I see it, her gaze softens. Her lips part, and though I don't really hear it, I know she's exhaled by the way her chest dips. And even though I'm not inside her head, I can see how long it takes for her gaze to shift upwards to my face again.

She stands up. Narrows her eyes. "I'm not following you into the shower," she announces in a tone that makes me realize she might have interpreted this as a move.

Screw you. That's the last thing I would ever do, make a move on someone like her.

I grab my towel and head into the shower.

CHAPTER SEVEN

HARPER

I walk out of the locker room thinking of all the many awkward situations I've been in, and Elias Cardoza stripping in front of me and not batting an eyelid has to be up there at the top.

I don't have him down for being a sleazebag. He's not a player. I can tell because I've been around guys who think they're God's gift to women. Elias isn't one of those guys, so the fact that he stripped off like that can only mean one thing; he doesn't like me poking around in his business. The guy doesn't want me here. Nobody thinks he's going to win and I can see the steely determination in his eyes. He wants to prove everyone wrong. If he loses, he's going to pin that on me.

This assignment is getting worse with each day, and I feel deflated.

"Any luck?" Ernesto asks me, as I sit back down at my small table. It's not even a proper desk, and it wobbles, and this adds to my frustration, but I manage to smile at Ernesto and tell him, "Yes, thanks." It's enough to have him go about his business, this time with a toolkit in his hands. He seems to be the handyman around here, fixing everything that's broken. There's not a day that I've seen him not fixing anything. On closer inspection, the gym is falling to pieces. Paint is peeling from the walls, and the wooden floors and doors look as if they've seen better days. Even the equipment is old and shabby. It is nothing compared to the high-tech bright and shiny gym that's around the corner from my apartment. Hard to see a place like this spawning a world champion, but Ernesto told me that Lou had trained another champion, a middleweight, many years ago. He reckons he can do it all over again but with Eli, and this time for the heavyweight title.

A few days later, Gerry wants to meet up to see how I'm getting along. Ernesto recommended a place which is a stone's throw from the gym, so that's where we decide to meet.

It's lunchtime and the place is busy. It takes a while for us to place our order and in the meantime Gerry wants to know what it's like being at the gym. I play down the friction I'm feeling from Eli, but hint that it's not easy.

"You can't get him to open up?" Gerry asks, as if this is a big surprise.

"He's a stubborn little shit."

"Shit?" Gerry raises an eyebrow. "You're not supposed to say that about the person you're interviewing."

I shrug and place my hand around my glass of lemonade. "Well, he is."

"Merv and I thought you'd be in awe of him."

I shoot my gaze up at him. "Why?"

He gives me an isn't-it-obvious look. "Look at him. He's a boxer. Isn't that appealing to you young ladies?"

I shake my head. "Not really." Gerry doesn't need to know that Eli's physical appearance makes me go weak at the knees.

I suppose I should be grateful that the guy is stone cold towards me. It helps keep me grounded. And a one-way attraction helps. Even if my attraction to him is steeped in hate most of the time.

"He must have given you something?"

An eyeful. The locker room scene is still vivid in my head. Eli's body is beautiful; every inch of it and it's an image I can't seem to shake from my head.

I could get carried away with my fantasies if he showed me even a molecule of niceness. Instead, I've gotten only a few short sentences from the guy. "Not a lot," I reply, gritting my teeth together.

This isn't working out, really it isn't. Merv is going to come down on me like a ton of bricks. Maybe that's why he put me here in the first place.

And then I see him. He's sitting a few stalls down on the across the aisle, and he's with someone. A woman. I catch her staring at me staring at Eli, and I look away. Is she his girlfriend? And I don't know why that annoys me a little.

ELI

I noticed her dirty blonde hair first when I walked in. She had her back to me and didn't see me, but she was sitting with a ginger-haired dude. I can't imagine he's her boyfriend, he looks way too old, but he's smartly dressed, and money talks.

I sit down a few tables ahead and across the aisle. Nina waits for me, if she knows I'm coming, so that we can eat together. It's a thing we have. It's not fixed, but she knows I'll come by around noon—if I'm going to eat—and she'll wait for me. It's one of the few times we get to catch up. Sometimes she'll invite me over in the evening, and eat early just so that it fits around my timetable.

"Who are you staring at?" she asks, when I glance over my shoulder. I assumed I was being discreet, but I forget how observant my sister can be.

I turn back around. "No one," I state, but Nina's gaze flicks over my shoulder.

"The blonde? You're checking out the blonde?"

"She's not blonde," I say quickly. "Wheat colored, more like."

"But you were checking her out."

I don't want to explain that I know Harper, so I move the conversation back to Nina.

"Have you decided on your next course?" She's recently finished a bookkeeping course and now wants to try her hand at something else. She attends a lot of night school classes and is always trying new things, but she hasn't yet settled on any one area of expertise. I see how we're similar in wanting to better ourselves. I chose boxing but Nina's still trying to find her vocation. For now, she's happy to waitress at Frankie's Kitchen until she can turn things around.

"Not yet. I need to save up, but I'm thinking maybe I'll try theoretical physics."

I chortle. "What the hell is that?"

"Don't know yet. I'll find out when I take the course."

"It sounds painful. And shouldn't you be doing courses in stuff you can get a job in?"

"It sounds interesting. Besides, it's not as if I'm giving up the waitressing."

I wish I could lend her money. I wish I could make things easier for her, but I don't have much myself. Even after this fight, I don't imagine that the winnings will be super huge, especially when everyone else has had their cut. But at least I'll get something.

She won't need to worry about money too much once I hit the big leagues, and Trent Garrison is my ticket into that world.

"I can help you out after the fight," I tell her. "After I win."

She grins. "Of course you'll win, and I will ask you then."

Nina looks at me and nods proudly. I love her for that. She always looks at me as if she's immensely proud of me. Most people don't see much when they look at me, actually, that's not so true now, especially when people find out I'm in this fight, but before it was always the case. Nina was always the sweet, quiet one, and I was always the troublemaker. I was disruptive at school. We came close to being adopted a few times, but the foster families always backed off. Many couldn't believe we were brother and sister. I couldn't help it. Rage can't be contained. It needs an outlet.

"Come and watch," I say, because it would mean a lot to me. I'm not scared about going to New York, or stepping into that ring at The Garden with the whole world watching. It doesn't faze me that ninety-nine percent of the audience will be on Garrison's side. What will faze me is not having anyone there. Lou and Santos and Jake will be, they're my entourage and they're the only family I have, aside from Nina, but to have her there would mean the world to me.

She winces, and it's obvious that I'll never be able to convince her. She shakes her head. "I can't, Elias. I can't watch you get hit."

I note she didn't say 'beat'. She believes in me, and that's all I need.

I avoid looking at her and mash up my baked potato. "Don't worry about it. I'll call you as soon as it's over."

She won't even watch the fight on TV and refuses to go to her friends' places or go out and watch it on the big screen. It can't be easy, I understand that. We only have each other, and she can't watch another man beat the crap out of me. It was bad enough when my aunt's boyfriend used to do that.

Nobody understands how big this is for me—to be given this chance, a fluke chance at that—and for me to end up in this fight against the heavyweight champion of the world. It would never have happened had the two fighters before not messed up. One failed a drug test, and the other threw his shoulder out in an injury. I was the third choice. They reckon I don't have a chance, that I'll be a pushover for Garrison, but time will tell what a big mistake he made getting into the ring with me.

We change the subject quickly. My sister doesn't like that I'm a boxer, but it's the only way I can earn money. It's the only thing I'm good at.

I glance over my shoulder again. Harper is so engrossed in her conversation with the ginger dude that she still hasn't seen me.

"She's new," Nina replies, when I turn back.

When I raise my eyebrow, questioning, she elaborates.

"I know everybody who comes in here. She's new. I haven't seen her here before."

"She's a journalist, and she's been hanging around the gym. Going to be there up until the fight."

"When did she start?"

"Over a week ago."

"And this is the first time you mention it?" Nina smirks. "Are you hiding something from me, Elias?"

This time I grab a couple of thin and crispy fries from Nina's plate. "She wants my story."

Nina's neck stretches like a giraffe's and she takes a good look. I can feel Harper staring back, because Nina's stare is so pointed. She makes it *so* obvious.

"Can you not do that?" I hiss.

"She smiled at me."

I rub my forehead in irritation. The last thing I want is for Miss Busybody to come over, but Nina does it again. She smiles in Harper's direction. I don't dare turn to look. "Stop staring," I hiss again.

Nina makes a face, like she always does when she doesn't want to do something.

I can tell what she's thinking and I shoot that idea down immediately. "She's not my type, and girls are off limits to me for now."

"She's been at your gym and she's writing your story, and you didn't think to mention it to me," she states. "What are you hiding?"

"Nothing."

"What's she writing? A book about you?"

I shake my head and snort. "Something for the local paper. Some long-ass piece on me."

"About time, too."

"The fight is a hot story. Whether Garrison wins or I

win is a moot point. But, *we* both know I'm going to win."

"Of course you're going to win. This belt has your name written all over it. Maybe I'll look into a journalism course next time," says Nina, as if the idea suddenly appeals to her. "But what if I don't like it?"

"You're way too overqualified to be working as a waitress. Why don't you try to get a job using whatever it is you've learned at night school?"

"Because employers want experience."

One day, she's not going to need to work at all, because I'm going to take care of her, but since I can't do that right now, I keep my mouth shut.

"I should go," says Nina, wiping her mouth on her napkin. "My lunchbreak ended twelve minutes ago."

"Hey." I hear Harper's voice over my left shoulder and I stiffen and stare at Nina. This is her fault. I'm usually receptive to people coming up to me, even when I'm eating or talking to someone. It's started to happen more and more recently, and I don't mind, but I have an aversion to Harper interrupting me. I don't know why it is I loathe her so much. I sense it's because she's nosing around in my business, and wants to know about the stuff I want to forget.

"Hi," says Nina, perking up as if she's my PR person. "I'm Nina, Elias's sister."

"Oh, *you're* the sister?" Harper lets out a little laugh and moves so that she's standing in the middle of us. "I noticed we kept catching one another's eye."

"Elias says you're doing a story on him," Nina answers.

"I'm supposed to be," Miss Busybody replies, "but I can't seem to get him to talk to me."

"He takes some getting used to," Nina tells her. "I wouldn't take it personally."

The ginger-haired dude stands beside Harper and looks at me as if he isn't sure what to say.

"I'm Gerry." He has the audacity to stick out his hand. Thank fuck I'm not eating anymore; I'm always wary of shaking people's hands because I never know where they've been. But I take this guy's hand and shake it, because it's the right thing to do and because Nina would only tell me off afterwards if I was rude.

It's awkward, because I don't want to talk, and Nina isn't going to say much, and Harper and her friend are waiting for us to lead the conversation and we're not going to. It takes a few more seconds for the awkwardness to ratchet up to another level, and then Harper says, "bye, nice meeting you," and she and her date shuffle out the door.

I assume he's her date.

"That was strange," Nina comments.

"I don't know what to say around her. She's writing an article on me and it makes me want to avoid her even more."

Nina pats my hand. "Lighten up, Elias. You're famous now, in Chicago at least, and in a few weeks' time you'll be famous everywhere."

I smile. Nina has so much faith in me. "I'm starting to get recognized," I tell her, wanting to switch the subject.

"Everyone in here knows you. Frankie uses you to drum up more business."

I groan inwardly.

"Your friend looked uncomfortable just now."

"If you think she looked uncomfortable, you should have seen her in the—" I stop mid-sentence. I want to tell her how uncomfortable Harper was the other day when I stripped right down, but I don't, not only because it's not something Nina would find funny, but because, she's my sister, and I can't tell her stuff like that.

She fixes me with a stern look. "What did you do?"

"Nothing. I didn't do anything."

"Two denials. Confess, Elias. What did you do?"

I clasp my hands together. "She says I haven't been helpful. I haven't been forthcoming with answers."

"Understandable." Nina has her demons too about our childhood years. Like me, she wants to forget.

"I don't like her sticking her nose in where it's not wanted."

"She's trying to do her job, Elias, like we all are."

I pick up my bottle of water and drink from it, not because I'm thirsty, but because she's right and I don't want to accept that fact. And then, just as I knew she would, she elaborates, in case I missed her point. "How do you think I feel when someone's being lousy to me? When they don't give good tips, or don't tip at all? Or when someone complains about the food I've given them, and then I have to be the go-between for them and the chef?"

I place my bottle down slowly, seeing that she's on her soapbox now. She's my sister, and though she's only a year older than me, she's always looked after me. We got left alone at home a lot, usually by our mom, since our dad didn't figure in our life much. He flitted in and out like a flea. I don't remember either of them much, and Nina doesn't either, but our aunt, my mom's sister, used to tell us things about them, and that's how we know.

Nina and I have had our fair share of adventures, but she's always looked after me the way any decent mother would have.

"I hear you," I say, and I wish she'd stop already. "But she doesn't need to work, and I don't know why she does."

"Elias! That's sexist, I'm disgusted."

I try not to roll my eyes. Ernesto told me all about

Harper and how she went to some fancy college, and how she lives in Lakeview, one of the most expensive parts of Chicago.

The princess and I are worlds apart.

"I don't mean it like that."

"Then how do you mean it?"

"She knows nothing about boxing, and she's messing with my head by being around. I have the most important fight of my life coming up, and I can't mess up, and I have this airhead of a woman—"

"How do you know she's an airhead? She got that job because she deserves it. She's trying to do her best, so don't be a jerk and get in her way."

I swallow. I don't think Garrison's punch would sting as much as my sister's reprimands.

"She didn't get where she is on her own. Her parents helped her."

"Good for her," my sister cries. "It means she has parents who care, and who want a better life for her, and parents who have money," she adds, as an afterthought.

"It's an accident of birth and she got lucky," I say with bitterness.

We fall silent then, because we often ponder about this very point. We had none of those things. We didn't even have the basics; food, or a goodnight hug and kiss, or story time. I see that shit on TV all the time, in sitcoms and in those Hallmark movies that my last girlfriend used to binge watch so much. Those are fairytale families with fairytale happy endings, and they are bullshit.

We talk about the accident of birth a lot, me and Nina. We pretend how different things might have been if we had been born to nice parents, parents who cared, who were together and lived in a nice suburban house, and made nice suburban meals, and who did our homework with us.

"And it's an accident of birth that Harper is where she is. She can't help that, so be nice to her, Elias."

"Okay," I reply, begrudgingly. But all the same, I can't help but think how different our lives would have been. I probably wouldn't have become a boxer then. There wouldn't have been any anger inside me.

"Promise?"

"I'll try." I frown at her. "Since when did she become your best friend?"

CHAPTER EIGHT

ELI

I'm in the ring sparring with Santos when I notice
Princess walk in. This is something recent, me noticing
her around, or maybe I'm not as good at shutting her out. I
blame it on the diner incident. I feel as if I've been forced to
be nice to her, and nice in my case is to acknowledge her.

Santos and I finish our session, and I take off my
headgear and gloves, and see Harper looking my way. We
lock gazes at the same time, and I nod in acknowledgment. I
still have Nina's words in my head, about being nice to
Harper, and letting her get on with her job. This time, I
decide to go over to her.

"I can answer any questions you might have," I say. She
looks up at me, and I see the surprise flickering across her
eyes. They're dark green, I notice, for the first time.

"That's good. Great." She moves her papers out of the
way and looks around, presumably to see if there's a chair

for me. Of course, I'd grab my own chair, but that's not the point. This isn't about to happen now. I have errands to run.

"Not now," I tell her. "When I get back. I have a few things to take care of in town."

Disappointment washes over her, and it's so easy to see. She doesn't hide her emotions. Probably because she never had to. "When?"

"Maybe in an hour."

She scratches her neck, seems to consider this. "I have a meeting with my boss."

I frown, unsure as to why she thinks I need to know that.

"Mind if I come with you?" she asks.

I don't suppose I have a choice. "I need to take a shower," I tell her, and then, because I can, because I know it gets her all ruffled up, I say, "You're welcome to interview me in the locker room again."

Her cheeks start to turn pink, and I walk away feeling pretty pleased with myself because I was responsible for that.

Not long after, we're in the cab together. She's up against one side of the car, and I'm at the other, and her handbag lies between us. It's a big expensive-looking one, with an ugly-as-fuck shiny gold buckle.

"So," she says, tilting her body slightly to face me. But then her cell phone goes off, and she looks at it, and then apologizes before answering it.

It sounds as if she's talking to her old man. I don't even remember ever having a conversation with my old man. I have no early memories of him, or what he looked like. I vaguely remember my mom, but it's more of an essence I have about her, rather than a picture in my head.

I know what my parents look like because of the few photos my aunt showed us.

To hear Harper's conversation is like wickedly eavesdropping on something alien. It sounds as if her dad's pissed that he hasn't seen her. She sounds as if she's trying to get off the phone.

Eventually she manages it. "Sorry, that was my dad."

"I figured."

"So," she says, starting again. "What made you go into boxing?"

"Survival, and making sure people stayed away from me."

"You don't need to put on a pair of boxing gloves to do that," she says, and tries to shift back slightly only she can't because she's already pressed up against the car door.

"Do I scare you?" I want to know. I already know I have some effect on her.

"It's not that you scare me. I just don't find you easy to approach," she replies.

I'm not trying to scare her. People like her aren't the ones I need to scare off.

The thing is, I'm not comfortable with this interview taking place anyway, and least of all in a cab. The last thing I want is for the taxi driver to go and spill my private stuff everywhere. Harper's going to write and publish it anyway, and Lou wants me to cooperate, and Nina wants me to be nice, but Princess doesn't need to know all of my business. I'm already cautious and watch what I tell her, and to that extent I can control what goes out there, but my story is not for others to know. Or Nina. It would break her heart.

"You were a troublemaker at school?" she asks.

"Aren't most boys?" I throw back, but then I remember

she must have gone to a really preppy school, and her idea of troublemakers is probably different than mine.

"But you're not like most boys," she replies, as if she's trying to dig for answers. I hate that she's digging, so I don't reply.

"Why do I feel as if our conversations never get anywhere?" she says finally, when silence fills the air. I can hear the exasperation in her voice.

"What is it that you want to know?"

"I want to know what makes you tick, what makes you climb into the ring and hit so hard."

"You want to know a lot of things."

"You're an interesting guy."

"You think so?"

"Not *me*, personally," she replies quickly.

I stare at her, because any talk about personal stuff, with me looking at her like that, is going to make her blush. I wait for it, and sure enough, she blushes. "Not *you* personally?" I question.

"I have no interest in boxing, or in you, Mr. Cardoza."

This makes me chuckle. "Mr. Cardoza, is it now?" She's desperate to put some distance between me and her. I find her discomfort amusing. "What happened to Eli?" I ask, making her blush a little more.

"This proves my point. I'm no better off, information-wise, than before. We go around and around in circles. My interest in you is purely work-related, *Eli*," she emphasizes. "It's for the article, and frankly, right now, the stuff I have on you is what I can get from the internet. I was hoping for more, but you seem to be a busy man who does his best to avoid me."

"I have a fight coming up, in case you hadn't noticed, and I don't have a *dad* to bail me out when times get hard."

She presses her lips together as if this pisses her off. Is it Daddy issues or rich-girl issues that she has? I can't tell.

"Tell me about Grampton House," she says. The request makes my insides sink.

Luckily, I'm near where I need to be to get out. I tap the cab driver on the shoulder. "Hey, man, can you pull over? I need to get out."

"Already?" She looks disappointed. I can see why. I hardly gave her anything.

"I've got things to take care of at the bank."

Her lips pinch together and she doesn't look happy at all. "Is this all it's going to be?" she asks, as I get ready to climb out.

"How much do I owe you?" I ask, pulling out my wallet.

"Don't worry about the cost. I've got this."

"You sure?"

She shakes her head, as if she's still pissed off at me.

"Could I get your autograph?" the cab driver asks. I'm secretly thrilled that he's recognized me. It's a new experience, and it's happened a few times lately, but each time it takes me back and I have to almost pinch myself to know that it is real.

"Sure you can," I say. He whips out a grubby little notepad and shoves it in my face.

"What's your name?"

"Al."

I scribble a short message to Al, and pass the notebook back to him. His face lights up. "You show Garrison what you're made of," he says, holding up his fist.

"I plan to."

"Good luck, man."

"Thanks."

I glance over at the back, and see Harper's tight face. "Where are you going?" I ask, out of curiosity.

"To see my boss, and to tell him that I have nothing on you. No story, no nothing. He's not going to be happy."

I remember Nina's words. Even if she's a preppy Princess, I guess she has a job to do. "Why don't you call me when you're done?" I ask, surprising myself.

"For what?"

"We can talk later," I offer.

Her face perks up. "What's your number?" She pulls out her phone. I tell her, and she taps it in and then I hear my cell phone go off. "Oh," she says in a tone that indicates surprise. "It's the right number."

"Did you think I'd give you the wrong number?" I ask her, pulling out my phone to check.

"Right now, I wouldn't put anything past you."

She really doesn't trust me, and this makes me smile. It's not that I like being such a pain in the butt, but when it comes to girls like Harper, it's more fun. "Maybe I'll surprise you and give you a call in a couple of hours," I tell her.

"I'll wait and see."

I grin as I walk away. She doesn't trust me at all.

CHAPTER NINE

HARPER

"I can't get inside his head."

"I'm not asking you to have sex with him," Merv shoots back. I don't like the way he throws that into the conversation. The 'Perv' tag is justified, and I cross my legs and clasp my hands together on my lap.

"He's closed off. Doesn't want to talk much."

"You're supposed to be a journalist. It's your job to get him to talk."

Merv's angry face stares back at me, and I'm at a loss for what to say. I'd been dreading this meeting all day, and my queasy stomach is evidence of that.

"He knows the deal. His manager knows the deal."

"Maybe he's got a lot on his mind," I volunteer, not understanding why I'm taking Eli's side when I'm in this mess all because of him. "With this big fight not so far off, his only focus is on the training."

"He must eat? He must stop to grab some water, or go to

the bathroom? I'm sure you can accost him en route? Use your initiative, Harper."

I want to tell him I've followed him into the locker room and it still didn't turn out well, but I decide to keep that to myself.

I feel like suggesting that maybe I switch with Gerry. That maybe he comes over to the boxing gym and interviews Eli. I have a feeling that Eli would probably be nicer and more receptive to Gerry than he is to me.

"I have background details on him and I've been talking to Ernesto."

"Who the hell is Ernesto?"

"He's a handyman."

Merv looks pained. "Are you cut out for this?"

I sit taller, snapping to attention at those doubting words. "Yes," I reply indignantly. "It's only been a few weeks, Merv. It was always going to take time for me to get settled in and win his trust." He has no idea how much I'm flailing.

"Do you think you can go any faster?" His tone is nothing short of patronizing.

"I'm working on it."

"Yeah, well, hurry the hell up. We don't often do articles like this one, and you're lucky that Gerry put you forward to run with this when he could have done a better job in one-tenth of the time. Sometimes that guy is too altruistic for his own good."

I leave his office in a bad mood, even worse than the one I came in with. I return to my desk and decide to go through a few things now that I'm here.

My cell phone vibrates. I'd set it to silent mode when I went into the meeting with Merv.

I glance at the incoming call. It's Eli.

"I'm done," he announces. I blink and it takes me a moment to make sense of what he means. I'm also probably in a little shock at the idea that he actually called me.

"What do you mean?" I ask, confused.

"I can meet. If you want to continue with the interview."

I place a hand on my stomach because it still feels weird. Surely, Eli's voice can't make me feel this unsettled? "Do you know The Weston?" It's a nice hotel and not far from town. It will be better for us to meet there.

"Yeah."

"I'll meet you in there for drinks. Give me twenty minutes."

"Okay." He hangs up and I sigh loudly. I'm suddenly not ready for the meeting, and I'm not feeling so good, but Eli's given me an in, and I'd be silly not to take it.

I quickly finish off the work I was in the middle of, then freshen my makeup and jump into a cab, even though the hotel isn't too far away.

By the time the cab pulls up outside the hotel, I see Eli standing outside, as if he's a doorman, minus the uniform.

"What are you doing out here?" I ask as I walk towards him. "You should have gone inside."

He shakes his head in disgust, it looks like. "This fancy place? No thanks."

I'm about to ask him what he's talking about, but then I take a mental step back and understand. It hadn't even occurred to me that he might feel out of place here, when he clearly had no reason to.

"We can go someplace else, if you prefer," I offer. A woman and her teenage boy walk past and I see them faltering, then they stop, and the woman prods the boy with her elbow. Eli notices them.

"He's too shy to ask," the mother says, and before the boy can say another word, Eli smiles at him. "You can't be shy, man," he coaxes. "Ask me. Don't ask, don't get in this world."

The boy hesitates. His mother whispers something to him.

"How are you ever going to ask a girl out?" Eli says to the boy who shrugs in typical teenager fashion.

"Can I have your autograph?" the boy finally asks.

The mother pulls out a notebook and pen and hands it to Eli.

"What's your name?"

"Chris."

He scribbles something down. "Here you go, Chris."

"Thanks."

"How about a selfie?" Eli offers.

"Sure!"

The kids pulls out his phone, and Eli faces the cell phone, then puts his arm around the kid. "This okay with you?"

The boy nods, looking as if it absolutely is more than okay. "Thanks," he says, and they both walk away.

Having never seen this side to Eli, I am impressed. "That was nice of you."

"I have my moments," he replies.

"You surprised me."

We're still hovering outside the main doors of The Weston. "Why didn't you wait for me inside? Was it because you'd get bothered by people?"

"It's because I hate these types of places. All money and no soul." He pulls the door open for me, but I still don't walk through.

"We can go someplace else. You choose," I tell him. "Show me where you hang out."

"Is this where you hang out?" he asks, still holding the door open.

"Sometimes. We can go somewhere else," I repeat, wanting to put him at ease.

A young and fashionably dressed couple walk through, and the woman does a double take when she sees Eli.

"Do you want the interview or not?" Clearly I do, so I walk through and he follows.

I choose a table all the way towards the end of the bar, in a corner where I feel there will be more privacy.

We both sit down and stare at one another. I haven't prepared for this, and the meeting with Merv has deflated my mood. Seeing Eli has lifted it somewhat, but I'm in for a tough time, and I'm not up to it.

"Ask away," he says, sitting back effortlessly. He eyes me like a lion.

"Let's continue from where we were," I say.

"We didn't get very far at all, from what I remember."

"Then maybe you can make it up to me," I shoot back. It wasn't meant to be laced with any intent, but I find my voice shaking as I speak. His dark eyes staring back at me might have something to do with the wobble in my voice. "What made you get into boxing?" I've asked him this question a few times now, and I've yet to get a decent answer.

"Survival instincts."

I turn on my voice recorder, then see the look of trepidation in his eyes. "What are you doing?"

"It's so that I don't miss anything."

He looks as if he doesn't trust me, as if a switch flicked on in his brain. "I can put it away if you want."

He suddenly looks so uncomfortable, that I switch it off. "We can do without," I say.

He slumps back in his seat, his brow smooth.

"Survival instincts?" I repeat, hoping he will start talking. But he presses his lips together, as if this is hard for him. I wonder why he had a change of attitude earlier, why he came up to me in the gym earlier today and said I could ask him anything.

"I used to get into a lot of fights," he starts to say, but a server interrupts to take our drink orders.

"What are you having?" I ask Eli.

"Water."

I angle my head. Friday night in the trendy bar of a chic hotel, and he's having water. "I'll get this," I offer, in case that helps.

"It's still water," he says.

I turn to the server. "I'll have a glass of dry white wine, and a bottle of still water, please."

I hear him chortle. "What's so funny?" I ask.

"I meant it's *still* water, my choice. I wasn't going to change it just because you're picking up the tab."

I laugh. "Did you want sparkling?"

"No, it's still still."

We both smile at the infantile joke. It seems to have pierced the tension in the air. "Why did you decide to talk to me?" I'm curious to know what made him change his mind.

"My sister said I should give you a chance."

"Your sister?"

"At the diner the other day when you were with that ginger-haired guy."

"Nina?"

He nods.

He cares what his sister thinks. I make a mental note of this. "Is she older or younger?"

"Older, by one year. She's always looked out for me."

He's volunteering information. "What about your parents?" I have to tread carefully here because I'm well aware that this is his Achilles heel.

"Didn't really have much parental support."

"No?"

"No."

I want to pry deeper, and I remind myself that he said I could ask anything, that he was the one who suggested we talk, but I back off, for some reason I don't fully understand.

"Apparently, my parents had a volatile relationship, even before we were born, and it got worse once we came along. My dad was always disappearing for long periods of time, then showing up unexpectedly. As for my mom, well, let's just say she didn't cope so well."

"What do you mean—?"

But before he can answer, the server arrives with our drinks and we turn silent again.

"Are you sure you don't want anything to drink?" I ask, as I lift my glass. For me on a Friday night, a glass of wine signifies the end of the week.

"I'm training."

"That you are. So, it means you can only drink water?"

"It means no alcohol. I need to be at the top of my game."

"And you certainly are that." When he doesn't say anything, I rattle off his impressive wins. "That's a pretty good record. Unbeaten in twenty-seven fights, one loss, one draw."

"Thanks." He unscrews his bottle top and pours water

into his glass. I sense that if we weren't in this place, he'd drink it straight from the bottle.

"Your career's been on an upward trajectory."

"Comes with training, a shit ton of hard work, and never giving up."

"Did your mom teach you that?" I ask, eager to probe into that part of his life.

He laughs, but it's not a happy laugh. "No, she didn't, but she might have been the reason I learned how to survive —*we* learned how to survive—from an early age."

"Why's that?"

"Our aunt told us that when Nina was four and I was three, my mom left us alone for the entire weekend. It was a time when our dad had gone AWOL again for months. We managed to survive on ketchup, raw eggs, and mayonnaise which we squeezed out from the bottles. There wasn't much food around. When the police broke down the door, because the neighbors could hear us crying, they said I was trying to drink the water from the toilet bowl, and Nina was asleep on the kitchen floor. I remember trying to scoop water out of the toilet."

The shock of his words hits me hard and I almost drop the glass in my hand,

"Social services would have taken us then had my aunt not stepped in." He's speaking so calmly, so matter-of-factly about it, as if he's telling me about the time he went to the beach, only I don't think Eli has those types of childhood memories.

"I'm so sorry," I put the glass down untouched. Images flash through my head of Eli as a toddler. My heart is beating, and I fall into his story as deeply as if it were my own. My childhood was a blissfully happy one, and I can't get to grips with the fact that this man had the type of life I can't even begin to imagine.

"Why are you sorry?" he asks, his voice hard, like a warning. "You don't know me."

"I... I feel sorry for you." It slips out before I can take it back.

"I don't want you to feel sorry for me."

"I don't mean it like that."

"Then don't say stuff like that because I don't want your pity."

"I'm not offering you my pity, and I'm sorry if it comes across like that." No wonder he wears that stay-the-hell-away-from-me body suit. His looks, his reputation, his demeanor; they all say 'keep away'.

Now I understand what makes him ruthless and makes him step into a ring and beat the life out of his opponent.

I can't help it though. And once again, my reaction to this man surprises me. I have so many images of him in my head, of him in the ring, ruthlessly attacking his opponent, of him in the locker room, of his tattoos with the sweat trickling down his steel-hard muscles. And now I have images of Eli trying to drink water out of a toilet.

"And then what happened?" I ask, trying to remain focused, trying not to let my feelings get in the way.

"My aunt took us in."

An aunt is a good second choice, I tell myself. She can never replace a mother, because nothing can, but this news fills me with some relief. "That must have been something?"

He nods again. The voice recorder wouldn't have helped because this man's expressions say more than his words. "Boxing is my salvation."

"Your salvation?" Boxing is rough, ruthless, dog-eat-dog.

Salvation is the last word that comes to mind when I think of this barbaric sport.

He doesn't say anything, so I go back to questioning him about the boxing, and the training, about Lou and Ernesto. His past is off limits, and I back off for now. I'll worm my way back to that another time.

Like Merv says, I need the story.

I order another glass of wine, and he still has his bottle of water. I'm debating whether we should get something to eat, especially when the mood lightens and we talk about current events, reality TV shows and the latest movies—all safe and common ground.

I'm enjoying his company, and every once in a while my gaze drops down to his sweatshirt. I can't help it. But it happens enough that I catch myself doing it. Once or twice Eli sees me do it, and my gaze flutters to meet his.

He fills out a sweatshirt well. Not too big and bulky that he reminds me of The Hulk, yet nicely ripped that I am curious about him all the same.

"You moved up levels," I say, when he catches me ogling him a third time. I point out that I was checking his body out because I had an important journalistic point to make about his size.

"I started off at flyweight when I first started out. I was a scrawny little thing."

He looks at his watch then announces that it's getting late.

"It's not. The night has barely begun," I reply, but he reminds me that he gets up at the crack of dawn and goes for a run before hitting the gym.

His training schedule sounds like my worst nightmare.

I want to ask him to stay longer, because I've enjoyed his company. The more I sit here and stare into his eyes, and find out about him, the more I warm towards him. It's been a while since I was out with a nice-looking guy. Odd, because I've never thought of Eli as nice-looking before. I've always thought of him as dangerous, with a to-be-avoided-at-all-costs label attached to his chest.

But my impression of him has changed. Despite his smooth skin and unlined face, and those mesmerizing brown eyes, he's got an edge to him. A roughness, and a meanness. Yet tonight I've seen another side of him, and it's hard not to find myself wanting to stay here with him, when the alternative is to go home to an empty apartment. It's too late to call my friends and meet up with them, and I still don't feel so great, but this I can do; sit with Eli and try to unveil his deepest, darkest secrets. I'm sure he has them.

"I was going to ask you about Grampton House," I say, forgetting my earlier resolve not to talk about his past.

"That's a topic for another day." He takes out his wallet, but I'm not going to take any money for water. "I said I'd get this."

"You sure?" he asks.

"I'm sure."

"Maybe next time I'll show you where to go to get a proper drink."

"I'll hold you to it," I say.

"Do that."

There's no point in me staying here if he's leaving, and since I don't feel great anyway, I decide to leave as well.

CHAPTER TEN

ELI

I could stay here talking to her for a while longer, but I decide now's the time to take my leave.

Harper isn't the type of woman I usually hang around with, and this place isn't the kind of establishment I like to frequent. I'm feeling a little claustrophobic as the bar fills up, and I really can't drink any more water. I also think she's eager to get to my life story. I don't want that. I wish she'd stick to the boxing.

She hasn't asked me about my love life, yet. That's a surprise because most women tend to get to that question real quick.

But I see her checking out my arms when she thinks I don't notice, and when I catch her at it, she hides it well— but there's a tell in her eyes, like a double-blink, and then she looks away and pretends she's thinking up a new question.

She was definitely checking me out. I find myself trying

to guess how old she is; I could easily do a search on her online. She looks like the type to have multiple social media accounts just so that she can tell people what her lunch looked like and show off the cool cocktail she's drinking. It's losers like her who give a shit about stuff like that.

But I'm not about to look her up online because I'm not interested. She's not my type, and, even if she was, there's no point. No sexy times, Lou has warned me. Not until the fight is over. So I don't even go there. Not even in my head. I haven't been with a woman for months, and I can't afford to have any distraction, especially this close to the fight.

I don't usually give people a chance because I trust no one, but, surprisingly, Harper's easygoing when we get talking.

She looks disappointed when I tell her I need to leave. I can see that she's trying to hide it, and I sense that she'd like to stay here for longer. She's partial to her white wine. I'm sure this is her third, although she's only had a sip of it.

She decides to leave with me, which makes sense because I doubt any woman would want to be left on her own for other men to hit on her.

"I can hop on the train," I tell her when she offers to get a cab.

She asks me where I live, and I tell her. "I'll be fine with the train," I insist, but she's not having it.

"There's no need to, and you're not putting me out because you get off first."

"Are you hoping to get some more information out of me?" I ask.

"No, I'm not." Her tone is serious, and I wonder if she's lonely. "Don't worry about the cost," she says, as if that's the deciding factor as to whether I'll share a cab with her or not.

"I'm not."

"Then what's the problem?"

"There isn't one. I'll share a cab with you."

She flags down a cab and we get in. This time, maybe it's because she thinks we're friends, or that we might have crossed the line from strangers over to friends, but she doesn't put her handbag between us, and she's not squeezed up against the door of the cab.

Neither am I, for that matter.

We talk, not nosy questions this time. Instead she asks me what plans I have for tomorrow. I tell her my gym routine and she makes all the usual admiring noises.

I ask her what she's doing, and she tells me she's meeting her girlfriends for brunch on Saturday, and meeting her dad for lunch on Sunday.

So far, she hasn't mentioned a boyfriend. "Who's the ginger-haired dude?" I ask, curious. But she doesn't answer, and has her head out of the half open window, as if she's trying to suck in bags of air. "What's wrong?" I ask, tapping her shoulder.

"I'm going to be sick," she whispers, closing her eyes, and dry heaving.

"What?" I hiss back, then stare over at the rearview mirror. The cab driver is oblivious to the drama taking place behind him.

Harper fans her face. "Oh," she groans, low and weak. "I'm going to... I'm going to be..."

Quick as a flash, I position my body to block out the cab driver's view. I've sectioned Harper in the corner. "In here," I say, and hold my gym bag open, not even stopping to think about the stupidity of what I'm doing.

Tired green eyes stare at me, she shakes her head, then promptly throws up right inside my bag.

I look away, otherwise I will want to throw up too.

"What's going on back there?" the cab driver asks. I glance over my shoulder.

"Her contact lens fell out. She's trying to put it back in."

He looks suitably suspicious, and trains his eyes on the road again. When I turn back around to face her, Harper throws up a second time. The stench hits my nostrils and I lean over to open the window fully. She wipes her mouth with the back of her hand, and slumps back against the seat again.

"Any more?" I ask quietly.

She looks deeply embarrassed and says nothing. I close the bag, wincing as the stench fills the air. I open the window some more.

I've been in gyms that smell worse than this, but knowing my gym bag is full of vomit makes me want to retch.

I gingerly place the bag on the floor of the car and tell the cab driver to bypass my place and go straight to Harper's. He nods his agreement.

I don't think Harper even hears, because she's staring out. She looks smaller, as if she's trying to sink back and disappear into the seat. I understand her feeling of humiliation and I want to tell her not to worry about it, but the cab is starting to smell and I'm worried the cab driver is going to say something. Strangely, he doesn't seem to have noticed.

We sit in silence for a while, until Harper pipes up. "Weren't you supposed to get off at your place?"

"We're going to yours."

"Why?"

"Why do you think?" I reply, lowering my voice.

She looks out of the window again, and we travel in silence.

The cab soon pulls up outside an upscale apartment building.

Holy shit.

She lives here?

She must get paid some serious shit ton of money. Or could this be because of Daddy's fund?

She's quick on the draw and has her wallet out, then slips the driver some notes and tells him to keep the change.

We get out of the cab, and I follow her, holding the gym bag in front of me at arm's length.

"You didn't have to see me home," she says.

I'm a gentleman, despite what she may think. Also, I'd like to think that if this ever happened to my sister, that the person with her would have the decency to make sure she got home okay. "Someone's got to clean up after you, if you throw up again." I'm joking, but it's the only way I know to shut her up.

We get in the elevator and silently ascend. Harper looks pale, and she seems embarrassed because she doesn't look me in the eye. I want to tell her not to worry, that it's okay if she got drunk and her stomach couldn't handle it, but I figure she doesn't want to talk about it.

When the elevator stops, I follow her along a hallway to her apartment. She opens the door, excuses herself and rushes off.

I walk in and my eyes nearly bounce out of their sockets. This place looks bigger than mine by a factor of at least four.

This princess really does live in another world.

CHAPTER ELEVEN

HARPER

I've never been more embarrassed in my life. As soon as we get to my apartment, I rush away, desperate to clean myself up. I stink, and look gross. Worse, Eli saw me throw up. And even worse than that, I threw up in his bag. Twice.

I will *never* live this down. Eli thinks I'm too drunk and that I can't be trusted to get home safely. He won't believe that I've had an upset stomach. I blame the sandwich I bought from the deli.

I stare in shock at the mirror, at my blotchy face. He can't have remained unscathed. I'm certain he has splashes of my vomit over his clothing.

The thought makes me cringe all over again. I splash cold water on my face, and wish I could wash away the last few hours.

Eli's outside, waiting in my apartment, and while I feel better now, and the queasiness has gone, I am still sick to my stomach about how the evening has ended. He will judge me, and that bothers me. He thinks I'm a lightweight who can't hold her alcohol. That's not it at all.

So, I quickly freshen up and rush into my room to change my top. By the time I get back to my living room, Eli's walking around, checking out my paintings and the view from the window. It is a lovely view, and this is a beautiful apartment. I wonder what thoughts are racing through his mind.

He turns around when he hears my footsteps.

"I should go," he says, his eyes noting that I've changed my top.

"Sorry about that," I say. I'm not entirely sure what 'that' refers to. I half point to his clothes, but I mean the entire evening. "I had an upset stomach, and I shouldn't have had any alcohol."

He nods, and it infuriates me, because when he doesn't say anything, I take it as a sign that he doesn't believe me. "I'm sorry about your clothes, too. Did you want to change out of that?" I ask, pointing to his shirt. Not that I'll have anything big enough for him to fit into.

He nods again. "I'll be fine. I'm used to the smell now."

If that's supposed to make me feel better, it doesn't. I don't have the heart to say I'm worried I might have splashed him with my retching.

He walks up to take the bag which he'd left lying by the door.

"I'll take care of that," I say, rushing towards it.

"Hey, it's fine. I'll take care of it. It's got my things inside."

"Please," I beg. "This is beyond embarrassing for me. I can't have you going home and cleaning this mess up."

"I'm going to throw it away."

"Then leave it here," I say, partly because I don't believe him. I sense he's crazy enough, and maybe broke enough to wash it all out, and I don't want him washing my vomit away.

"Don't worry about it," he insists.

"This is really, *really* humiliating for me, Eli. Let me at least deal with this."

He shrugs and walks towards the door. "If you insist. Take care," he says, and doesn't even glance over his shoulder as he walks out of the door.

I'm more than embarrassed, and it feels as if he's got the upper hand right now.

I stare at the bag and I don't have the stomach to go through it now. But then I worry that he might have something valuable in there, like his boxing gloves, or phone and wallet. I wrap a scarf around my mouth and put on my cleaning gloves, and gingerly go through his bag as much as I can, without touching anything inside. There's nothing but gym clothes. There definitely are no boxing gloves.

Tomorrow I'll buy him a new bag and clothes.

———

I canceled brunch with my friends yesterday because I wasn't in the mood to socialize. I am still humiliated by the fact that I threw up in front of Eli, in his bag, in a cab. All three of these things are bad enough, taken individually, but the fact that they all happened in one car ride, with the hot guy who loathes me, makes things a million times worse. So, yeah, I wasn't in the mood to meet with my friends.

Instead I went shopping and managed to buy a

replacement bag and gym clothes for Eli. I did the best I could, and hope he'll like them.

The lunch with my father still goes ahead the next day. My father tries to make a point to meet up with me at least once a month. It could because he feels guilty or it could be that 'Meet Harper' is an item to cross off his to-do list.

"Is Mervyn taking care of you?" he asks as he's cutting into his steak.

"He's my boss, Dad, not my babysitter." I don't like that he's on a first-name basis with my boss. It makes me nervous that he might be keeping an eye on Merv and making sure I get interesting work. I'm not sure Merv would be amenable to such bribes, or persuasion, but I hate the thought of it nonetheless.

I hate that all my father has to do is pull strings and I get a job that many would kill for. I want to think that I got it on my own merit, but I really don't know.

No wonder Merv looks at me like he wants to gouge my eyes out every time.

I stab an olive and lift the fork to my mouth. "If you're asking how my job's going, it's going great."

"It's only a phase, Harper," he tells me, smugly. "You don't need to work."

"Mom works," I say with admiration. She's a law professor at a college in Boston. I'm immensely proud of her, and I don't understand how she and my father ever got together. They split up when I was in high school, and I lived with my mom and spent the holidays with my dad up until I went to college. During that time, he got married and divorced again, and is now dating a woman who's twenty years younger than him.

She could be my older sister, and that thought makes

me sick. Thank goodness I'm an only child. The new girlfriend also has a lot of fake parts, despite being so young; boob and butt implants, fillers and expensive veneers.

I avoid going to their house for dinner. His girlfriend hates me and I hate her. My dad is our common ground, and therefore, meeting outside of the house is how we see one another without too much drama

But it means I have to listen to his 'advice' on these occasions. My father constantly tells me that I don't have to do this if I don't want to—he's talking about me working. And he often reminds me that I have a trust fund to fall back on if things get too difficult.

I don't want a helping hand. I don't want him to pave the way for me. It might sound ungrateful, me talking like this, but after learning about Eli and his childhood, I appreciate how lucky I am. I completely understand that I sound like a spoiled brat as we sit here, having a ridiculously overpriced lunch. My dad ordered a bottle of wine that cost two hundred dollars.

It's insane.

I don't want that type of life.

I want to earn it my way.

Being a rich man's daughter isn't as easy as most people like to think, and I probably deserve a slap for saying this, but it's the truth. I don't fully approve of my father's lifestyle, and getting a job and wanting to earn my living is my way of telling him that.

I did try to get a job by myself, but after a month of looking and not finding anything suitable, my father stepped in and put in a word for me with Merv. I understand that this is privilege, but next time I will try to do it on my own. This was just to help me get my foot in the door.

"What have they got you investigating this time?" my father asks.

"It's not an investigation. I'm doing an article about a boxer."

"Ugh." My father's face crinkles with disgust "Why did he give you that? Maybe I should have a word with Mervyn and see if he can't have you doing something more glamorous."

"Stop it, Dad," I say harshly.

"I don't see why you can't cover the Oscars, or the Golden Globes."

"Dad!" I cry out in exasperation. He has no idea how any of this works. "I'm a junior journalist. And I'm working for a *newspaper*, not a glossy magazine, and I don't host a show on TV."

"I could speak to someone about that."

I put down my cutlery with as much control as I can muster. He's not even joking. That's the sad part about all of this. "Please don't interfere, Dad. I'm at the bottom of the ladder and I have to climb my way to the top."

"You're a Lindstrom," he says, giving me a stern look as he raises his expensive wine to his lips. "We are *never* at the bottom of anything. And don't you forget that." He circles his glass in the air, vaguely gesturing at me. "This is a phase," he tells me, in his smug, I-know-better-than-you tone.

"Please don't meddle," I plead. I hate to think what Merv would make of this.

"But, still, a boxer?" he asks, visibly disgusted. "What do you even know about boxing?"

"I'm learning about it," I reply. "There's a big fight happening soon, for the title of the world heavyweight champion. Trent Garrison is the current champion," I say, trying to read my father's face for traces of recognition. I see none. "He's fighting some unknown guy who nobody thinks has a chance." I look at my father with a smile. "I'm with the unknown at his gym, charting his progress. He's a Chicago guy, hence the local interest."

"What's his name?"

"Elias Cardoza."

My father's face remains impassive. He barely blinks. "Never heard of him," And then, to drive the knife home, he adds, "He's probably some low-life scum. You know what these people are like."

"What people?" I ask.

"The ones who end up boxing." He laughs because I look so angry. "They're obviously desperate down-and-outs, they have to be, if the only way to make a living is by getting beaten up."

I don't like the way he's talking. Even though Eli has been nasty to me in the past, I still don't like it. My father sees the world through a different filter than most, seeing only the champagne, the yachts, and the good life.

I think of Nina and how she works at the diner doing such long shifts, and how she attends night school a couple of times a week. Eli told me this, on a rare day when he was feeling especially giving. Most people live like this, I discover, now that I'm here, deep in the trenches, seeking out stories from the average person in the street.

Except that Eli is no average person.

Everyone else thinks he is, but being around him, watching him fight and train, I see a tenacity I've never seen before.

A killer instinct.

These things are alien to me—boxing and beating, and

fighting—but Eli does this for a living, and he's not afraid to hit and get hit.

I imagine that my father does stuff like this, too, only he probably does it with dirty money, and insider dealings and other seemingly innocuous trades.

Eli and my father are different sides of the same coin.

CHAPTER TWELVE

ELI

I tell Nina about the evening with Harper and her throwing up.

"You went on a date?" she asks.

"Not a date," I clarify quickly. "I took your advice. You said to be nice to her, so I was."

"How nice?" Nina asks, her eyes glinting with mischief.

I snort, because I know what she's implying, and even though my evening with Harper wasn't as awkward as it could have been, there was definitely no attraction there. "She's not my type."

"She's pretty."

"Pretty uptight," I reply, even though this isn't true. "She's not the kind of girl I go for." Everything about her is upscale. I'm from someplace she would never recognize. She's groomed. I'm rough. She's rich, I am not.

"Why can't you be friendly?" Nina sounds as if she feels sorry for her. "Is she okay?"

"She was fine when I left."

"What about now? Did you call to check?"

"I hardly know her."

Nina looks at me in disbelief. "She's been at your gym for weeks, you went out with her on Friday, she's doing a great write-up on you—"

"How do you know it's going to be great?"

"It's her job. You're Chicago's New—"

"Don't," I say. I hate labels, and that bullshit label is one that doesn't sit well with me. This city holds a lot of bad memories for me, and if I had money, and if I'd been in a position to, I would have turned my back on it and left.

I would never have missed it.

But Nina seems more settled. Each time I talked about leaving here, she didn't like it, and life had other plans for me.

Lou found me and said he saw I had raw talent. I owe him my life. He saved me. Nobody else looked at me and saw that. That's why the moment I was put forward for the Garrison fight, and was picked, it was not only unreal, and surreal, it was my moment.

I want to make Lou proud.

I go on to tell Nina about Harper throwing up in the cab and how I saw her back to her apartment.

"That must have been so embarrassing for her." I've had dinner at Nina's place and I'm cleaning up for her. It's only fair seeing that she cooked. I don't have time to cook, so I eat either at Frankie's Kitchen, or at Nina's place most times.

"It was. She couldn't stop apologizing." I would be the same way if I were in her shoes, but I'd never get that drunk, though to be fair, she did say it was something she'd eaten. I'm inclined to believe her even though I don't know her too well, but my initial impressions about her have started to come apart. Friday evening wasn't so bad, even though I was vomited on. I caught splashes of it on my sweatshirt, but I didn't want to own up to it because it would only heighten Harper's shame.

I had made assumptions about Harper, and some of them were definitely true. Walking into her apartment confirmed some of them, but she was easy to talk to. She tried to get information out of me, and when I pushed back, she didn't persist. She backed off, and I liked that. She seems to give me my space.

I'd expected her to be one of those pushy in-your-face journalists, but she's not. There's a kindness about her, a touch of the humane, and I'm a sucker for people who have that. I don't trust many people, and I don't know many people who exhibit that trait, but Harper shows signs of it and it makes me mistrust her a little less.

"You should have seen her apartment," I tell Nina. I'm washing the dishes, and she's sitting at the table looking through a magazine.

"Yeah?" Nina seems distracted, as if she's reading something interesting. So I let her read in peace.

Lakeview is a beautiful part of the city. When I win this fight, I'll move into one of the more expensive parts of town. Because then I'll feel that I've moved up, clawed my way out of the gutter.

HARPER

It's Monday morning and I've had the weekend to get over the episode from Friday night. I head towards the gym and I don't know how I will face Eli today. My hesitation makes me head for the diner instead. I can grab a cup of coffee to steady my nerves. It won't matter if I'm slightly later than usual to get to the gym.

The first person I see as I push through the doors is Eli's sister. I wasn't expecting that, and I'm silently surprised. She's behind the counter, serving another customer, so I walk over and get a seat by the window. It's early morning, and the place isn't that busy. Frankie's Kitchen fills up more around lunchtime.

I put my bag on the seat next to me along with the new bag I bought for Eli. It's got his new gym clothes inside.

I can't decide if I'm hungry, or if I'm putting off going into the gym, but I've barely had time to check out the menu when Nina comes up to me.

"Good morning!" she says. "It's Harper, isn't it?" Her greeting is like a ray of sunshine, and I momentarily forget my worry about seeing her brother.

"Yes. Hi." I didn't think she and Eli looked too alike before, but now that I'm seeing her for the second time and because I know she's Eli's sister, I can see a definite similarity. They both have the same brown eyes, and the same lips.

We make small talk about it being the first day back after the weekend. She tells me she worked two shifts over the weekend.

"Don't you get any time off?"

"I get a day during the week. But I prefer to work weekends," she leans towards me and whispers. "The tips are better."

I stare back and try to wonder what a wreck I'd be if I had to work my weekends. I take work home sometimes to proofread or edit, but it's nothing compared to waitressing.

"How are you feeling? Eli said you were sick."

I feel as if I've been punched in the stomach, because I'm surprised that he mentioned that fact to his sister. He has no loyalty to me, and therefore has no need to keep it a secret.

"I had something dodgy to eat from the deli, I'm sure of it. Smolensky's," I say, when she frowns.

She looks relieved now. "I was worried it might have been something you ate here."

"I haven't gotten sick after eating here," I tell her. We smile. She's nice, and easy to talk to, and she's so different than Eli. Come to think of it, Eli on Friday was a different Eli than the one I'd known prior to that evening. He's slowly growing on me.

"What can I get you?"

"Just a coffee, please. A filter coffee, no sugar."

I want to ask her more questions, but she nods and rushes back towards the kitchen before I can say anything.

A short while later, she comes over with an empty cup and a small jug of milk, and pours me a cup of coffee.

I decide to take my chances, seeing that I haven't been successful with Eli so far. "We were talking," I say, adding milk to my cup, "and Eli mentioned that you were both at Grampton House."

"He spoke about that?"

"Among other things. I was shocked to hear about you two being left home alone at such a young age."

Nina looks startled for a few seconds, and then it passes. "It was a long time ago."

"You were probably too young to remember being taken into foster care?"

She folds her arms. "Our aunt, my mom's sister, took care of us while my mother tried to get her life back together, and when that failed, we ended up living with her, and when that failed, we went into foster care." She scratches her ear. "Did Eli tell you all this, or did you read up about it?"

"He told me," I reply, and part of that statement is true. This is nothing new, it's information I have on him online, and he did tell me about the time their mother left them at home for the entire weekend.

I'm not making any of it up, yet I feel slimy asking her these things. I have no choice, I tell myself, in an effort to make myself feel better. Eli said I could ask him anything, but when I've pressed him for information, he's backed off. I can't go into another meeting with Merv and not have something more than last time.

"If your aunt took care of you, why were you taken away?"

"She couldn't cope, and her boyfriend at that time didn't like Eli. He used to beat him."

I blink in shock. "Beat him?" This is news to me, and it gets filed along with the images I have of Eli and Nina as toddlers being left home alone for two days.

Nina continues before I can tell her that I didn't know this.

"He would take out his belt and whip Elias, usually for no reason. Our parents came from dysfunctional families. Grampton House didn't seem like such a bad place."

She looks up as more people file into the diner, then she tells me to have a good day, and leaves.

My heart is in splinters at the news she has shared. I feel sorry for Eli now, and for the little boy that used to be Eli then. I feel sorry for both him and his sister.

I don't want to finish the coffee. My craving for it has

vanished. There's only one place to go now, back to the gym, but I'm still not ready to face Eli, and for different reasons this time.

vanished. There's only one place to go now, back to the gym, but I'm still not ready to face Eli, and for different reasons this time.

CHAPTER THIRTEEN

ELI

Harper's late today. She's usually here by now, pretending not to watch me when I'm training.

I glance at her desk one more time, and this time my sparring partner strikes a blow to my chest so hard it knocks me back.

"Not so hard, Jake," Lou roars. "You're not supposed to injure him before the fight," and to me, "Where's your head, Eli?"

I hit back, and land a ferocious uppercut with more force than I'd intended. It slams under Jake's chin. He staggers back, then falls against the ropes. His eyes are full of anger.

I'm not supposed to hit hard, but that came as a reaction. I hold my hand up in an apologetic gesture.

"Take a break from this, and go for a run later," Lou orders.

I nod in response. I'm hot and sweaty, and feel like I've

gone ten rounds in the ring. I need a shower. Then Harper walks in. She glances at me, then looks away.

I get out of the ring, then take off my gloves and headgear; it gives me something to focus on so that I look busy.

But she's coming towards me, and she's carrying a bag that doesn't look like mine.

"Hi," she says, in a voice that is softer and more familiar. I can see why she would make this mistake. "This is for you."

I eye the bag with suspicion. "That's not my bag."

"It's new. I hope you like it."

"But that was my lucky bag," I say, trying to look serious. "It's how I won fights." Her face crinkles and her mouth falls open. I notice she's wearing lipstick this morning. "Oh, shit." Now she looks worried. Like, *really* worried.

I can't keep up the pretense. "I'm kidding with you. It wasn't a lucky bag, but the gloves were. They're in there, right? Tell me you didn't throw them away."

She narrows her eyes. "You did not have any gloves in there. You didn't. I checked."

"You checked?" I'm surprised. I can't imagine Princess going through the bag. "I don't believe you."

"I checked. No gloves. Nothing but your gym clothes."

I've been caught out and as we stand there, half-grinning, half-wary of one another, the tension between us feels lighter. Her throwing up on me that evening changed our dynamics in some way.

She holds the bag up in front of me obviously eager for me to take it. "I couldn't bring myself to clean the other one, so I got you a new one."

"You couldn't clean *your* own vomit?" I peer at the bag

and I'm not sure I like it. It looks expensive, and I bet it was. Some people like to flaunt their money.

"I'm sorry I ruined your other one."

I take the bag and murmur a 'thanks' then open it up and look inside. She's replaced the clothing, it looks like. I now have a new pair of boxing shorts, boxer briefs, and a gym shirt. I hold up the boxing shorts and briefs. "I hope you got the extra-large size," I say.

As expected, she blushes and her cheeks tinge the color of her pale lipstick. Her eyes turn dark just like that. For a reason I can't explain, her reaction shoots through me, and something stirs inside me. We both stare at one another, but she's the first to look away. "I'm pretty sure I got the right size." And then she walks away quickly, just as I was getting ready to give her a few moments of my time.

By the time I come back from my six-mile run, I see Harper in Lou's office. I'm curious to know what type of piece she's doing on me, and why she's here for so long. Maybe I'll ask her next time we get a moment to talk.

But after my shower, I'm starving and I need protein, so I go to the diner.

Nina brings my lunch and then sits down across the table and has her lunch too. "I saw Harper earlier," she tells me.

My head lifts up. "When?"

"This morning."

"Yeah?" I say, wondering why Harper didn't mention it when she gave me the new bag. At least I now know why she was late to the gym.

"She was asking about Grampton House. Did you talk about it?" She has that sad look on her face again.

"I didn't say anything." Nina and I have a deal. It's unspoken. We don't talk about that place much. It was a holding place for us, when family gave up on us. For me it had its darker moments, but Nina doesn't know that. We don't have good memories of when we were young, and Grampton House is a symbol of our abandonment. I hate that Harper stirred up these murky memories when she needs to mind her own business and butt out of mine.

"Really? She said you mentioned it," Nina insists.

"*She* mentioned it, more than once in fact. I never gave her a proper answer."

Nina puts down her fork. "That's strange, because she acted as if you'd told her things."

"Told her what?"

"Like when mom left us home alone, when child services took us away."

I can barely eat, my stomach is empty, and I need this plate of protein, but my appetite has gone.

I don't know how I get through the next half hour not flipping my shit, but all I can think about is going to the gym and having it out with the princess. Who the hell does she think she is, lying to my sister and snooping around? There are things she shouldn't be sticking her fucking nose in.

CHAPTER FOURTEEN

HARPER

I've been talking to Lou quite a bit. "Is it normal for you to be his trainer and manager?" I ask him, wondering if there might be a conflict of interest at some point.

"It's not a problem for Elias, and I don't see why it should be a problem for you."

"It's not a problem for me," I tell him, noting the defensive tone in his voice. "I'm after a story. It's why I'm here."

"Elias is the story," he says, pointing his finger at me. "That kid is going places, and you," he points again, "I hope you'll give him the write-up he deserves."

"I'm working on it. Lucky you found him when you did." I've read up some more about Eli's start in boxing, and how he joined an underground fight club. Some of the injuries sustained by the fighters make for horrific reading.

"He was young then, doing what he had to do. This kid didn't get where he is today from learning it all in a gym. He came from the streets, and I don't care if he was fighting in those illegal fight clubs. I'm glad I found him when I did, else God knows what might have happened to him. I found him, saw his talent and convinced him to come and train in my gym. But his lethal punches, that's not something you learn; hitting the way he does, as if he wants to kill someone, that comes from a place deep inside him."

"He hits hard," I comment, remembering something I read about him from some old newspapers.

Lou chuckles. "That kid came out of his mother's womb fighting. It's going to be a good fight," he says. "That kid has a meanness to him that even Dwayne Banks didn't have."

When I frown, Lou reminds me. "He was the middleweight champion about twenty years ago. Dwayne did it, and I know Eli can. He's young, and virile, and that body... the women go crazy for him. I wouldn't be surprised if as many women as men watch the fight. Eli's easy on the eye."

That annoys me, for some reason. He is easy on the eye, and he probably has a huge legion of female followers.

Lou clears his throat. "We're going away soon; me, Eli and the boys, for about eight to ten days. You'll be finished by then, I assume?"

"Going where?"

Lou looks uncomfortable. "To... a... a training facility in Wisconsin. It's Dwayne Banks' place, except he's not going to be there. He's agreed to let us have it to do some pre-fight training. It will be good for Eli to get out of this place. The kid's been stuck in here too long."

"I should be finished with my assignment by then."

I barely register the sharp knock at the door before it opens and Eli walks in. "I need to speak to you," he says, giving me a look that freezes my blood. Then he storms off.

"What have you done to him now?" Lou asks.

"I only have to breathe and that does it," I mutter as I rise. The familiar throbbing in my chest amplifies. "I'd better go see him before he breaks a wall down."

I catch sight of Eli barreling through the locker room door. There's no question of whether I ought to go in there or not, because I can tell from his body language, and his tone just now that he's about to kill someone. And that someone is me.

"What is the—" I begin to ask, as I turn to face him, but his fingers encircle my wrists and he pushes me up against the wall. I try to figure out why my head didn't hit the wall as hard, given that he pushed me so hard against the hard stone wall. "What the fuck do you think you're doing sneaking around behind my back and asking my sister all sorts of questions?"

My heart is thundering, and his grip is tight. Not so tight that he's hurting me, but tight as in the way he's pinned me against the wall.

"I passed by this morning," I pant out, "I had a coffee. We got talking."

His eyes are cold, and he stares back at me as if he'd rather spit at me. "You were asking questions."

"Since when was that a sin?"

"You never said a word about it."

"I forgot."

"You're going behind my back and upsetting my sister."

Now I'm surprised. "I upset her?" This is news to me. I try to straighten up, but's it hard to do that since he's in my face. His body, hard as steel, isn't pressed against me, yet I feel the heat that comes off it. He's not touching me, except for the grip he has on my wrists, but I'm breathless almost, and I have no reason to be. Then I realize it's not from fear, it's from something else.

"Yes, you *fucking* upset her."

Something sizzles in the empty two-inch gap between us. His breath is warm, and sweet, and his scent, and the aura he gives off, has nothing to do with expensive cologne or body spray. It's natural, something altogether wild and raw; a supercharged concoction of sexiness and danger, if it's possible to bottle these things up.

I should be afraid, but I'm more turned on than anything else. "She didn't look upset to me."

"How would you know? You don't know Nina, just like you don't know me."

This wounds me more than his grip on me.

"I didn't mean to upset her, and if I did, I'm sorry."

"You were being sneaky. You lied. I thought you were different than the other nosy journalists."

"I'll apologize to Nina. I honestly didn't mean to upset her." I'm confused now. I had no idea that I had upset her. As it was, I didn't get much from her, and Eli's reaction tells me there is more.

And then he leans against me, and for a moment his eyes turn dark. My nerves start to jangle. Eli stares at me, and the rage in his eyes disappears for a fleeting second. It's replaced by something else, not hate, but more a look of possession. He moves his face inches from mine. "Stay away, Princess. Go fuck up someone else's life."

My eyes widen in surprise. "I'm... I'm not trying to mess up anything." I don't understand what he means. I don't understand how that simple conversation with Nina could lead to this. And then an image of Eli as a toddler flashes through me. My heart softens and I want to put my arms around him.

Whatever his nightmares are made of, I want to make him feel better. I never meant to cause him more pain. "I'm sorry," I whisper, and suddenly I don't want him to let go of me. I want him to press all of his body further against mine. We barely touch, but it's enough for me to want more, and I pray that he will grind his hips into mine.

Hussy that I am, that I become, when this man is around.

And then I feel it against my belly; subtle at first that I'm not sure, but it can only be one thing. His hardness. We become aware of this at the same time, because he pulls away. Random wicked thoughts swoop through my head and I stare at his lips. I'm well aware of his fingers around my wrists. "Eli," I whisper, and lift my head towards him. "I don't know what I've done, but I'm sorry."

In answer he moves his head forward, as if he's going to kiss me. "Keep away from my sister," he warns, and then he leaves me.

I miss his touch.

I miss his fingers around my wrists.

He has his back to me, and I want to run up behind him and throw my arms around him. But it's not to hug him. I want to touch him, and feel him all over.

And that's a bad thought to have.

It's not a thought I have about people I barely know. I've thrown up on him, and so, in that respect, we are not complete strangers.

"I'm sorry," I say, because I don't want to leave. I don't even care about the story. I want to make it better for him. I want his sister to like me. He's messing with my head and he doesn't even know it.

"Get out," he growls.

I'm stunned. "Bu—"

"Now!" He's talking to me like I'm a nuisance, and it hits me then. I'm aroused. Being around him has done that to me, even though he sees me as a nuisance. This is not good.

I don't wait to be told again.

CHAPTER FIFTEEN

ELI

Jake nods in acknowledgement as he walks out of the toilet stall. He's holding his hands up. "I didn't hear a thing. You good?"

I dismiss him with a nod but say nothing. I'm not good. I *was*. But I'm not good now. I don't need that shit from my past in my head. I need to keep my head clear. I was lucky to get this fight. I might not get so lucky again, and if I've learned anything in my life, it's that you've got to take a chance when you get it.

Some of us don't have rich dads to help us when we're in trouble.

I don't know why Lou agreed to have a reporter here at all. He claims it's for the publicity, but I'd rather do without that than have her snooping around and upsetting my sister. Our past is our past and we want to keep it there.

Harper's messing things up. She's messing with my head, and making me lose my focus.

. . .

HARPER

I go back to my desk, feeling wretched. I don't know what happened just now. I don't understand what Eli's talking about. Nina didn't look upset to me, and I feel bad if she is. I'll apologize.

But Eli being mad at me like that? It's humiliating and unfair. I've never been treated like that before by anyone.

Lou comes over to me. "What's going on?"

"Eli wanted to talk to me about something. It's nothing major." I try to sound light and breezy because he looks concerned, then I flash him a smile and pretend that everything is okay. But it's not.

It's so not.

I don't even know what I feel.

In there, in the locker room with Eli pushing me against the wall—I was a mixture of surprise, and anger, and shock. But he awakened something else in me. A longing for him. Elias evokes reactions in me which take me by surprise.

Things have changed. At first I saw him as someone untamed, a fighter with a body that's hard to ignore; the type of guy who might catch my eye in the gym, but that's all. The type of guy whose pecs and deltoids might make me drool over them, even though he's not someone I would pay any more attention to.

But now my skin prickles when he's near me, and I can tell when he's around, even if he's behind me, and out of sight. I can sense his presence without seeing him.

It is attraction, and it has crept up on me. It might be

tied into the things I'm learning about his past, the things that horrify me, and fill my heart with compassion. Maybe this is what draws me to him. He's a broken man, despite the tough-as-steel exterior.

I don't understand it, but as I sit here pretending to look at my screen, at this piece I'm supposed to be writing on him, my body is still tingling from where his body touched mine.

And now I feel sorry for myself.

He told me to get out. He told me to stay away and mess up someone else's life. I don't understand. He also called me Princess, and the way he said it he made it sound like a derogatory term.

I wonder who else might have been in the locker room and would have heard that. My anger starts to build. What gives him the right to treat me like this? I was only doing my job, and I wasn't being a complete sneak.

I'll put my head down and work, but I need to talk to someone, to get this off my chest. I call Gerry, and ask him to meet me at The Weston, the same hotel where I met Eli that night I threw up on him. Gerry would never pass up the chance to get together.

A few hours later I meet him there. He's waiting for me on one of the sofas in the lounge area outside the bar. We nod at one another, and I feel ridiculously grateful to see a friendly face. I rush towards him.

"Hey," he says, staring at me as if he's assessing me. "Why the SOS?"

"What SOS?" I exclaim as I plant myself down in the comfy single-seater adjacent to him. Its softness is a salve for my tired body and emotionally bruised ego, and I allow myself to sink into it even more.

"You don't call me to meet unless you need something."

That stinging comment snaps me to attention. "That can't be true," I say out loud, while thinking over the past few times when I've called him to meet. It's never ever been about a personal matter, and it's always been work-related. Like the time I was freaking out because of a deadline I didn't think I was going to be able to meet and I feared that Merv would skin me alive, metaphorically, if I turned in the assignment late. Or the time when I was late with an article that was going to press, and Gerry helped me out.

"I'm offended," I reply, feeling a little sore at the remark.

He laughs. "Hey, I don't mind being used in this way. Tell me what's wrong?" And that's what I like about Gerry.

He's kind and gentle and always willing to help, and he often takes my side when Merv has something to say about an article I've written. He's like the gay friend most women love to have, only he's not gay, but he's safe, in that he'd never hit on anyone.

He's recently divorced. His wife left him after seven years of marriage. No children. I have a sneaky feeling that he's still in love with her and he's finding it hard to adjust to single life. That's what I gauge from the small pieces of information he's given me. I feel sorry for him because he's a good guy.

"I wanted to meet you for a drink. Can't I do that?" I ask.

"You know you can. I'm glad you called. Merv's in a mood."

I groan. "What is it now?"

He tells me about some minor headaches in the office. "I'm glad I escaped," he says, "Tell me about the boxing gym. What's the latest with your boxer?"

"He's not my boxer," I retort, glancing around at the bar. I don't really want to talk about Eli. That would put a sour mood on the evening. This sofa is so comfortable that I'm inclined to want to kick my sneakers off and stick my legs up. And yet a dry white wine is exactly the tonic I need after a day like this, and I can't be sitting on a comfy sofa having one of those.

"Shall we sit there?" I say, pointing to an empty table in the bar.

"Whatever you want."

We move over to the bar. Warm orange sconces are spaced around the walls and rich red glass domes hang along the bar area. It's cozy, and discreet, and the chatter of people in the background is a comforting hum.

"You were going to tell me about Elias," Gerry prompts.

"Was I?" I peruse the drink menu even though I already know what I want. "I can't get anything out of that guy."

"*That* guy," says Gerry. "That doesn't sound too good."

"I can't get any rapport with him."

"I'm surprised a woman like you can't get him to open up."

I frown in response, because that sounds sexist, and I don't expect that from Gerry.

"You'd probably have better luck," I reply. I really do believe he would. Eli would respond better to a guy. He's so changeable, and I don't know how to handle him. We seemed to be getting along fine the other evening, until I messed things up by throwing up, and just as I thought we had reached some sort of happy medium, I've managed to upset his sister and now I've angered him beyond belief. How am I supposed to get information when our personalities clash the way they do?

"You have to make him trust you, Harper. Boxers aren't known for being open and easygoing. They can't be because of what they do. You have to remember this guy is a nobody and he's going up against a seasoned pro. He's going to get his ass kicked in the first few rounds. It must take serious guts for Cardoza to step into a ring where the odds are stacked against him, but this is what he's going to do. He's not going to willingly offer up information to you because he couldn't care less about what you need. You have to work at it."

I consider his advice. Gerry's right, as usual. Any other journalist would know she'd pressed a hot button, that she'd touched on pain buried so deep beneath his soul that the pain was still so evident in his face. Eli's hurting and I sense there's stuff I need to delve deeper into. My ego is hurt and bruised from the way he spoke to me. It's odd that I don't mind so much the way he handled me—shameless hussy that I am—and that I'm more put out by the tone he used and the way he spoke to me.

I don't tell Gerry any of this, or of the vomiting episode. That would only make me look unprofessional in his eyes.

We order our drinks, which arrive surprisingly quickly. A lemonade for Gerry and a cocktail for me. I need something to pick me up after what happened today.

"Mery is sending me to the fight in New York," he says. I feel fine about that. I've never been to a boxing match before, and I don't watch these things on TV either, so I'm more than happy for him to go.

"You'll appreciate it," I tell him.

"Don't you want to see it? You've been shadowing this guy, don't you want to see it through?"

I make a face. "Not really." When I first started this

assignment, the fight seemed so far away but it seems to be creeping closer all the time. I hadn't even thought about watching it live. I'm not entirely sure that Merv would want me to go, especially if Gerry's going. I can run with the story up until then and leave Gerry to report on the fight.

Win or lose, Eli will be a great story.

"Think about it," he offers, "and if you want to—I personally think you should go—I'll have a word with Merv."

I make a face because I can imagine Merv's reaction to that request. "Merv already thinks I have a ticket into this job, he's not going to send me off on a trip to New York."

"We'll see what he says."

"He hates me, doesn't he?"

Gerry's lips pinch together and when he doesn't reply, I ask, "What does he hate more, that my dad helped me get this job, or that he couldn't give it to his nephew?"

"The former led to the latter."

"I wish my dad would butt out sometimes," I say. I can sense that others in the team don't exactly warm to me, and that Gerry's the only one who makes an effort with me. It sucks to be me sometimes.

"Stay for one more?" Gerry asks when I finish my cocktail. He strikes me as being lonely. But even though I feel sorry for him, I want to go home and have an early night. Plus I have notes to write up, yet I feel obligated to stay and keep him company.

"I don't want to hog your evening."

"You're not hogging me," he replies, looking happier. "It's good to have some company. I can only spend so many hours working late nights."

I smile in return.

It seems as if we've both had a bad day.

I've also decided to stay away from the gym for a few days and return to the office. Right now, putting up with Merv at the office doesn't seems as bad as facing Eli in the gym.

CHAPTER SIXTEEN

———

ELI

"E lias!" My sister's eyebrows shoot upwards, and her eyes widen. "What did you have to go and do that for?"

"She was snooping around you." I knew she would be pissed when I told her that I'd had words with Harper. I don't tell her that I might have been a little rough with her, I only told her that I had said some words. She doesn't need to know the exact details.

Though I don't know why I told her. Maybe it's because Harper hasn't been in at the gym for the past three days and I feel guilty.

"She wasn't snooping around me," Nina counters.

"That's not what you said the other day."

Nina looks confused for a moment, and I feel like a traitor. "No, I didn't. I said she'd been asking questions, that's all."

I bite my tongue. I tried to find out from Lou earlier

today, in a roundabout way, when I asked where the journalist was. He told me to focus on the boxing and quit worrying about everything else. Then I asked Ernesto, and he immediately asked me what I'd done to her. He thinks he was joking, but he has no idea how close he got to the truth.

"She'll be back."

"Back?" Nina looks horrified. "What do you mean she'll be back? I hope you didn't get her fired."

"Relax," I say. "I'm not that thoughtless. She hasn't been at the gym for a few days, that's all."

"Since you spoke to her?"

"Yeah."

"What did you say?" Nina asks.

I wince. "I might have gotten a little angry."

"Elias!" my sister cries. "That temper of yours is going to get you in trouble one of these days."

"Too late for that," I reply. My temper *is* the thing that got me in trouble; always has, probably always will. It wasn't enough that Nina and I were born to parents who should never have had children, but we were then passed onto my aunt who changed boyfriends the way most people change their wallpaper. My anger spilled out into the streets as I grew older, and school became impossible. When my aunt could no longer take care of us, we were sent to Grampton House before being passed around from foster home to foster home.

No one really wanted us, not both of us together, not *me*. I was a troubled child. But the state didn't want to separate us, so we went through lots of different foster homes.

We would never have parted.

Ever.

We told one another we'd rather have gone homeless

than be split up, and later on we almost did. As soon as she could, when she was out of the foster care system, Nina got a job and managed to get a room. A year later, I followed, and we got a small place in a dangerous neighborhood. She worked all the time, and when she was in danger of not being able to make the rent, I started fighting in the underground fight clubs to help make money to pay the rent.

Then Lou found me.

Now she's mad at me because I told a nosy journalist to quit hassling her. "You're not making things easy for her."

"Don't waste your time worrying about her," I shoot back.

"I like her. She was nice."

"That's not what you said the other day."

"What did I say?" Nina asks, planting her hands on her hips as if she's getting ready to fight me.

I say nothing.

"You always jump to the wrong conclusions, Elias. What did you say to her?"

I don't tell her everything. "I told her to quit poking around."

My sister's frown makes me reconsider. I might have been a little harsh. A princess like that isn't used to being handled or spoken to like that, the way I did. It was a shock to her system, I can tell.

Maybe Nina has a point. I have anger issues but my anger is what makes me lethal. It's my fire, and my fuel. Take that away and you might as well castrate me.

"You should apologize."

"How can I when she's not around?"

"This is work, and she'll be back, so make sure you do when she does come back."

CHAPTER SEVENTEEN

HARPER

"Are you still here?" Merv asks. I've been at the office for a few days and I'm starting to wonder if he gave me this assignment purely because I'd be based in another location.

"I'm writing up my assignment, and fact-checking a few things."

"Let me take a look at what you've got so far."

It needs more, much more than I've currently got. "I will, when it's ready for your eyes."

"Gerry's going to the fight," he tells me, and of course, I already know this, but I'm not about to tell him that Gerry suggests I come along.

"Your boy is going away to a training camp in Wisconsin."

I resent the term he's using. "He's not my boy."

"I've suggested to Lou that it makes sense for you to tag along."

I'm not keen on the idea. "I don't think Lou wants me there." That day when I was talking to him, I got the distinct feeling that Lou would have told me if he'd wanted me to come along.

"You can't cover half of a story. They're training in Dwayne Banks' place. You do know who he is, don't you?"

"The middleweight champion nineteen years ago," I reply calmly. "Lou thinks he has a chance of repeating that success with Eli now."

"And if they're going all that way and training, it makes sense for you to go with them."

"Eight to ten days?" I balk at the idea. The only reason I can put up with the boxing gym here is because I can go home every evening and take my mind off Eli. I can recover. I shudder to think of what it would be like being stuck with him for days.

"I can't let you go for that long. Four days. That should give you enough time to flesh out what you have."

He walks away and I ponder how awkward things are going to be. I am already dreading the training camp but I don't have much time to think about it because I have a lot of things to look through. I had planned to visit Grampton House later today but found out that it's closed down. Reports of neglect and incompetence have circulated for years. There were other rumors too, but they weren't substantiated. I shuddered when I found out that this was the place where Eli and Nina ended up in when they were seven and eight years old.

I return to the boxing gym the next day and Eli's back is the first thing I see as I walk in.

He's hitting the speedbag. There's a certain rhythm to it, one I couldn't get the hang of when I tried. Ernesto laughed at my feeble attempts.

Eli makes it look so easy. I try not to stare but he moves slightly and I see the side of his face now as he casually, almost lazily, taps the speedball. It's not a brute force, or strength, but rhythm, Ernesto said, and as I slide into my chair, I'm still riveted by the way Eli's hitting that thing.

It's hypnotic.

And then he turns and throws a glance in my direction, as if he can tell I'm watching. It's odd how we both do that. How, across the floor of the musty, smelly gym full of people, he can sense that I'm here.

When I escaped to the office, it wasn't only because I was angry at him, it was because I needed to get away. I'm not sure what's going on with me, or why my belly tingles when Eli's around, but something happens to me that I can't control. I can't fight this feeling, but I need to because his feelings for me are completely different than my feelings for him.

ELI

I'm sweaty and grimy, and I could leave it until I've showered, but I don't want this hanging over my head and I'd rather get it over and done with now. I go up to Harper.

"Haven't seen you around here lately," I say, taking my gloves off.

She looks up, surprise flickering in her eyes. "I was working from the office."

She's cold and has an edge now. Nothing like how she was before, and I can't blame her. I don't suppose anyone's ever answered back to this princess or treated her the way I did the other day. It must have been a huge shock to the system.

Nina's words reverberate around in my head and I force myself to make the apology. "I'm sorry," I say, "about the other day." Funnily enough, my apology sounds softer than it did in my head. It almost sounds sincere.

She stares right at me but doesn't say anything. I can't tell if she's surprised or still pissed at me, but because there's nothing but silence between us, and because I've had to make the move and come to her, I can't walk away. "I didn't mean to get so angry."

"I don't suppose you can help it."

That stuns me for a moment. "I can't, but I shouldn't have taken it out on you."

Now she's the one who seems to hesitate. "It's okay," she says finally. "You've got a lot going on. It's a big fight. You don't need me to mess things up for you."

She didn't have to say that, but I'm pleased she did. She understands me more than I give her credit for. "Is that why you stayed away? Because of me?"

The way her mouth shuts tight, I can detect her struggle to answer the question. I'm thinking 'yes' and that she's not about to own up to it. She's too proud to admit to certain things. We both are.

"You hurt me," she replies, knocking me back as sure as Garrison's left hook would.

"I did what?" I didn't hold her wrists that hard.

"What you said. I wasn't expecting that. I didn't know I'd overstepped a line. I own up, I might have pushed the conversation in a certain direction with your sister. I'm sorry if you thought I had maliciously tried to seek her confidence, but the level of your anger was something I wasn't prepared for."

I'm still trying to process this.

"I stayed away because I needed to get work done and..." She looks at me with her sad green eyes. "I'm not having the best time with this assignment. I don't have a boxing bone in me. I don't know this sport, and my boss is breathing down my neck. He hates me because my dad pulled some strings to get me this job, but I'm not a privileged brat. I work hard, and I'm trying to do my best to get this story, but you make it so difficult. I needed to take a break from you."

Holy crap. I'm stunned. She's let it all pour out, and I kind of feel sorry for her. Nina was right. She's trying to do her job. I'm the obstacle.

"Are you coming to the fight?" That's the first thing that pops into my head, because she'll get the story of her life if she's there to see me win the title.

"I don't know if Merv will let me."

"Merv?"

"Merv the Perv," she says, scratching her neck the way she does when she's nervous or thinking about something. "My boss."

My gut tightens. "Merv the *Perv*?" I ask, not liking the connotations of that label. "He's a perv?"

"No," she shakes her head. "I don't think he is. He just hates me. People call him that behind his back, but I don't know if there's anything to it. It's a name that's stuck."

"Don't you want to see me win?" I ask, finding it strange that she's been hanging around here for a while, and yet on the fight night, the big one, she's bowing out.

"Gerry might do that."

"Gerry?" Now I can't tell if that's a work decision, but

her answer soon makes that clear. "I really can't handle a boxing match. I would be a mess watching it at the ringside."

"You're at the gym to watch me and write about me, and you wimp out on the big night?"

She runs a hand through her wavy hair. "I don't know if Merv will let me." I'm convinced that he thinks me being here so long is a good enough break in itself.

"Come with me to the diner," I say on the spur of the moment. "We can talk there." This has been our longest and most civil conversation yet, and I feel as if I owe it to her to give up something of my story. Plus, if I take her to the diner, Nina will know I made it up to her.

"At the diner?" she asks, sounding shocked and suspicious at the same time. "Now?"

I take a step back, and note her gaze run down my chest, and then back up to my eyes. I caught her looking again. Most women don't hide their blatant appreciation of my body, but Princess here looks ashamed that I caught her. I breathe in, and pull myself up so that I'm standing taller, I even go so far as to puff my chest out a little. Her gaze is pinned on my eyes now, and I would bet anything that she's itching to let it slide.

"I need to shower first."

CHAPTER EIGHTEEN

HARPER

That was an odd exchange; Eli asking me to go to the diner with him. Who am I to say 'no'?

But did he have to tell me he was going to take a shower? He's left me with that picture of his back as he walks away in his boxing shorts. My eager eye takes in every muscle, every curve, every inch.

"We missed you," Ernesto says, his voice jerking me out of the Eli soft-porn movie that's started to play in my head.

"I missed you," I tell him truthfully. I'm happy to see him. He sets down his toolkit and wipes his brow with a small white handkerchief. "What did you fix now?" I ask him.

"The sink was leaking in the bathroom."

"You're a real DIYer, aren't you?"

"Someone's got to take care of things. This place is falling apart." He scrunches up the hankie and shoves it into his pocket. "Where have you been?"

"I had some work to do from the office."

"Did you?" he asks, looking at me as if he doesn't believe me. "Or is that an excuse?"

I lean back in my chair and fold my arms.

"I was fixing one of the showerheads in the locker room that day. I heard everything."

I press my lips together. "Then you know why I needed to stay away for a few days."

Ernesto's face turns somber. "That boy needs to control his temper. He treats everyone as if they're his opponent."

I smile at him, glad that he has my back. "He's apologized."

"That's a start. Glad to have you back," he says, then picks up his toolkit again.

I get back to work and a short while later, Eli comes up to me and announces that he's ready.

Ten minutes later, we walk to the diner and things feel a little strange. It's not because of the people who turn to look at him, or that kids shout out encouraging words to him, it's because the tables have turned. He's being extra nice, maybe *nice* is not the right word, but he's trying to make conversation and I'm holding back. I'm doing that because I find myself in a peculiar position. I am well aware of the effect Eli has on me, or rather on my body. My mind is trying to be in serious journalistic mode but my body is getting ready for good times.

Ever since he strode over to me earlier, wearing nothing but his boxing shorts, and sweat, and a smile, my mind has started playing games. Now that we're together, out of the familiar confines of the gym, my pulse races and my heart starts to beat faster. It's annoying, and exhilarating, and all the myriad of emotions in between, and I hate this because I don't like being out of control.

He wants to know if he can read the stuff I've written on him. "You haven't given me anything," I retort.

"Ask me anything you want," he dares, then pushes the door of the diner open for me. I'm in front and as I scan around the half-full room, trying to decide where to sit, people look up, and the sudden silence is followed by a hum slowly moving through the diner as the customers realize he's here.

"They know I'm Nina's brother," he explains, and saunters over to where he wants to sit; in a booth over by the window, where Gerry and I sat last time. I follow and watch as people high-five him and smile at him and greet him along the way.

"Hey," Nina approaches us as we sit down.

"Hi." I smile at her.

She looks from me to Eli, and then looks stumped for a moment. "A working lunch?" she asks me.

"I'm not sure," I reply, because the truth is, I have no idea what brought this on.

"I told him to be nice to you."

I look at Eli, then at Nina. "So I have you to thank for this?"

"Yes," Eli confirms, then glances at the menu in his hands.

"How refreshing, a boxer who cares what his sister thinks of him."

"I've always looked up to her," he says. "She's looked out for me my entire life."

"Someone had to," replies Nina. Though she says it as if it's funny, almost a dismissive comment, I start to think there might be something weightier under those words. "What can I get you?" she asks, getting ready to take our order.

We place our orders, and then stare at one another when Nina leaves. Eli seems to take up his entire seat, and it's not because he's huge. He isn't built like a grotesque bodybuilder, but his persona takes up more space that his physical body. I feel a little shy around him, and it's not something I should be feeling at my age. It's definitely not something I've felt outside of my teens, so the fact that I feel it now throws me. This happens more and more, I realize. Eli unnerves me, and it's not just because of his displays of anger. He excites me as well, and he's making me feel like a teen right now. I blame it on his pheromones; they roll off this man like dust.

I'm eager to make some conversation. "This is why you're being nice to me?" I say, with a grin. "Because Nina asked you to? I assumed it was because you'd softened towards me."

"Nina did ask me to apologize, and I could have left it at that, but I feel I owe you. I don't want to get you in trouble with your boss."

"I'm not in trouble with him."

"You said I'd made it difficult for you to get your article written."

"You haven't exactly made it easy." If ever there was a guy who didn't want to talk about himself, it's him. "You were going to tell me about your meteoric rise to the top."

"It's not meteoric yet," he states. "I know how this fight is being promoted. Most people don't think I'll go the distance, let alone make a dent, but I will, and then they'll be talking about my rise to the top."

"I believe in you," I say, sitting forward, because I do. I've seen Eli's different faces, some of them, but I've got a jagged jigsaw-pieced picture of his past. I believe in him because I want to and because he thinks nobody else does, outside of his boxing family and Nina.

"Where do you want me to start?"

"At the beginning."

So he starts, allegedly at the beginning and tells me about his absent father, and the struggles of his mother, and how after that weekend where she left her two toddlers home alone, they were taken away from her until she cleaned her act up. How his aunt took care of them, and how his mother never did manage to get over her problems. "She died of a drug overdose a few years later. She never managed to clean up her act."

My body slumps at the news, at how much strife this man has known. "I'm sorry, Eli." I want to comfort him in some way, but it's hard to know what to do, and how to do it. We have such a tricky dynamic; I don't know how I'm supposed to react around him most of the time. He doesn't like too much emotion yet how can I rein it in when I hear such awful things about his childhood years?

He lowers his voice each time Nina walks past. I sense he doesn't like talking about it especially when she's around, but I dare not suggest we go someplace else.

"My aunt had no choice but to take care of us. I guess she hoped that my dad would come back and take over, but he went back to Panama."

"Did you ever see him again?"

"He died a few years after my mom, but he never came back here. We never saw him again. I have no proper recollection of either of my parents."

"How long were you with your aunt and uncle for?"

He shakes his head. "There was no uncle. She had a series of boyfriends over the years. The last one didn't like me much."

I remember what Nina said about the beatings.

"He had a temper on him. Liked his belt too much."

I force myself to remain composed, but it's hard not to wince or jolt at the images that his words paint.

"She couldn't take care of us as time went on. She was struggling and had two little kids of her own by then. We got taken away by CPS then, and ended up at this place where we stayed while they tried to find us foster families."

"Grampton House?"

Nina brings the food over and Eli turns silent.

"That's the place," he says, when Nina leaves.

"It closed down years ago."

"It should have been razed to the ground."

I push my salad around on the plate, and he barely touches his brown rice and veg. The conversation dies.

"But you must have gone to school and made friends?" I ask, desperate to hear about something good in his life, something normal.

"I hated school. I couldn't sit still or pay attention. I'd play hooky, and get into trouble. Hang out with the wrong kids. Get up to no good. Teachers always said I'd amount to nothing. That I was a waste of space, come to think of it, that's the message most people drummed into me most of the time."

"Is it respect you're after?" I ask, wondering if that was what he sought, the thrill of winning a fight, and proving his physical strength and ability.

"Respect?" He says it with such derision that I know it's not that. "I want to prove that I am worthy."

"To who?" His family? Nina?

"To myself," he says, as if I've asked him a silly question. "I've grown up with people telling me I was a useless, worthless piece of shit. Now's my chance to prove that I'm not."

I look at him, at the defiance in his dark eyes, but I'm too choked up to say anything.

"Everyone wants to prove something, Harper. Don't you want to prove something?"

"I want the story."

"And I want the belt."

These are simple things to want, but not so simple to get.

"You can give me the story," I say, wanting to see his reaction to my request. "But I can't give you the belt."

"I'm going to get that myself, don't you worry."

"I have every confidence in you." He looks up and throws me a look as if he doesn't believe me. But I mean what I say and I'm not saying this to pay him lip service. I don't care what everyone says about Garrison. Eli wants this title more than life itself and I want, with all my heart, for him to get it.

We haven't eaten much, and our plates look mostly untouched.

"What's wrong with your food?" Nina asks when we get the bill.

"Nothing," I say brightly. "We just got talking too much."

"I'm not hungry," Eli replies.

Nina snorts in disbelief. "That's a first. You must be coming down with something."

I get the bill, and tell Eli that I'm going to charge it to my workplace, and then I give Nina a generous tip which puts a huge smile on her face. She thanks me. "You should come to Waquito's," she says, as if she's suddenly had a bright idea.

"Where?"

"Didn't you tell her about it, Elias?"

Obviously not. I look at Eli's face because I have no idea what they're talking about.

"Waquito's," Eli replies. "It's a bar where I used to work as a security guard at the door. They're throwing a small party for me."

"You should come," Nina insists excitedly.

"I don't know anything about it," I reply. But something else concerns me. Eli doesn't exactly look like he wants me to come. If he had, he would have told me without needing Nina to prompt him to.

"It's next week, Friday night," he continues.

"Our friends grouped together and they're throwing him a party," explains Nina.

"I've never heard of it." Because I haven't, and I notice that neither of them have even told me where it is. Talk about being vague.

"You wouldn't have," Eli shoots back quickly. "It's not your kind of place."

I raise my eyebrow. "Maybe it's time I had a look at your type of place."

I tell myself that I'm going in the name of research and because it will give me more information about Eli. But the truth is, I'm also curious to know about the type of place Eli hangs out at.

CHAPTER NINETEEN

ELI

I decide that Harper's not so bad. That's one thing I've learned about life as I've grown up; most people aren't so bad once you get to know them.

Some are. Some are monsters, but on the whole, a lot more of them are nicer than not. I've also realized that most people aren't who we first see. We have our own preconceptions of them at first glance, and these are often wrong.

It's taken me a while to come to this conclusion, because I'm wary about meeting new people and trusting them. I keep them at a distance until I can properly suss them out.

There's a reason for this. When we were young, Nina and I trusted people, and each time we'd get allocated to a foster family, it was like starting over. We didn't know them, and they didn't know us. But they must have been good people because they took us in, right? Most were. I can't fault them, but a couple weren't so great. I reckon they went in for the fostering side of things because it was a way for them to get more money.

But those first days when we'd be in yet another strange house, and these people would be staring at us with plastic smiles, they were hard. We were too young to know any better, and this was the only life we knew.

It's why I look out for Nina, because I can now. I'm protective of the people who are important to me. That's why I'll always look out for her, and that's why I lost my shit when Harper snooped around.

But the more I get to know Harper, the more I see a different side to her. Thinking about it, she probably didn't change. It's my perception of her that's changed. I'm sure she had her own ideas about me, and I wasn't the nicest person when we first met, but things seem different now. It's like we were in the ring and I was trying to keep her from coming near me.

I don't see her as someone to steer clear of anymore. I don't see her as someone who is a threat.

Unlike my opponents in the ring. I see them as a threat because then I know I have to deal with them. I don't humanize them. I can't humanize them. To do so would be to put myself at a disadvantage. It wouldn't be so easy then to land a punch at a man's face and watch blood water-fountain from his nose after the crunch of my punch connecting to it. I couldn't then land an uppercut in his ribs and send him crashing into the ropes.

"I'm moving the training camp forward by a few days," Lou informs me.

"Why?" I've pushed it out of my mind until now.

"So that you have a longer time to recover before the fight. I want you to ease off the training when we get back," he explains. "You can't push your body too hard before the fight. Garrison will have you for breakfast if you do."

"Garrison isn't going to last twelve rounds." I'm sure of that. I feel like I'm still improving and that by the day of the fight, I'll be in peak condition. I'm also eager to get to that day. I'm sick of eating brown rice. I'm sick of tuna and potato. I crave butter, and ice cream, cakes, and donuts—all the bad food I'm not allowed to have and it haunts my dreams. I'm sick of the same training, the same gym. It's funny that I don't miss the sex much, in comparison, though lately I've had my weaker moments.

A change of scenery could be the thing I need.

"When do we leave?"

"On Sunday."

Sunday is good. I won't miss the party at Waquito's, though it's going to be a pretty dry party given that I can't drink or have any fun. But I'm looking forward to the training camp. I've never been to Dwayne Banks' place before and I'm eager to see what kind of place a middleweight champion can buy with his winnings. I never had a role model to look up to before, but I figure it's not too late to start now.

Lou stares at me as if he wants to say something. "I notice you and Harper are getting along better now."

"I'm being nice like you asked me to be."

Lou scratches his chin.

"What?" I ask, when he still hesitates.

"She's coming to the camp, but only for a few days."

My nostrils begin to flare. I should be annoyed. A tiny part of me is, because she distracts me. I've been able to block her out most of the time but lately... not so good. I blame it on not having had any pussy for a while.

Lately, having Harper around makes me think about sex

even more. "Does she need to be there?" I ask, because if I can stop this right now, I can kill the chances of any temptation.

"Her boss suggested that it might be a good idea for her to get an insight into your routine out there. Don't worry, the stuff she's writing on you isn't going to press until right up before the fight. Garrison won't discover any of your training or preparation secrets."

It's not Garrison I'm worried about.

"If it's any help," Lou continues, "she'll only be there for a few days, plus she can keep Margrit company."

Margrit is Lou's wife, and I can't really complain about Harper coming now.

We've been around one another for weeks and I don't assume for one second that I'm the only one thinking about sex. It's natural. Princess is a good-looking woman, and I'm not gay. Can't help it if my mind wanders sometimes. It's not just me. I see the way she looks at me, and I see the way she blushes. I'm not sure her coming with us is a good idea, but it will test my resolve. I'm already worked up enough, like a bomb waiting to explode.

I know Harper a little better now but I still don't want her to be around. She will be a distraction. But if her boss thinks it will be a good idea, and Lou promises me she'll only be there for three to four days, I can't do anything but accept it.

HARPER

"It's Wisconsin. I don't know if you'll be up for it, but your boss seems to think it would be a good idea, so maybe you should come." Lou hunches his shoulders in an it's-up-to-you fashion.

He doesn't sound too eager for me to come along, but if Merv suggested it, I can't see how I can refuse to go.

But also, things seem calmer between me and Eli now. If we hadn't gone to the diner, if Eli hadn't made an effort to make things right, I might not have been so eager to go.

He isn't the easiest of people to be around but he'd be deep in his training and I'd get another angle into this piece I'm writing.

CHAPTER TWENTY

HARPER

I t's the evening of the party at the bar where Eli used to work part-time up until a few years ago.

They've all decided—Eli, Jake and Santos—to go straight from the gym. It's okay for them, since they get to shower and freshen up, but I've been in my work clothes all day. Still, I suppose it's better not to go home and get changed because then I wouldn't be sure of what to wear. I'd feel pretty foolish if I showed up overdressed.

I've never been to this bar, and I don't know what it's going to be like. I remember Eli didn't like the bar at The Weston because he thought it was too upscale for him. I have no idea what to expect from this place.

We get two cabs there, and as soon as we pull up outside, there's crowd of people on the street. Eli gets out and he's immediately surrounded by people.

We head towards the bar, or rather, we try to. The crowd is thick. Eli, Santos and Jake lead the way while Nina and I follow behind. Everyone wants his autograph and a selfie with him.

It's like he's suddenly become a rock star. I can't see his face, so I can't gauge what he makes of this. Nina looks at me and raises her eyebrows as if she's also surprised by this response.

I'm taken aback. I don't know why, but I had always assumed that he was a loner. He's never talked about having friends. Boxing is his life. Aside from his team at the gym and his sister, I hadn't considered that Eli might have another life.

We go sit at a table nearby, and leave Eli to work the room with Santos and Jake at his side.

Luckily, the music isn't too loud and it's not dark. It's possible for me and Nina to make small talk.

The atmosphere is lively and noisy, and happy. Everyone is happy. It's as if the name Eli hates, Chicago's New Hope, is the perfect manifestation of what Eli is to all his friends here.

We don't see much of him for most of the evening, but it's not a problem. It's nice for me to get out and I like Nina. In fact, I've come to like all of them, even Jake and Santos who I haven't spoken to much, but we're always in the gym together so I kind of know them better than I know the other regulars there.

Eli and I have been getting along a lot better lately. I don't know if what I feel for him is something that only I have, or whether he feels it too. I can't tell and maybe that's a good thing because it's obviously a passing phase. Staring at a half-naked man with a body as beautiful as his is bound to have some effect on me. I'll soon forget about him when I move back to the office.

For now I'm content to site and observe and sip my

wine. Eli is continually surrounded by stunning women who all vie for his attention.

I didn't even think to touch up my makeup because I was mindful not to look as if I'd made a special effort to look good. I managed to retouch my lipstick but that's about it.

I begin to feel slightly out of place, as if I don't belong, and the situation is compounded because I don't know anybody here. All I can do is watch, and silently hope that Eli might come over at some point and talk to me.

Nina has left my side and is talking to some friends on the next table. Jake and Santos are laughing at something on one of their cell phones. Eli hasn't returned to our table, and the chances of us having a conversation tonight look increasingly bleak.

My hope deflates. I'm embarrassed by the idea that I had been harboring thoughts of having him to myself for a while.

But he doesn't see me. How can he when he's surrounded by such gorgeous women? There are lots of pretty young things here; dark-haired Latinas with their long hair and beautifully made-up faces, their tight tops and dresses and curvaceous figures. They're throwing themselves at him, circling him like sharks around a helpless survivor, even though there is nothing helpless about Eli.

He's the hero even though he hasn't won the fight yet. Even if Eli lost, he'd still be the local hero. He'd still be a catch.

I look away because I can't bear to watch him talking and laughing with these girls as if he's known them all his life. More than that, I feel pathetic and lonely sitting here by myself. It's hard to look happy on your own. Thankfully, Nina soon slips into the chair next to me.

There's food laid out on a table at one end, but I'm not

in the mood to eat, and I still have the drink which Santos bought.

Then, Eli comes over and sits down, and within minutes Santos and Jake return to the table.

"So many girls, so little time," Jake says, with a mischievous smile.

"Plenty of time for plenty of girls after," Santos adds.

Eli grins but doesn't give an answer. He glances at me before he lifts his glass. I feel as if he's about to speak, but someone taps him on the shoulder and grabs his attention.

Nina and the boys are laughing about something and I feel increasingly lonely even now when our table is full.

I've been meaning to let Eli know that I'm coming to the training camp next week, but I'm not sure if he knows or not because he hasn't said a word to me about it.

He must know, because Lou would have told him, so I find it surprising that he hasn't mentioned it to me at all. The only reason I can think of is that he's not happy about me being there. He's already told me in the past about his focus and how he blocks all distractions. I made the mistake of assuming that all the access I've had to him lately—with him being good with answering my questions—is because he felt sorry for me when I had my little outburst and told him that Merv was coming down hard on me.

I don't think Eli's kindness and accessibility extends to the training camp, and the reason he hasn't mentioned it to me is because he doesn't want me to be there.

I wish Merv would stop butting in and hadn't insisted that I go. Gerry seems to think it would be a good idea and he's eager for me to go.

So I am going.

Only I'm not sure I should.

The one thing that consoles me is that I only have a few

days left at the gym after I get back. I'll likely have a few things to finish up, and after that, everything about Eli's life I'll probably only read about in the papers.

That makes me feel reflective.

"What are you doing sitting here by yourself?" he asks suddenly. Disappointed that he hadn't even spoken to me, I'd turned to my cell phone and luckily was engrossed in checking my messages.

"You were... busy," I say, pushing away the snarky comment that bubbles up and sits on the tip of my tongue. I was going to joke about his harem of women, but with the fight looming, and his self-imposed celibacy soon to be over, I don't want to hear him talking about his conquests.

"There are so many people that I haven't seen in a while," he replies. "I'm catching up. It's been a while since I socialized."

I can see that. The place is so full of people, and I'm certain there's still a big crowd outside. I already feel invisible compared to some of these beauties surrounding him.

"Want a drink, Lover Boy?" Santos asks. Eli shakes his head. I notice he hasn't touched a drop of drink or eaten anything. His resolve is obviously strong.

"I see girls are throwing their numbers at you like confetti at a wedding," Jake comments. "Any numbers you don't want, pass on to me."

"Or me," says Santos, then adds, "No getting up to anything tonight. Lou told us we had to keep an eye on you."

"Lou should know me better than that," Eli replies, rolling his eyes.

"You've only got to be good for a few more weeks," Jake reminds him. "Get through the training camp and the fight, and then we're going to par-tay!" He rubs his hands together as if he's about to make fire.

Nina stares at me and gives me a boys-will-be-boys look. I smile back at her to acknowledge it, but I don't really feel like smiling.

"Are you going to the training camp?" Nina asks me.

"Yes," I reply.

Jake and Santos say something in response, and seem glad, but I don't pay attention because I'm looking at my wineglass and waiting for Eli to make a comment.

But I don't get a response from him. And when I look up—because I need to see the expression on his face—I catch his eye and he quickly looks away.

It's like he suddenly feels uncomfortable and in that moment my worst fears are confirmed.

"Dude," Santos says, tapping him on the shoulder, then leans in and whispers something in his ear. For a stupid, misguided moment I assume they're talking about me, until I hear Nina groan.

"Ugh, I knew she'd make a play for him," she murmurs low enough but I hear it.

"Who?" I whisper.

"His ex. I can't stand the leech."

A beautiful creature glides over to our table. She is tall, her skin and hair golden-brown, her figure straight out of a lingerie magazine. "Elias," she drawls, and he takes her hand, and gets up.

"Athena," he says, and I'm not sure whether it's me being paranoid, or if he's deliberately being louder than is necessary. He takes her over to the corner and they stand face to face, talking deeply.

This is someone he's known on an intimate level. I know that from watching their body language.

I feel as if I've been slapped.

And now I want to leave.

Jake and Santos get up and walk over to the bar.

"She was his last girlfriend," says Nina, her eyes still trained on Eli and the gazelle.

I struggle to breathe. "They look very much together," I manage to say.

"Don't be fooled by that," Nina replies. There's a note of disapproval in her voice, and I like that. Or I could be imagining it. "They had a volatile relationship."

My heart lifts. "Did they?"

"She's been itching to get her claws back into him. Thank goodness he got the fight. He ditched her as soon as he got short-listed."

"Maybe they'll get back together after the fight?" I say, not because that's what I want—I want to yank Eli's ex out of here by her hair—but I ask in order to get more information.

"Eli has been known to do stupid things, so I wouldn't discount that idea." She excuses herself and gets up to leave.

Nina's reply burns into my skin and sinks deeper, like acid. I want to leave, and I haven't even been here that long, but my heart is sinking. Seeing Eli with the girl makes it harder for me to sit here and pretend I don't care.

It was bad enough watching Eli's reaction to the training camp news. I was already upset before his beautiful ex-girlfriend showed up.

Eli doesn't want me at the training camp and if I was unclear about where we both stood, I now have my answer.

He and his ex will get back together again after the fight. The way she's standing, facing him, I know they will.

And I am so thankful that I will finish this assignment soon.

I can't do this any longer, so I get my jacket and bag and walk over to Nina, who is talking to a guy. "Sorry," I say, when I tap her on the shoulder and she turns to me, mid-conversation. I feel bad for her because she feels as if she has to keep an eye on me. I'm a burden, and there's no need to mess up her evening just because my own has been messed up.

"I'm leaving," I tell her.

"Already? We only just got here."

"I need to go. My dad called earlier so I'd better see if he's okay," I lie.

"Is that why you're going?" Nina asks in disbelief. "Because you have to call your dad?"

"I have stuff to do," I insist. "*You* stay," I tell her, then lean in and whisper into her ear. "He looks cute."

She gives me puppy-dog eyes, then kisses me on the cheek.

I start to push through the heavy crowd and make my way towards the entrance, but I'm stopped by Callum.

"Hello, gorgeous," he says, resting his hand across my lower back. I flinch at the unwanted familiarity.

"I didn't know you were here," I exclaim. Although I see him often at the boxing gym, we don't talk much aside from the casual greetings.

"Eli invited me. There are a few of us here from the gym."

I nod, because I hadn't noticed. I haven't been people-watching as much as I've been casually Eli-watching. "We go back a long way, me and Eli."

This catches my attention. "How long?"

"From the fight club days."

"You were also fighting there?"

"I was desperate. Needed the money."

"I was just leaving," I tell him, "But I'd love to hear more about your days at the club."

"Yeah?" That seems to put a smile on his face.

"But I was leaving," I tell him to prepare him for the fact that I'm not staying long. In the corner, I can still see Athena with her paws on Eli's arm. It annoys me. Like, *really* annoys me. I can't bear to watch this show any longer, and now I don't even care to hear about the fight club days.

"Let's talk," Callum suggests, but I'm ready to split.

"It's too noisy, and too hot, and I've been here too long." I feel claustrophobic.

"Let's go outside," he offers. "There are plenty of people hanging around outside."

I could do that. Hear what he has to say and then go.

"That's a good idea."

CHAPTER TWENTY-ONE

ELI

I was hoping it wouldn't come up, I was hoping nobody would bring it up but when Nina asked Harper about the training camp, I didn't jump for joy.

I can't lie.

But Harper knows I wasn't ecstatic about it.

Santos and Jake aren't stepping into the ring, I am. The trip to Dwayne's place will be a small vacation for them. They have to help me train, but their neck isn't on the line.

Mine is.

I sense Harper knows I'm not over the moon about it. It's hard to do, to create this distance between us, but it will help me in the long run.

It's been an insane evening, and everyone wants a piece of me. It's only Harper who stays distant. She watches me, and I react in the moment. Friends come up to me, girls I've met before, and their friends, some of whom I've never seen before, but they all want something; an autograph or a picture with me. They get all territorial with their hands all over me. I swear, some of them even squeeze my muscles and their hands linger longer than is appropriate over my back or on my shoulder. If the roles were reversed, if these were guys doing this to a woman, there would be outrage.

But then again, I can handle it. This is new to me, and I'm humbled. Hard not to get carried away when there's so much attention leveled at you.

I wonder what Harper's thinking. This place is like a beauty pageant minus the swimsuits. Working here as a security guard was crazy. I was always getting hit on, and if I hadn't been so singularly dedicated to boxing, I could have had a different woman every single night I worked here.

I see Harper sitting alone and she looks uncomfortable. Nina's close by and keeping an eye on her, and the boys are hovering around, only they keep getting distracted. I sense that Harper feels as out of place here as I did at The Weston.

I want to go up to her and rescue her, but I also know I shouldn't. This wasn't such a problem a few weeks ago, and I don't know why it is now.

Ever since Lou told me she's coming to the training camp, I know I have to do it again; I have to shut her out just like I shut out Athena.

Except that Athena's back, and boy, does she look good. Better than I remember. It's been months since I've seen her, but she looks hotter than ever. I can feel Harper checking us out. Athena bends down to kiss me on the cheek, and I steal a glimpse of her breasts. Memories of our nights together come flooding back.

We were good together.

At least the sex was.

And I miss that.

When Athena reaches for my hand, I let her take it. I want Harper to see. I want to knock away any ideas she might have of how things have changed between us.

She has feelings for me, I know that. She can't hide what she feels and I already knew that from the first moment I saw her.

But it's my feelings I have to hide now.

So I let Athena take my hand and we walk away so that we can talk in private.

I don't want my training week to be messed up, and ignoring Harper tonight will make things easier for me later on.

I turn away when Athena puts her hand on my arm. She thinks we have a chance to get back together again. She couldn't be more wrong. I look away in exasperation, and that's when I see Harper talking to Callum. He's a smooth talker, that one. I can see he might want to take a shot at Harper. He probably thinks she's in his league.

"You're not listening to me," Athena wails, and she pulls my face so that I'm looking at her. I hate her talons on my skin, and I'm about to tell her to go to hell, but she doesn't always hear such requests. She's still in denial about the fact that I split up with her.

Out of the corner of my eye, I see Harper making her way towards the door. She got the hint and she's finally leaving.

So why do I feel bad?

It's done the trick because she's going, but a part of me wishes she wasn't because Athena is talking shit and I'd rather be talking to Harper instead.

I turn my attention to Athena and bide my time but I keep glancing in Harper's direction because she's still talking to Callum.

It annoys me.

I should ignore them, but I can't, and when they both leave together, I narrow my eyes. I don't want Harper to leave, not with Callum. I excuse myself from Athena, and move to follow Harper, but people stop me along the way. I talk to them and tell them I'll be back.

When I leave the bar, I see that people have spilled out onto the street. This both surprises me and makes me happy, especially when they all turn and get excited to see me. They pat my back, and shake my hand, and shower me with good wishes.

But I see Harper and Callum talking not too far from me and it's like a pinprick in my skin. I can ignore it, or I can choose to focus on it, and make it bigger than it is.

They're talking, nothing more.

She's doing what I did with Athena.

But this feels like a hundred fucking pinpricks and I know it shouldn't.

Harper shouldn't be a blip on my radar.

And I hate that she is.

I should have ignored Nina and never apologized to Harper. I hate that she turned the tables just now. I used Athena, and Harper's using Callum except she's not even bothered by Athena, and she has no idea that I'm irritated enough to follow her.

I blame Callum. That guy is a smooth operator. I've seen him work on women before. I also know that Harper wouldn't be interested in someone like him.

She's not, because I've seen the way she looks at me.

Then why does standing here watching her and Callum laugh make me want to walk over and interrupt them?

I'm about to, except that one of my oldest friends gives me a bear hug.

And when I look up, Callum and Harper are getting into a cab.

CHAPTER TWENTY-TWO

ELI

Thank fuck I don't have to see her for a few days, and thank fuck my mind's solely on the training camp.

We left on Sunday and arrived here late in the evening. Lou tells me that Harper isn't going to be here for a few days yet, and that's enough time for me to get my head out of her business, and switch my attention back to my training.

The six-mile run is easy. I've been up since 5:00 a.m., doing my morning exercises. No big change there. Food-wise it's still lean chicken or tuna, brown rice and pasta, maybe a potato. I'm sick of it, but when I look in the mirror, and when Lou and the guys show me pictures of how I looked even as little as one month ago, I can see the difference.

It's huge. I'm chiseled to the max. There's not a millimeter of saggy skin, or soft muscle on my body.

Lou has me doing these six-mile runs after each hard

training session. He wants to build up my endurance, my stamina, and it helps, but what he doesn't know is that I was born with stamina.

Real fighters are made outside the ring, when there are other things at stake and not just a boxer's purse, not the fame or the adulation. Real fighters are built through necessity, through the need to survive, through the need to keep predators at bay. Strength, boxing, speed, and agility can be learned, and improved upon, but the steel grit, the don't-mess-with-me attitude, that comes from a deeper place.

HARPER

"You made it?" Lou asks. He walks out towards me. I called him to let him know I'd arrived, but I didn't expect him to answer the door. I couldn't see where to knock or ring the bell, so I called him on his cell phone instead.

This place is huge. Like *colossal*. I was half expecting a maid or butler to open the door.

Lou looks genuinely pleased to see me, though, which eases my worry a little.

"It was such a long drive, but I made it." I lift out my small suitcase and pull out the handle, waiting for him to lead the way. "This place is amazing." I look around at the huge building in front of me. It doesn't look like a home, nestled here high above the hills. It looks like a shiny building from Silicon Valley; like a beetle, with its shiny, hard surface. "This Dwayne Banks guy owns this?"

"He sure does. And if he plays his cards right, Eli will be living in a place like this before long."

I force a smile.

Eli is very much the underdog. Not many people believe that he can do this. He does. And I do. I believe in him.

"Come on in, the gang's all up and it's business as usual. You'll have a proper desk all to yourself in your room."

"A proper desk, my own room." I'm secretly thrilled.

"Let me at least show you around this floor," he says, "Leave your luggage here. I'll get Margrit to show you to your room later."

"Margrit?"

"My wife. She's the only cook we could afford." He howls with laughter.

"Your wife's here?" I exclaim in surprise, and partly relieved knowing that I won't be the only woman, and I might have someone to talk to for the few days I'm here.

"She's a helluva cook. Garrison might have a nutritionist and a chef, and a twenty-strong entourage to take him through the boxing regimen, but Eli has me and my wife, and a couple of guys from the gym. We're his support network, and that's what we're here for. I hope you're here to support him too."

I shake my head, confused by this sudden turn in conversation. "Of course."

"I hope you'll do credit to him in what you're writing. Eli doesn't have the type of money Garrison has. He can't afford a publicist. He has no PR show. Hell, he doesn't even have a nickname—"

"He's Chicago's New Hope."

Lou scrunches his face in disapproval. "That's not a

nickname. It sounds like a TV soap opera. You know why he doesn't have one?"

"Why?" I never asked Eli this, but I will, next time we get a chance to talk.

"Because that's not his focus. His focus is on that fight. That's all he wants. The belt, the title. It means a lot to him. It means everything to every boxer who ever went the distance and lost blood for it, but this kid," Lou waggles a finger at me. He does this every time he wants to make a point, "This kid wants it even more than Dwayne Banks did when he was in his prime and took the title. So make sure you do good by him."

"Don't worry. I'll only write good stuff about him."

"I need to get back to him. Follow me," he says and I do. Now I know why he was so pleased to see me. I don't mind. The knowledge that his wife is here soothes me, and I don't feel so anxious anymore.

I follow Lou into the building. Curiosity builds in my belly. It's hard to tell what this place is like inside, and I feel anxious and giddy all at once, knowing that Eli is inside.

Lou's phone rings and he steps away to answer it. I stand there feeling nervous. I don't know why I feel like this.

It's silly, and I shouldn't, but I haven't seen Eli since that night at the bar, and now I don't know what I feel; hurt, or jealous, or plain curious. That night when I left Waquito's, Callum accosted me and we ended up sharing a cab together but only because I assumed he was going to tell me about his days with Eli at the fight club. But as our ride progressed, my head was with Athena and Eli, and Callum's voice was just background noise. He wanted to go for a drink at another bar, but I wanted to go home and bury my head in my pillow. I was hurting because of Eli. I'm weak when it comes to him. I feel so much for him that my heart hurts to see him with another woman.

I hate that I, a strong and independent woman, go to pieces when he's around. I have to get my act together and forget this nonsense.

I stand in the hallway and look around me, waiting for Lou to finish his call. This place isn't homey at all. It looks more like an office building. There are floors, and corridors, and doors all around. There's nothing remotely warm and comforting about it.

I feel cold all of a sudden, and miss the dingy little boxing gym. At least that place had character. Beaten up, with the paper peeling from the walls, and the water leaking in the bathrooms every so often, the gym was like the people it gave home to, like its boxers, its down-and-outs, people who'd been beaten in life and needed a fresh new start, just like the gym needed a fresh new lick of paint and good makeover.

A trembling feeling floats in my stomach, as if butterflies are skittering inside it. I'm anxious and a little excited. I want to see Eli, and I don't.

He takes me through another set of double doors which open into a huge gym area. I see two boxing rings, and in the furthest one from me, at the far end, is Eli.

The hairs on my neck lift.

I recognize him by his back. It's funny because I don't see his face, only the back of his head, and he's sparring with Jake who is almost as built as him so that it could be easy to mix up who is who.

The tattoo on Eli's back is a giveaway, and it only confirms what my heart already knows—that is Eli. Even if he didn't have the ink, I would know *that* back.

My breathing slows down, enough that I notice it

because my eyes are drawn to his body. He swings out at this opponent, but it's his muscles my beady eyes narrow in on.

My fingers tingle. My senses snap, and he's done nothing, yet.

Yet.

As if it would ever come to that. I remind myself that I'm supposed to be getting over him; over this crazy, stupid obsession that seems to have consumed me.

The closest thrill I had was him gripping my wrists in the locker room. What he doesn't know is how I've replayed that scene back hundreds of times since then. And it doesn't end with him walking away naked.

I don't remember him being so sculpted before, or so big. He seems bigger, and yet I only saw him a few days ago. I think about him when he's not near me, it's like I put him on a pedestal and see the better side of him, but when I'm near him, I doubt myself again, and when he looks at me with such loathing, I know I mean nothing to him.

I can't help that he has this effect on me, but this is not a way to live.

Eli stops just like that in mid-fight. He turns around and sees me. There's a tiny delay, a micro-second maybe, but it's enough for his opponent to punch him. Eli falls to the mat.

"Don't worry about what's going on out here," Lou shouts. "Think!" He taps a finger to his head. "Now get back in there!"

But Eli's not looking at Lou. He's staring at me, and he gets up like a cat, slow and stealthy. He doesn't smile. He doesn't look pleased.

My heart slams to a stop and splinters into a million pieces.

He turns his back on me again, as if I wasn't even there,

as if he'd forgotten about me in an instant. Instead, he faces his partner and dances around the ring. Even though I can't read his expression, I can tell he's completely blocked off. He's got nothing further to say.

I don't understand his anger. I don't understand what happened between last week and now. I'd made myself believe that he wanted me to come here, but it couldn't be further from the truth.

"Don't worry about him," Lou says, throwing a glance at me. Then he turns to watch Eli again. I forget to swallow. I forget to talk. I forget my defense because I'm ripped into pieces.

Eli dances around the ring, and cuts me another dirty look. He's wearing his headgear, but everything about his posture tells me he's not pleased. And then he lands the mother of all punches at Jake.

SMACK!

The blow is so hard, I hear it and feel it in my bones.

His opponent crashes to the floor.

"That's my boy!" Lou cries. "Do that a couple of times on the night and we'll have one of the biggest upsets in boxing history."

I had something to do with the rage in that blow, I just know it.

But I don't understand it.

I thought we were friends. We hardly got to talk at Waquito's that night and he has no idea how I felt when I left. If there's anyone who should be mad, it should be me.

The level of his rage surprises me.

I turn around and start to walk back out because I don't want to be here. I should have listened to my instinct and made an excuse about coming here. I'd rather deal with Merv's sarcasm than Eli's wrath.

Lou rushes up to me as I leave, and it's a silly move because I don't know my way around this place. "Don't mind him," Lou says.

"I don't. I know what Eli's like."

"He's pumped up because of the fight," Lou says. "He's going to have moments when he blows up; he can't hide his emotions like a normal person can."

Because he's not normal, I think to myself. I feel out of place again, and I'm convinced that it was a mistake coming here.

"I'll get Margrit to show you to your room," he says, because clearly he's busy. I'm the nuisance from the paper. "Margrit!" he shouts. A few seconds later, I meet Lou's wife. She's short, and plump, and cuddly. There's a twinkle in her eye, and I lean towards the warmth I feel from her.

"Margrit?" I say, holding out my hand. She takes it between both of hers.

"Harper?"

I nod.

"Will you show Harper to her room?" Lou asks her. She replies with a smile.

"If I can remember the way there. The room next to ours?"

"That's the one." To me he says, "You don't want to stand here and watch this all day long, do you?"

"No." I most definitely don't want to be here. I need the distraction of my new room; something to make me forget what Eli just did, so that I don't dwell on why he's so angry.

Margrit jokes about how big the house is and how it's a maze of corridors and doors. I'm glad I'm not the only one who thinks this. She makes small talk and wants to know about my car trip here and I answer all her questions.

She shows me around. There's a movie theater room,

and a spa room with a huge hot tub right in the middle, and to the side, I see a door marked 'Sauna'.

There's also a swimming pool and a media room as well as so many rooms that I soon lose count of them all.

Finally we reach my room and she leaves me. I am grateful to be alone again.

A few hours later, I go down and offer to help her in the kitchen but she won't have any of it.

So I set the table in the dining room. It's a huge, long table that could easily seat twenty people. I put placemats down so that we only occupy the middle part and we face each other.

Eli and I haven't spoken at all since I got here.

We all eat together, and it's a jovial, relaxed atmosphere. Jake and Santos lighten the mood, and Margrit is sweet. Lou looks as if he has a lot on his mind and he eats quickly and quietly. I wish Ernesto had come along. That would have made all the difference.

But, I'm a grown-up and I can deal with the situation.

I don't join in the conversation much, because all they talk about is boxing. The guys are having a laugh, and I'm content to listen.

I can't bring myself to even look in Eli's direction. There's a reason we are sitting at opposite ends of the rectangular dining table. I'm at the end with Margrit to my left and then Lou next to her. Opposite us sit Eli, Jake and Santos. Eli is opposite Lou, so I'm the furthest distance away from him. It means I won't have to look at him.

It's all so different to how things have been during the week. I don't know what changed.

CHAPTER TWENTY-THREE

ELI

True to form, Harper's avoiding me all through dinner. I'm surprised she didn't go sit at the head of the table; at least that way she'd be even further away from me.

We eat together and she talks to Margrit, and joins in the conversation, but mostly she's quiet. We're talking about the training and my routine tomorrow, so it's only natural that she doesn't join in.

A couple of times I steal a look at her, and I can tell that she's not comfortable. Not like how she was in that swanky hotel bar the night she puked all over me.

I know what it's like to not belong. Not only that night at the hotel bar, but every time Nina and I turned up at a new foster place we'd been allocated to, it felt like that for a while. The foster parents would look at as, and I used to wonder if they really wanted us, or if they were only after the money they got for having us.

Seeing Harper wearing that same unsure expression

makes me feel sorry for her, but she's never been in the situations Nina and I have been in.

I can't figure out now if I hate her or pity her; my feelings where she's concerned seem to change like the wind. When I saw her earlier, I wanted to know if she'd ended up in Callum's bed.

Yeah, why the fuck am I thinking about that?

The fact that I am tells me Harper's already in my head even though I've been trying to build up my resistance to her in the days between Waquito's and now.

Clearly it hasn't worked because the moment I see her, I'm pissed off again.

And now I'm pissed off about being pissed off and not being able to keep my cool as I had intended. I'm supposed to be mentally bracing myself for Garrison, not feeling sorry for Harper just because she looks subdued, even if I might have had something to do with that.

But I can't help myself. I try to get a reaction.

"Can you pass the salt?" I ask, tilting my head forward and in her direction. She looks at me, her gaze defiant. She's so easy to read, and she is truly pissed off and holding onto that grudge again. I prod her some more. "The salt?" I ask again. The shaker is by her right hand, and I'm praying that Margrit or Santos aren't going to hand it to me instead.

"What's the magic word?" Harper asks, a thin line forming between her brows.

"Just give him the salt, Harper." Lou digs into his food and seems weary.

"I'm waiting for the magic word."

Jake and Santos snigger, as if this is petty or amusing, I don't know which, but I agree that this is childish behavior on both our parts.

She's staring at me with her steely eyes, and I can tell

she'd just as easily throw that shaker at me than she would hand it over.

We're locked in a checkmate. I refuse to say 'please', and she refuses to give it to me.

Then Lou nudges Margrit—he'd grab it himself if he could reach it. Margrit passes the salt over to me, and them mumbles something to Harper that I can't catch.

I know, I just know that if Margrit hadn't taken the salt from Harper's hands, Harper would never have given it to me until I said the magic word.

"I want an early night for you," Lou tells me.

"I always have an early night," I mutter.

"But first we're going to watch some of Garrison's old fights."

"Tonight?" Santos asks.

"Yes, tonight."

Jake looks as peeved as Santos. Those two probably wanted to head into town and see what's going on, but Lou has ruined their plans.

HARPER

I'm wide awake. I expected to be knocked out by now, especially after the long drive here, but I'm wide awake. I'm finishing off a few work emails. Merv is on my back again. I gave him a copy of the piece I've done on Eli so far but he says it's weak, it has no depth, it lacks interest. He wants a meeting as soon as I return.

I plan to leave here on Friday morning but can't see

myself reaching Chicago until late afternoon. Merv is adamant I do, so I punch in the meeting details into the calendar on my phone as a reminder. I get an email from Gerry asking me if I got here okay.

I smile, touched that he was concerned enough to ask. I reply quickly, and tell him a bit about this place. Then I put away my phone and laptop because all that blue light is only going to make it harder for me to sleep.

After dinner, the guys retired to the movie theater room. Margrit and I followed but there was only so much footage of old fights that we could sit through. We didn't stay for long and returned to our rooms.

Margrit showed me the leisure suite briefly earlier, and this is where I return to. There's a swimming pool here somewhere. I open the door, and see the light floating on the water. It's empty, and clinical, and scary, like a scene out of a horror movie. I close the door quickly and step away, walking back towards the way I came. I see the door on the left, the one labeled 'Spa', and it has the hot tub and the sauna room in it. I push it open and jump back. Eli's sitting in the hot tub, his arms spread out on either side of the rim. My heart flips in my chest. He doesn't see me because his eyes are closed and his head is laid back so that his face is upturned towards the ceiling. The water's up to his shoulders, covering all of his tattoos and he's low down, as if he's got his knees on the bottom.

I am frozen, and I don't know what to do.

I need to shuffle back slowly, and leave, but I can't move. I'm rooted to the spot. Eli looks so peaceful. It's one of the rare times that I've seen him look like that. I find myself staring at him, taking my fill. His strong sinewy arms are a temptation. I want to run my hands all over them. I want to run my fingers over his muscles, over his biceps and triceps and deltoids, and I want to trace every ridge, every dip and every curve.

I don't want to leave, and I must, for my own sake, but at the very moment I step back, his eyes snap open, and he turns his head and stares right at me.

I'm having a cardiac arrest.

He pulls something out of his ear. A wireless earphone.

"You been watching me?" he asks.

"I..I haven't..." It's no use lying about it because what else was I doing standing here salivating at the sight of him? "I was looking around..." I point behind me, as if this will convince him. "I saw the pool and I got curious." I shuffle back another step. "I'll leave you to it."

"Don't go," he says. "We need to talk." My defenses sink. They'd been compromised the moment I saw him. Ordinarily I wouldn't have listened, I would've turned defiantly on my heel, my chin high, my moral code intact, but I have no barriers to protect me right now, and it will take a few moments, possibly hours, before I find my willpower again.

So I step towards the hot tub. There's an odd look in Eli's eyes. They're dark; darker than usual. For a moment I wonder if he's high, if he's taken something because he looks laidback and relaxed, a rarity for him. But I've been around him long enough, and I've seen how dedicated he is, so I know he wouldn't touch anything like that.

"What?" I ask. At least, I think that's what I said, but I didn't hear my voice out loud. He looks up at me, his brown eyes, the color of rich chocolate. His gaze is softer than I've seen it in days.

It turns my legs to jelly. They were pretty boneless from

the moment he asked me to stay, and I have no idea how I managed to walk over to him just now.

"We got off to a bad start," he says. I think I know what he's talking about, but he's being vague, and I want to play devil's advocate.

"You mean about the salt shaker, or you mean generally, from the first moment I met you?"

He frowns. "Today, when you first showed up."

"You didn't look too happy. You don't like me being here. I get the message."

"I'm sorry."

His quick and unexpected apology surprises me. It's almost as if the Eli I was beginning to know, before the night at Waquito's changed things again, is back.

"You're so changeable," I say, voicing my thoughts out loud.

"Can't help it. It's in my genes."

"I understand," I say, throwing him a carrot. I want him to open up to me without me prodding too much, because I know from before that the more I pry, the harder it is to extract information from him. It's better when he volunteers information willingly. "I never know where I stand with you."

Being around Eli means being on edge. That's why I savored looking at him without him knowing that I was. And now that I'm talking to him, now that he's being nice again, and different—he's so soft and gentle right now—I want to stay here all night and talk to him like this.

It's in this moment that I am reminded I like him so much that it hurts.

"Don't just stand there, get in."

I swallow. My body wants to be in that hot tub with him, but my head tells me to back off.

Stay away.

Eli is wild and unpredictable, and I can't get involved. I'm in two pieces, and as a result, I do nothing but stare back at him vacantly.

"You know you want to." His voice is raspy, tempting too. I'm beginning to feel hot and sticky. I pinch and pull my T-shirt so as to get some air between the fabric and my skin. "No," I state, but with less conviction than I intended.

I can't do this.

I want to, but I can't.

I shouldn't.

Yet my gaze still shifts to his chest. He's straightened up and the water comes up to his nipples. I can see more of his beautiful body now.

"No?"

"I don't … I didn't bring any clothes."

"You don't need any clothes."

He's playing with me. His tongue glides over his lower lip, wetting it. I'm riveted by the sight, and decide that I want my mouth on his. I want to feel his lips with mine.

I pinch my T-shirt again because the temperature's suddenly shooting upwards.

"Feeling hot?" he asks, splaying his arms out on either side of him again, putting his football-shaped biceps on parade.

"A little," I say, running my hand over my neck.

"Take a dip with me, Harper. Cool down."

"Uh… " The invite is loaded like a gun. I'm aware that I need to say something but words fail me. "Cool down?" I manage to say.

"It's a warm night. Actually, it's a *hot* night. I couldn't sleep so here I am."

I have so much to lose if I accept. This man can keep his

cool, but I can't. I lose my wits around him. Sense flies out of the window.

This verbal foreplay will be my undoing and if I stay here any longer talking to him, I'll get into that hot tub, and then I'll want all of him. He could use me like a plaything, and I would happily let him.

But the reasoning side of my brain reminds me that Eli does nothing even when surrounded by a harem of women. I know this from watching him at Waquito's.

It's only a dip in the tub.

And then my heart tells me he's not the problem. I am.

I want him to touch me. I want him to kiss me. I want him to do so many unspeakable things to me, and I can't believe I'm having this conversation in my head when all he's asked me to do is to take a dip with him.

"I didn't bring my bikini."

"I didn't bring my swim shorts either."

Now I lick my lower lip.

"Strip to your underwear," he tells me. It's the most suggestive and sexiest thing he's ever said to me. This is a different Eli, and I don't know what brought this on. Before I can formulate a reply, an objection, a denial, he says, "I'm not wearing anything either."

My mouth goes dry, as if his words sucked all the moisture out of it. I'm a boneless, vibrating, throbbing mass of blood and tissue, and what I do next will either define me, or ruin me.

He watches me with amusement, then starts to slowly rise. I stumble back a few steps, bracing myself. Even though I have seen him naked before—and I revisit that scene every night in my bed—seeing him stand up punches the breath clean out of my chest.

Shock and anticipation mix together like an aphrodisiac

cocktail. Palpitations go off in my heart like firecrackers. "See," he says, splaying out his hands as if he's shown me a magic trick. "I was kidding." Turns out he lied, and he's wearing his swim shorts.

He's also wearing what looks like a humungous boner. Breath escapes from my lips, part admiration, part desire. I can't decide if I want my mouth around him, or if I want him inside me.

Or both.

"Ooops," he says, looking down and seeing his tented shorts. He sits down slowly, as if it's painful to. "I must have been thinking about you."

I jolt and gulp in air at this, then I examine his face for signs of amusement, but I see none. He looks serious. Or he's pretending to be. Any moment now he'll tell me he's kidding again.

He hated me a few hours ago, and now he's telling me something else. I want to believe this notion that he finds me attractive. It makes me want to yell for joy, and cry with relief.

I gave him a boner.

Me.

He treats me with disdain, and pretends to put up with me because his sister told him to be nice to me, and now he tells that the bulge in his shorts is because of me?

Hard to believe.

It's a trick to get me into the hot tub, and this forwardness on Eli's part startles me. I seriously consider the possibility that he is high.

"I don't mean in *that* way," he says, eyes wide open now. "I meant that I was thinking about you because of the way I treated you before."

Oh. His words are a slap to my newfound euphoria, and my hopes deflate like a lead balloon.

"Before? You mean from the very first time when we met or earlier today when I arrived here, because you looked pretty annoyed then."

"When I was sparring? I had headgear on. How could you tell?"

"So you *were* annoyed?"

"How could you tell?" he repeats.

"I don't need to see your face to know that. It's in your gait, in your posture, in the air around you."

A smile spreads across his beautiful face. "You've been keeping a close eye on me, huh?"

"I have an assignment to do, and I'm trying to do it."

"I know. I haven't made it easy, even though I've tried." His voice is softer and he sits up and folds his arms. My eyes fall to his shoulders and I have this urge to smother his wet skin with kisses. It killed me to see him surrounded by all those wanton women at the party. I hated Athena and I hated that Eli gave her so much attention.

I hate that I barely got two words from him. I've spent the past few nights torturing myself with those images, and now I have him all to myself.

I'm honored that he's talking to me as if he cares, and I'm also wary because of his chameleon-like personality. I don't know if he's being sincere or if he's playing with me.

I don't know what to say because I don't know Elias Cardoza despite having spent weeks with him. What does that say about me? Or him? Or us?

"I tried to make it up to you over dinner," he says.

"By asking me to pass the salt?"

"I was trying to make conversation."

"*That* was your attempt?"

"I didn't hear you try," he remarks.

"I didn't have any reason to make it up to you because I haven't done anything wrong as far as I can tell."

Our gazes lock. He lifts his chin and looks as if he's unsure of what to say. I would give anything to know what's running through that mind of his.

"Have I done something wrong?" I want to know, and since this is the closest we've ever come to having this type of conversation, I figure this could be my best chance.

His face hardens. His expression turns to stone. "Showing up at the gym maybe?"

He just lost me again. "I had a job to do."

"Snooping around in people's lives?"

"You're a person of interest."

"Would you like it if I snooped around in your life, Princess?"

What did he call me? I fold my arms and I'm about to ask him this very thing, but he reaches for his earphone and inserts it into his ear. He's closed off to me again, and that flirty, light banter vanishes.

A coldness lies in the space between us.

Maybe that's not a bad thing.

I wouldn't have been able to resist him for much longer. I would have joined him in the tub and then he would have claimed my soul.

Eli has already done that. It's a one-sided infatuation because he barely knows I exist. I'm reminded of those beautiful creatures we bumped into that night at Waquito's and I know the type of woman he likes.

And I'm not it.

He wasn't my type of guy either, not before, but this man has made my body do things that are out of my control.

The throbbing in my heart reverberates outwards and moves in between my legs. It tells me everything.

I have to make an effort to shift my body, to move back towards the door, even though I've been dismissed. He's closed his eyes again, and he's listening to his music.

CHAPTER TWENTY-FOUR

ELI

I dismiss her and get back to listening to my music, but the truth is I am so hard, I can't sit here much longer.

The look on her face has been priceless the entire time. I didn't realize until now how much of a good time I have playing around with Harper; making her uncomfortable and joking with her to come into the hot tub with me. Her expression when I stood up after telling her I was completely naked—you can't put a monetary value on that. My mouth curls up in amusement just thinking about it, especially knowing that I haven't even laid a finger on her.

I'm not going to, but it's not as if I haven't thought about it.

What I told her was true. I was thinking about her. I was thinking about that time she was at Waquito's talking to Callum. I didn't like it, and I've been trying to figure out why ever since. I block things out, but seeing her with someone else brought it to the fore. I think I've figured it out. The thing with Harper is that she doesn't fall at my feet. She doesn't throw herself at me like Athena does. But it's also that I've told her more than I ever intended to about my past, my life, my childhood.

I should have known better, and I don't understand why I did that. She's a fucking journalist, for Christ's sake. And yet, getting that crap off my chest has been enlightening.

I sense that I can trust her, and she surprises me on every level. It's her unpredictability that puts her in my head and keeps her there.

I didn't want her to show up, but I knew she'd be coming. But seeing her when she turned up made it real. I knew then that it would be tough keeping her out. It's not as if I don't have enough to contend with. The fight is only two weeks away. How the hell am I supposed to concentrate with Harper around? I slipped in my earphone, and hoped it would send her the message.

When I opened my eyes, she was gone.

HARPER

As surprising as it seemed, I managed to sleep last night after leaving Eli in the hot tub. The long drive, and the long day and the tsunami of emotions that swept over me just from talking to him left me exhausted.

The next day in between his boxing sessions and his exercises, Eli comes over and asks me how I am.

It takes me by surprise on many levels, but I manage to

give him a proper reply. I tell him I'm okay. Before he has a chance to say anything else, Lou calls him over and he disappears, much to my relief.

Lou seems to be harder on him here. He has him doing a lot of runs to build up his stamina. He shouts more too.

I get the lowdown on the training regimen from Santos and Jake, who are a minefield of information, and this means I have lots to add to my piece.

My dad calls me while I'm writing up my notes. I take the call away from the gym area and walk out into the hallway. This place is a maze of doors and corridors. Nothing like a home. I want to find a window to look out of, but there isn't one.

"Where are you?" he asks. It's the first thing he says, and the lack of a greeting tells me he's annoyed.

"In Wisconsin, at the training camp."

Before I get a chance to elaborate, he asks, "What training camp?"

I realize I haven't told him. I explain, and the disapproving sound he emits makes me wish I hadn't said anything. I wish I had lied and told him I was covering a gala event in the city.

"When are you coming back?"

I'm quickly on alert. "Why?"

"I haven't seen you in a while," he tells me.

"I'll be back at the end of the week."

"We'll meet for dinner one evening," he suggests, putting on a casual tone, but I know he hasn't called me for nothing.

"What is it, Dad?"

"Nothing. I want to see my daughter. I'm allowed to, aren't I? Call me when you're back."

"Okay, I will. Love you."

Later that day, I find out that we're all going out to eat, to save Margrit from doing the cooking. And, Lou says, we could all do with a change of scenery.

They all came up a few days before I did and I'm not surprised they feel claustrophobic. I feel like this and it's only my second day. He tells us that there's a nice restaurant nearby that Dwayne recommended. So we go out.

Santos drives the SUV that's big enough to accommodate all of us.

Unfortunately, I'm in the back with Eli, and our knees knock together from time to time. I shuffle away, as if his touch is poisonous. It's not. It's electric, and explosive, and it puts me on edge again.

The music is on, and in front of us, Lou and Margrit are talking, so it's not as if anyone can eavesdrop in on our conversation, but neither of us mentions last night. Instead we keep making small talk, like *really small* small talk, about his training, and Nina, and the fight. I don't know how long the ride will be, but I'm conscious of his knee, and his scent, and everything about him.

It's hard for me to erase the image of him in the hot tub, and to forget the conversation we had. It's especially hard for me to control the way my heart thumps against my ribcage.

When we get out, I make a dive for Lou and Margrit and manage to sit in between them at the restaurant. I don't think I can take sitting next to Eli during the whole of dinner.

It's a small Italian restaurant, and the food is homemade deliciousness. Authentic Italian cooking, the chef tells us. It's small enough that he comes out and talks to his customers, while ordering his waiters around like minions.

When he finds out that we're staying at Dwayne Banks' house, and that Dwayne recommended we eat here, he becomes even more animated.

Soon, the other customers in the restaurant discover who Eli is and when talk spreads that he's in the big fight with Garrison, they all want pictures with him. He willingly obliges.

Watching him, I conclude that he's good with people. It's just me he's not so good with.

Thankfully, the meal is quick, and Lou and Margrit don't want to linger. They want to go home. I don't want to be left here with the three guys, and so I say that I want to go back with them. It's still early enough that I can get back to my room and check my emails and tend to work business, and then have a bit of the evening left to unwind.

"No drinking and no women, you hear me?" Lou says to Eli.

"As if I would," he replies.

"And don't make it a late night either. I'm going to switch up your training tomorrow."

"Isn't it a bit late to be telling me that now?" Eli asks. "What are you changing up?"

"I'm still thinking about it."

"Great," I hear Eli mutter as I walk past.

"Why are you leaving?" he asks in a low voice as he grabs my hand to stop me. He lets it go as soon as I turn to answer.

"Because I want to go back."

"Stay."

His request surprises me. "For what? So you can shoot me down again like you did yesterday?"

Jake and Santos hear our conversation and chime in.

They also want me to stay, and say that we can have a few shots, and Eli can watch.

"Just because he can't have fun, doesn't mean we can't," says Santos.

"That's tempting," I reply with a grin, just to show Eli that I like the other guys, it's only him I have a problem with.

"Then stay," Jake insists.

"Yeah, stay," Santos says. "You'll have more fun with us than you will with Lou."

He and Jake laugh as if he's made a silly joke. Eli doesn't. His face stiffens. I wait for him to ask me again, but he doesn't say a thing. I wouldn't have stayed even if he had. The roller-coaster ride of being around Eli isn't good for my blood pressure.

"Are you coming?" Lou shouts, sticking his head back through the door.

"I'm coming."

I rush out and we drive home. I'm more relaxed on this ride than I was on the way here.

When we get back to the training camp, Lou and Margrit retire and I return to my room and then reply to a few emails.

I lay back on the bed and flip on the TV, but nothing appeals to me. I decide to make the most of the evening, given that the guys are out. I decide to make use of the hot tub, or the sauna, or maybe both.

Because I don't have a bikini or a swimsuit, I take my towel, and still in my jeans and T-shirt, I make my way to the spa room.

The room is empty. I hadn't expected that Lou or Margrit would be in here, but it's still reassuring to know that it's empty.

I walk past the hot tub, and over to the sauna. There's a window in here which looks onto the hot tub, and I push my face against it to take a look inside but I can't see much. This is what I wanted to check out yesterday but Eli being here prevented me.

I push the door open, then switch on the light. It's tubular shaped and wooden inside. Long, rather than wide, with two benches facing one another. It's enough for two people to lie toe-to-toe on each bench.

I can't decide where I want to go. I glance over at the hot tub, and the water looks still and cold. The sauna looks more appealing, and it's a clear winner.

I decide to heat myself up, and then cool off in the hot tub. So I close the sauna door and turn on the switch to get the steam running. And it does, slowly. Though it feels silly to be undressing in here, I do. I take off my clothes leaving nothing but my panties on, and I wrap the towel around me, then sit down. The heat has been building slowly, and soon the room is misty with searing steam. I turn it down a little, because I don't want to steam cook myself.

I bunch my hair high into a bun, and lean back against the wooden wall. I close my eyes as the heat swirls and heats my skin. It feels wonderful to finally have some time to myself.

Today has been pretty intense. Being around Eli always is, even when he's not talking to me directly, even when he's minding his own business and sparring or training.

He can cold-shoulder me easily. I wish I could do the same thing back to him but this assignment doesn't make that possible.

Right now though, I feel as if I'm in paradise. My body is loose, and the tension rolls away from my neck and shoulders.

The heat makes sweat trickle down my face, and my arms, and neck and shoulders. I get up and turn the dial down some more. Dots of moisture spring up all over my body. It's thick heat, but not suffocating, and it gives me the eerie sensation of being deep cleansed

I am sinking, and falling, and floating.

CHAPTER TWENTY-FIVE

ELI

I should be tired. I *should* be, because it's been a long day of training.

I'm usually knocked out by now, but Lou changed up my routine, insisting that we go out to eat. I think he did that because he wanted to give Margrit a day off, but I can't sleep because we ate later than I usually do and my routine is messed up. The food is still sitting in my stomach.

What sucks is that even though we went out to a nice place, I still ended up eating boring food—tuna and carbs, while the others dined out on dishes that made my mouth water. It was torture sitting in that small crowded place with the smell of garlic and butter floating in the air, and me knowing that I couldn't have any of it.

It kills me. It really does, watching everyone else eating all that lovely food that I can only dream of.

I stayed an hour at the bar in the restaurant, but when Jake and Santos announced that they wanted to go drinking,

I told them I was leaving. I reminded them that they're supposed to come running with me in the morning, but they laughed and told me I was a lightweight. They said it would only be for a couple of beers. But I wasn't drinking, and I didn't want to stay out late. I should have jumped in with Lou when he drove back.

I got a cab back alone, and left those two at the bar. They're probably still there right now even though Lou gave them a warning. It doesn't matter because they're not the ones who will step into the boxing ring opposite Garrison.

I will.

But I know what's at stake and I'm the one who wants the belt. I persevere because the biggest prize I could ever hope for is waiting for me at the end. And when I bring that belt back to Chicago, I know it will have been worth every sacrifice.

I signed autographs and had my pictures taken with some of the customers. It kept me distracted from the aroma of the food, and Harper.

Something happened yesterday; something that changed the dynamic between us. I noticed she was ignoring me today. Doing her best not to sit anywhere near me; we ended up together in the SUV on the way there and she didn't talk much.

Even at the restaurant, she sat in between Lou and Margrit, and then she left early. I would have expected her to stay late, get some more information out of me but she looked like she couldn't get out of there fast enough.

Which is odd, because this is the second time I've wanted her to stay. The first time was at Waquito's. I think that was the night I had an inkling that I might like her.

I hate thinking about Harper, especially when I'm tossing and turning so much at night in bed trying to sleep.

My sleep hasn't been that great for most of my life. I'm a light sleeper, and I often wake up for no reason. I tell myself there's nothing wrong. I have no problem, nothing to worry about, but the truth is there are thoughts which bubble up at night and confront me.

Thoughts which make it hard for me to breathe.

Thoughts that turn me into a helpless child once more.

The only thing to do is to find something to occupy me until I'm tired, so I put on my sweatpants and T-shirt, check the pockets of my sweatpants for my earphones, and head downstairs.

I briefly consider watching a movie, but when I open the door to the movie theater room and see the foreboding rows of empty plush red seats, I change my mind.

I head towards the spa because I have a better idea—relaxing in the hot tub. The warm water will help me to unwind and once I start listening to my music, I'll be able to get a good night's sleep. I'll be fully charged and ready for whatever new regimen Lou has in store for me tomorrow.

I walk into the spa and take off my sweatshirt and sweat pants next to the hot tub. That's when I notice that the light inside the sauna is on. The windows are steamed but when I look through the glass, it's empty inside.

I assume that Lou must have left it switched on, so I open the door, and it's like the flame from a blowtorch seared me.

But that's not all. My heart nearly jumps out of my chest because Harper's inside. She's sitting on the floor, looking as shocked as I am.

"What are you doing there?" I ask. Did she fall, or slip? And then I realize that there's no steam coming out of the vents, even though the room is hot.

She gets up slowly, clutching the towel around her as if

it's a life buoy and she's sinking in an ocean. She opens her mouth but nothing comes out. And then I understand. She's hiding from me.

This is the temptation I so badly didn't need.

She stares straight at me and blinks. Her hair is piled high on her head, and her skin is wet. I see her pile of discarded clothes on the bench.

Fuck.

This is a moment of many firsts. I don't know what to process first. That I can see her long, slim neck, or her bare, wet shoulders, or that underneath that towel, she's naked.

My cock hardens in an instant.

She's trying to hold the towel tight around her as if I could X-ray vision right through it.

I can't walk away now, but I should. I have a big fight and my neck is on the line; my reputation, my need to prove everyone wrong. My desire to claim the title—all of this is on the line.

I should walk away.

But my cock has other ideas.

My hand is on the doorknob, and I know my limits.

But I can still have some fun.

Not *that* type of fun. I can't get involved, but I can have a little fun with Harper. She looks so uptight right now, it would be the right thing for me to walk away.

But I always do the right thing. And now I don't want to.

So I close the door, and I stay.

CHAPTER TWENTY-SIX

HARPER

I want to vanish, just like the wisps of steam vanish into the air, but Eli is looking down on me as I slowly stand up. I feel stupid.

I dove onto the floor as soon as I saw him near the hot tub. He's the last person I expected to see, and I was so sure I had the place to myself. I'm surprised I'm not having a heart attack right now.

Now he's looking down at me as if I'm an idiot. He's not silly; he knows I was trying to hide from him.

"I dropped something," I say, and put a hand to my neck. "My necklace."

I crouch back down on the floor, and pretend to look for it, and I'm buying time trying to think of something smart to say.

He chuckles then sits on the wooden bench watching me. He doesn't believe me. *I* wouldn't believe me. So I get up, because there is no necklace, and because I need to stop digging myself deeper into this hole.

"Found it?" he asks with a twinkle in his eyes.

I'm not going to answer that because we both know the truth. "You said you weren't coming back until later," I say, securing the towel around me as if it's shrink-wrap. I sit across from him because he's taken my bench. Only, his body seems to take up half of it. Even though he isn't built like those grotesque body-builders with oversized muscles, to me he seems larger than life, bigger than he looks in the boxing ring. Maybe because the sauna is a confined space and he fills it beautifully.

"I changed my mind."

I try to look him directly in the eye, but it takes all my willpower to keep it trained on his face when my mind seems to take on a life of its own and my eyes want to drop to his bare chest and below. "Why?"

"Jake and Santos wanted to see the sights, and get friendly with the locals."

Breathing suddenly became harder. "And you didn't?" I fiddle around with the towel and makes sure it's still secure.

"I didn't want to watch them get drunk and hit on women."

The heat is dying down now, but it feels hotter than it should given that there's no steam coming out. Prickles break out up all over my body. Admittedly, the dying steam has nothing to do with it and it's all Eli's fault because he sits facing me in nothing but his boxer briefs.

I'm acutely aware that I'm naked under my towel except for my panties. My nipples have pebbled and I thank the Lord that the towel is thick and he can't see through it.

I wipe a hand over my face to wipe away the traces of sweat,

"Why you were sitting in here with no heat?" he asks.

"I turned it down. It got pretty hot."

"You *look* pretty hot."

I can't figure out if he's paying me a compliment or commenting about the heat. I can't tell with him. Eli has always been hard to read, and the strange thing is that the more I get to know him, the harder he gets to read. Still, I don't want to presume too much, so I assume he's not complimenting me. Meanwhile my heart continues to hammer like crazy. I place my hands over the top of my towel, convinced that Eli has superpowers and can see through it. "I was cooling down."

"Take a dip in the hot tub," he says.

My brain tells me this doesn't make sense, but we're not talking sense here. We're flirting, at least, I think he's flirting with me. Again, I don't want to presume too much. "Why don't *you* go ahead and get in the hot tub, like you were about to?" I suggest.

"Do you want me to leave?"

His question surprises me. It's a simple enough question, and while the proper answer would be to say 'yes'—the *only* sensible answer in this situation—I know that even if I said that, he's not going to listen to me. Eli does whatever the hell he wants to do.

"It's up to you. I can't stop you."

"Wouldn't you rather be in here, just the two of us talking, for a change, without any interruption?"

I see a playful, flirtatious side to Eli that I've only seen a few times. He's usually so angry and so intense, and now that he's flirting with me, I can't tell if he means it or if he finds it entertaining.

"I was going to go back to my room," I say, tucking a stray wisp of hair behind my ear. My hand lingers on my neck, then lowers, because I feel suddenly clammy. He's watching me. Amusement dances in his eyes and all over his stupid beautiful face. I could slap him right now for the way he's looking at me, for how he's making me feel, but if I did that, it would mean touching his skin, and knowing me, my hands would slip lower down, towards his neck and shoulders and then...

"You would really rather go back to your room?" he asks, interrupting the ridiculous running commentary in my head. I sit up straight and try to keep my wits about me.

"I have work stuff to do," I lie.

"Gerry?"

I frown. He always mentions Gerry with disdain. "He likes you."

This is the most absurd thing I've ever heard. "No, he doesn't," I exclaim. "Why would you say such a thing?" It's ridiculous.

"He does."

How Eli comes to this conclusion based on that one time they met at the diner is beyond me.

"He doesn't. He looks out for me. He's probably the only person at work who does."

"You watch," says Eli.

"You're paranoid," I throw back. He rests his back against the wall again, still appraising me slowly. His eyes run down the length of my body, and a tingly feeling spreads in my stomach.

"I'm not paranoid," he replies. His voice just got a million times huskier. "But you seem slightly tense."

"Me, tense? Well, I'm not." Aroused, maybe. He is too, I notice, because his boxer briefs are tented. It's hard to ignore an erection that big. He must know. But he doesn't seem embarrassed by it, and he doesn't try to hide it. He'd need a bucket to hide something like that.

My breath turns shorter, and I squeeze my legs together.

"Good, because I'm not going to do anything."

"Who says you were?" I ask.

"I'm not, but you look as if you're scared I'm going to make a move on you like Callum did."

My eyes widen in surprise. "Who?"

"Callum, the guy you left Waquito's with. The guy you've seen butt naked in the locker room."

It takes me a while to process what he's saying. I hear an accusation in his voice, maybe even a splice of jealousy.

I frown as I recall that night, when he and Athena were reconnecting, and I couldn't wait to get the hell out of that place. Eli was busy in conversation with his ex. "How do you know?"

"I saw you," he replies. His voice has a hard edge to it now.

"But you were in the bar with your girlfriend."

"My *ex*-girlfriend." The emphasis is slight, but I hear it.

"She had her claws into you that night, if I remember correctly. I'm surprised she allowed you to leave her side."

"Athena has no sway over me," he growls. His eyes narrow, and his languid demeanor slips.

"She looked like she was glued to your side."

"You were watching us?" he asks.

"Her desperation for you is hard to miss. It wouldn't surprise me if you ignored your no-sex ban and took her home." What does surprise me is that I said this out loud, but I couldn't keep it bottled in any longer. I've wondered since that night if she managed to ensnare him. Eli has resolve, but in the face of such jaw-dropping femininity, and that minx and her wily ways, I don't expect him to abstain. He's only a man, after all.

"Did you go home with him?" he asks, not bothering to respond to my comment.

I laugh out loud because that's insane. He's obviously trying to rile me up, first with Gerry, and now with Callum. "You are joking, aren't you?"

His silence tells me he isn't.

His silence tells me that he's been thinking the exact same thing about me as I was thinking about him and Athena.

It means he's jealous.

It means he feels something.

For me.

This preposterous idea makes me so incredibly happy because up until now I thought it was something in my head.

"You really think Callum and I...?" The sentence is too ludicrous to finish.

"You didn't?" he asks, as if he doesn't believe me.

"I hardly know him!" I exclaim, trying to inject as much indignation into my voice as I can, given the highly aroused state I am in.

I've been thinking about nobody but Eli for as many weeks as I've been around him, but I steel myself so that I don't give anything away.

"You've seen him in the buff. Maybe you liked what you saw?" he prompts.

My heart misses a beat or four. "I've seen you in the buff..." But I can't finish the sentence. I want to tell him I most definitely liked what I saw, that I *want* what I saw, that he makes me lose my mind, and my sensibility. But I cannot say a word. I should not say a word.

"Then what did you do, because you got into a cab together?" he asks, adding to my growing excitement, and hopes, and happiness.

"We talked on the way. I wanted to find out about your fight club days, but he was mostly talking about himself."

"That sounds about right for Callum."

"And then he got out, and I stayed in the cab until I got home. Why? What did *you* do? Last I saw, you and Athena were gazing dreamily into each other's eyes."

This makes him laugh. "It's easier to extricate myself from her if I let her think we might get back together."

"You might?"

"Hell, no. You're not listening, Princess."

"Why do you keep calling me that?"

"*Princess?*" he asks, and to my utter shock and delight, he scoots over and sits next to me. My displeasure at him using this term soon falls by the wayside. I'm in lust with Eli. I'm pretty sure I would do anything right now, give him anything right now, if he asked.

"What other name is more fitting for the woman who has everything?"

"Is that what you think? That I have everything?" His impression of me is warped. I understand why he'd think that though, but I had hoped he'd warmed to me given that we've spent a lot of time around one another.

"I have other nicknames for you," he tells me, as I concentrate on my breathing. He exudes an animal aura that makes my brain malfunction. I'm certain it stopped working the moment he stepped in here.

I stare at him blankly.

"Don't you want to know my nicknames for you?"

"What are they?" I ask.

"Miss Busybody, on account of your snooping around."

"I have a job to do."

"I know." The corners of his mouth curve up into a smile in understanding. "And Princess is because you're in a different league."

I stare at him in confusion. "A different league?"

"You looked lost that first day you walked into the gym. I was sure you were allergic to the dirt and falling-apart vibe of the place."

"Ernesto keeps it ticking over," I reply, fondly, thinking of the man who made me feel welcome.

"He does. He's a good man."

I remember that first day. "I did feel lost, and you didn't help."

"I probably didn't."

"You *definitely* didn't."

"I've tried to be helpful," he argues.

"And I have cherished those moments because they've been few and far between."

He nods this time, as if he's taking it in and analyzing it. "I've tried to block you out, Harper."

Now he's lost me.

"Is that why you were cold towards me when I got here yesterday?"

"You're not listening. I thought you and Callum might have gotten a bit too friendly."

"And that would bother you?" My elation skyrockets.

"I don't know why it would, but it did."

Right now I feel like a cheerleader on the winning team. I jump for joy with my imaginary pom-poms.

"I'm always after my story," I say, attempting a laugh.

"I figured." His voice is raspy. "I didn't mean to make you run away from the hot tub last night."

I stare at him defiantly. "You didn't," I insist, even

though I had to take a few breaths once I was out of the spa room. He's the epitome of relaxed seduction. His back is flat against the wood, and now he's slouching as if he's totally relaxed. He's confessed that he was jealous about Callum, and I don't know what to do with what he's just told me.

I'm sitting upright, my hands around my body, doubling up to keep the towel from falling apart. I'm on the edge of my seat, on high alert, trying to keep it together.

I want to leave, but I also don't want to leave. I'm excited, and I'm scared. I want to give in, and hold out.

I want him, and I know I can't have him.

I'm torn.

He strokes my shoulder. I don't flinch at his electric touch, as much as I welcome it.

"Your skin's cooled down real fast," he murmurs. "Are you cold?"

I nod my head, because I don't trust my voice.

"Would your boyfriend mind you being in here with me?" he asks, his eyes gleaming.

"I don't have a boyfriend." My voice doesn't seem like mine. Suddenly I'm not scared, but I don't trust myself. The towel feels tight around my body, and the nerves from my belly down to my thighs sizzle in anticipation. My breath feels ragged, and my fingers itch to roam over his skin. I've had sex where I've faked my orgasm and couldn't wait for it to be over with, but now I'm sitting next to Eli and I can already feel my orgasm building.

This man arouses me without even laying a finger on me.

"Then there's nothing wrong with us being in here like this." His voice is low, and deep, and it reaches every orifice of my body.

His thumb circles around my shoulder. It's a sexy

motion, and my skin responds with a rash of goosebumps. It's a surprise move coming from him, but I am so, so, so grateful for it. I turn and look at him in order to figure out if he's still playing with me, or being serious.

"What?" he asks, still thumbing my shoulder gently. "Want me to stop?" He sits forward and shifts his body so that he's twisted towards me.

"That depends," I reply slowly, trying to formulate a reply, "on what you'll do next." I can't believe what I've just said. It seems I shed my professional persona at the same time I shed my clothes.

"There's a couple of things we could do next," he says, and I'm too scared to look at him, or ask him to elaborate. Instead I look ahead. His fingers skate gently along my collarbone.

"I've wondered lately, what it might feel like to kiss you."

My insides explode at this. My shoulders might even have sagged under the weight of his words. "Do you want me to kiss you?" he asks when I say nothing.

Every part of my body comes together like a jury, and the verdict is a unanimous yes.

I don't manage to reply in words, as much as a weak moan.

"Is that a yes, Harper?"

"Yes."

"What's the magic word?"

"Now," I reply and turn to look at him. He smiles at that and my heart takes a dive. It's rare when he does that, but he's got such a beautiful smile, and my panties have truly melted off my skin. "That didn't work the other day," he reminds me.

"*Please*," I say.

"That's better, Princess." He could call me all sorts of things right now, it's not his words I need. He leans towards me, then brushes that same vagabond wisp of hair away from my face. "I like your hair up," he says, then skims his thumb down my face, from my forehead, down the side of my face, to my chin.

I'm breathless, and the throbbing between my legs is so intense that I'm quivering. I'm ready for his kiss, but his hand moves to my neck, then traces over my collarbone again. He is driving me batshit crazy with this lingering and delay.

"Your skin is so soft," he whispers, he's close enough now that his lips graze my ear. It's not only his fingers I feel on my skin, but his warm, sweet breath. The combination is a double hit to my erogenous zones. Then he kisses me, his lips brushing so gently at first, that I can't reconcile his soft touch with the boxer that he is.

I melt into him, as his soft and luscious lips claim my mouth ever so gently. His hands cups the back of my head, he angles his head, deepening the kiss.

We kiss for the longest time and the newness of his mouth, his lips, his tongue, all heighten every sensation. I moan, because I have hungered for his kiss for the longest time. We pull away briefly, to breathe and to stare at one another.

Only, he doesn't look as playful anymore. He's more serious. His moist lips make me want to kiss him all over again, but he doesn't move.

And to my horror, he scoots back a little. I can see the training kicking in; his determination, his focus, his fight.

But I am soaked, and desperate, and I won't lose this moment. I swoop towards him, and splay my hands over his chest. I finally get to put my hands on his body. It's the stuff of my dreams and I feel like a kid in a candy shop. I plant my lips over his, and explore his mouth. He snaps to it. His hands go around my waist and he pulls me towards him, as if he just made up his mind to go for it.

We kiss hard and fierce, as if the lust and longing, once tightly coiled in frustration, now has a release.

And then we hear something.

"Eli!" Lou's voice screeches from outside. In a flash we duck down, and stay close to the wall under the window, like I did when Eli found me.

We hear Lou mumbling something, and we hide like naughty schoolchildren. I'm breathing so hard, and I turn my head to look at Eli. He lifts his head towards the window, but doesn't try to sneak a peek.

Then the outside light turns off, and we hear the sound of a door closing.

Then, silence.

Eli lifts his head and steals a look out of the window. "All clear," he says, then stands up.

"He said he was going to bed. So did Margrit!"

"One of the guys must have told him I was on my way back. They're supposed to keep an eye on me."

"Won't Lou worry when he doesn't find you?"

"He'll see I made it back, because my phone and clothes are on the bed."

I'm still crouched on the floor, and only when his eyes fall to it, do I discover that my towel has come undone.

Crap.

I rush to pull it together again, but Eli's on the floor beside me, and he stops me. His eyes bore into mine as if he's looking for my reaction. He must see the hunger in them because he whips my towel off and tosses it to the bench along with my clothes. Then he scoots towards the wall, resting his back against it and with his legs straight out. "Take a seat," he orders, patting his thigh. His searing gaze takes in my naked breasts and I don't need to be told twice. I have an ache between my legs and I need to feel him against me.

No sooner do I do that than his hands are around my waist, and he pulls me towards him. We kiss again, hungrier than last time, our lust amplified by the interruption.

His hand kneads my breasts, pulling, and pinching my nipples. I am so highly aroused now that I could come just from his fondling and kissing. And just when I think I can't get enough of him, he slips his fingers past the fabric of my panties and slides them around, exploring and teasing. I gasp in surprise. If he doesn't know how wet I am for him, he will now.

"That's not sauna steam," he whispers into my ear.

"That's all you," I murmur, our lips brush as I savor the way he's stroking me. I am drowning in pleasure. His hands, his fingers, his lips are an assault on my senses. "I've dreamt of this," I tell him, not caring that my guard is down.

He moves away, jolting me cruelly, then stands up and lifts me as if I were nothing more than a feather floating on his thighs. My arms deadlock around his neck, and my legs wrap around his hips. I can feel his hardness and I grind into it.

"Easy," he says, laying me down on the bench before ripping my panties off as if they hadn't just melted anyway. I open my mouth to protest, but his finger slides into me, and all I can do is utter a dirty sigh.

"You're so wet," he moans, as if this gives him the greatest of pleasures. He dips another finger in and I bite my lip, arching my back because I am on the precipice, and he controls which way I fall. He clamps his mouth over mine, his tongue fighting for dominance as we kiss again, this time with an urgency. Eli pleasuring me at either end fogs my brain. I am in heaven, and I tremble, wavering on the edge of my release.

But he breaks the kiss off and moves away from me. My legs fall open, because I can't control a thing. This time he thumbs my clit with the other hand, while his fingers pump in and out, driving me into a frenzy. The pressure builds and spirals upwards and outwards from my core. With his expert touch and attention, I'm a mass of beating heart, throbbing pussy and swollen breasts.

He bends down and sucks my breast hard, first one, then the other, and he's still circling my clit. I open my legs wider, moaning as he suckles my nipple as if this was his first time. But I no longer want surface-level entertainment, I need more; something deeper, dirtier, more fulfilling.

His mouth is latched onto my breast, but I need his cock, and I'm desperate to relieve the ache between my legs. I reach out for his boxers and the steel pipe of his erection greets my needy hand. My fingers wrap around him and I marvel at the feel of him, at the size, and the hardness. I will die if I don't get him inside me right now.

But he moves my hand away. "No," he growls. His voice is coarse with need.

"I need you," I whimper.

"I'm not done with you yet."

Thank heaven. I could spend the whole night here with him. I try to pull his boxers down but I'm in a vulnerable position, lying on the bench, splayed out the way I am, and I can't get the grip I need.

Only he moves his mouth away from my breast and adjusts his position so that he's between my legs. Then he throws my leg over his shoulder, and spreads my legs wider.

"Fuck," he says, staring at my pussy. He makes a noise, a feral, raw noise deep in his throat, and then his mouth is on me, and his tongue rolls over me, licking and tasting my clit while his fingers move inside me.

I feel as if he's given me the most powerful aphrodisiac on the planet as heat surges through me and reaches every orifice in my body. Eli unravels me from the inside out, and I breathe out shakily. I have no control over my limbs, and I lay back, floating in nirvana, letting him take his fill. His greedy sucking lips make me see stars, but when he moves his fingers out and thrusts his tongue deep inside me, I shake and jerk to his touch.

My back arches off the bench, and I moan and squirm as he buries his face deeper in my pussy. I grab the wooden slats, desperate to grip hard onto something. The pleasure has been building for the longest time and I jolt, then cry out helplessly. The frustration of weeks of lusting after him finally releases with my orgasm. "Eli," I moan, and lift my hips up to free myself, but his mouth is still latched on, and he's still tunneling, and licking, and driving me wild.

"Eli!" I cry out, because my nerves jangle and tremble, and I feel ready to explode. "Oh...god, Eli!" I shudder with him at my most intimate place, but he doesn't move away. His mouth and fingers still work their magic. I feel as if I could die from too much pleasure. This exquisite combination is something I have never experienced, not like this.

I cry out, forgetting where we are, as my orgasm tears through me, leaving me breathless. Slowly, he lets go, and kisses my inner thighs gently. His lips trail slowly up my belly leaving kisses in their wake.

"Oh, god," I murmur, as he sucks my breast again. I rake

my hand through his hair and grab on, needing a piece of him to hold on to.

My insides are fluid, and the space between my legs still throbs. And still, he lets me finish at my own speed, while leaving tiny kisses all over my body.

CHAPTER TWENTY-SEVEN

ELI

I look down at her as she comes. Harper's professional exterior has vanished, and she's lying here open to me; vulnerable, and beautiful, and mine.

I hadn't intended for this to happen. I thought we would fool around a little, but I should have known better. I should have known that I was on shaky ground after our first kiss.

I blame Lou.

If he hadn't come in, I would have backed off after that first kiss, while I still could, but things got out of hand. Seeing her naked triggered it. And still I could have held back. I'm no stranger to resistance. I can close off my feelings at will. Taking in her naked body hit me hard, but I could have walked away.

Who am I kidding?

I haven't been able to get Princess out of my mind ever

since the night at Waquito's when I saw her with Callum. Why else would I tell her to sit on me? Why else would I make a move I knew I couldn't get out of. A move she couldn't avoid. We kissed and my defenses fell.

Hard to keep it together when her gorgeous tits were in my face, and my fingers sank into her silky folds. Up until then, I thought it was a game.

I don't know why I'm attracted to Harper, but I am. I've always been around women who let me know in no uncertain terms what they want from me. They fall for my physique. They like that I'm a boxer. Women like men with power, and physical power is the ultimate god. Some women like a man with money, but I bet most women want a man with a good body. When it comes to fucking, women want muscle. Doesn't matter if their sugar daddy is rich, in the heat of the moment they want to feel muscle.

Harper's no different.

Maybe it's because she and I have been cooped up around each other for weeks. Maybe it's because Callum and Athena showed us our real selves, but what happened just now was going to happen at some point.

It was only a matter of time.

I hated her at first, I own up to it. I hated her and everything she reminded me of. But she doesn't come at me like the others, like Athena and the many women like her.

Nor does Harper hide it as well as she thinks she does.

My gut instinct is my survival beacon. I knew she found me attractive almost from the first day, but she didn't give in to it, maybe because she's a professional, or because her daddy wouldn't approve of her taking up with someone like me. She didn't give in, and I admire that.

I sit back and watch her come down from her orgasm.

She's naked, and she lies panting, her hand on her chest. I could look at her naked all day long. I want her. My hard-on is going to hurt, my blue balls are painful, but I won't allow myself to do anything, even though I want to bury myself inside her. It takes all of my control to sit back and do nothing.

After a while, she slowly sits up, trying to cover her body with her hands. Too late because I've seen everything. Tasted everything. But I reach over for her towel, and hand it to her since she looks embarrassed.

"Why did you... stop?" she asks, staring at the hard-to-miss bulge in my shorts.

"You came."

"But you... you're not ... *done*."

"Watching you was as good as."

She opens her mouth then looks as if she can't bring herself to say anything, and instead wastes more time securing the towel around her. She looks uncomfortable, then tells me, "I wanted you."

This brings a smile to my face. "I can't get up to anything. You heard Lou."

"Isn't that a myth?"

"It could be, but I'm not willing to test it out, even if you tempt the hell out of me."

She has no idea how much I want her. "I didn't have a condom," I tell her. "I wasn't expecting to need one." I don't want her to think I didn't want to, or that I don't find her attractive, because I do. I want her badly.

Only just not *now*.

Having sex before a fight is going to take away my edge.

My hunger.

It will weaken me.

I've been building my mental discipline for months and I'm determined that not even Harper's naked body is going to make me falter.

Afterwards, though... that's another thing.

Her gaze slips to my boner again. We both want more. She has no idea how hard it was for me to stop when I did. What it took not to drive my cock inside her.

Her chest rises and falls, and I can see she's having trouble accepting this. She's caught in limbo, recovering from what just happened, and caught halfway between the lure of secret sex and at the same time aware of our professional relationship.

"I can reciprocate..." she says, scratching the back of her neck. That brings a smile to my lips.

"Hold that thought," I tell her, surprising myself. Now my chest rises and falls because she's placed an image in my head that I can't shake. She's got her mouth around me, and she's giving me the best head I've ever had.

She says nothing, and I close my eyes for a moment longer than is necessary.

"You have good restraint," she says.

"I want the belt." It's been my mantra ever since this fight was set up. Nothing takes my eyes off it, not even the offer Harper has made.

"And I want the story," she says, reminding me why we came together in the first place. She picks up her clothes from the bench.

"You'll get your story," I tell her.

"And you'll get your belt."

We're both standing now, and I want to kiss her again as I look down at her. Things have changed between us again, because of what just happened. We can't go back to what we were before, but I'm not sure that we can easily step into the future.

She puts her arms around me in a surprise move and nestles against my chest. I hesitate at first but when her dark green eyes stare up at me, I feel a connection. I wrap my arms around her and we stand and hold one another for a moment.

I open the sauna door and we file out silently. She goes her way, and I go mine.

I return to my room with the smell and taste of her all over me.

The next morning, Lou wakes me at 4:00 a.m., an hour earlier than usual.

"Where the hell where you last night?" he asks, turning on the lamp by the door. The glaring light makes me want to bury my head under the covers. I'm exhausted, but that's my fault because I couldn't sleep last night. I tossed and turned with images of a naked Harper in my head.

"Here," I say, forcing myself to climb out of bed. I mentally prepare myself for another brutal day.

"I knocked on your door. Santos called to say you were coming back early. I checked everywhere for you."

"I was in the movie theater," I say.

"No, you weren't. I checked. I hope you weren't up to no good."

I know what he's driving at. "You know me, Lou. I don't go there. Even if that journalist was hot—and she's not, she's not my type—but even if she was, I wouldn't go there. You know I'm a professional. If you'd checked the kitchen, you would have found me. I watched Garrison's last fight then I made myself a snack."

He seems satisfied with my report.

"Why am I up so early?"

"You're running a longer distance. Fifteen miles today."

"First thing in the morning?" I almost yell.

"Resistance and stamina, that's the only way you're going to get through twelve rounds with Garrison."

I wipe my hands over my face. "Okay," I reply. I've done everything Lou's ever told me, and even though I'm bone tired, and I hate the idea of going through yet another day like every day before it, I know this is what I have to do.

"Did you wake Jake and Santos?"

He grunts in disapproval. "They're wasted. They got back too late. I'll drive beside you and watch you run."

Great. That's all I need.

I'm out for a couple of hours, and then I get back and shower, and change, have a bite to eat, and it's back to training.

I see Harper in the kitchen with Margrit, but I barely look at her, just to keep things the same.

At lunchtime we all sit together and eat, and we still don't get a moment alone.

Hard to dismiss her when she's in front of me. She lifts her fork to her mouth, and joins in the conversation, but every once in a while she'll throw me a look, and it's enough.

Our hands brush together as we walk back to the gym. We're behind Lou and the others, and I grasp her fingers as we go through the double doors.

Then I go off and train some more, only I keep wondering if she'll be in the spa room tonight. It's a distraction, and one I didn't want to have, but it is hard to block that out when I have such vivid memories of yesterday still so fresh in my mind.

The evening finally draws to a close. We've watched more fight sequences in the movie theater room. Margrit and Harper are missing. Lou says that Margrit is reading in bed, and I have no idea where Harper is. I don't think she'll go anywhere near the spa room tonight.

Santos and Jake are staying in because after last night, and the fact that they couldn't get up this morning, Lou has them on a strict curfew.

I have another 4:00 a.m. start tomorrow morning.

CHAPTER TWENTY-EIGHT

HARPER

I have to stay away from him if I want to help him. I don't want Eli to lose this fight because of me. I shouldn't flatter myself, but I've had a hard time trying not to think about our night in the sauna room.

Each time I recall it, my body starts to heat.

For all his steel determination, I bet Eli's having as hard a time as me.

That's why I'm surprised when he texts me late at night.

He asks me what I'm doing, and when I say I'm about to go to bed, he tells me to come over.

I don't even pretend to fight this one. My good intentions of not being a distraction are discarded in an instant. He meets me in the hallway, and we tiptoe to his room—I wouldn't have been able to find it in this maze, and I've never been to his side of the house.

Once inside, we manage to close the door before we're

kissing again. We're not just kissing, he's lifted me up and I cling to him like a leech, my arms and legs around him, as if I'm sucking the life force out of him.

He claims my mouth with such hungry abandon that I know nothing except for the feel of his body against mine, and the warmth of his mouth.

Soon, we're on the bed, rolling around like teenagers.

Within seconds, I feel his arousal. I want this, and I ignore everything he told me, I reach for him, but he takes my hand away, and rolls us so that he's straddling me, only he's not completely resting on top of me because he'd flatten me. His strong hands pin my arms over my head and he smiles down at me.

This is a new Eli, and I love him.

"We can't do anything," he says. "Remember my commitment."

"You're not a monk," I counter, even though for all intents and purposes, he might as well be, for now.

I jiggle my hips, waiting for his magic fingers to roam all over me. I wait for his lips to savor my skin. He grins at me as if he knows what I'm thinking, then shakes his head. "You can help me stay on the straight and narrow."

I make a pouty face, but I'm up for the challenge. "Seriously? No fooling around?"

"You can help me."

I wonder why he called me to his room then, if he wasn't going to fool around, "You called me at this time of night to tell me this?"

"I called you because I wanted to fool around, because you've managed to chip away at my restraint—"

"Hey," I reply, trying to sit up but I can't because he's on top of me. "We both had a part in that yesterday."

"Simmer down," he says, as he sets my heart on edge

again. It's as if he's ditching me even before I've had the chance to become his girlfriend or lover. I hate that he has this power to make me feel happy or sad. Then he kisses me, confusing the heck out of me again, but I don't mind, in fact, I'll take whatever he gives me. His tongue swirls around my mouth and his hand cups the side of my face.

I love this.

My confusion gives way to elation, and we kiss like before, hard and rough, as if we're new to it. I sigh with contentment and hold onto his shoulders as if they belong to me. I savor every beautiful second of this; Eli, in a good mood, desiring me. All that's missing is the sex but, like a dog thrown a bone, I'll take this over nothing.

After a long kissing session that has me grinding my hips against him in a subtle effort to wrest more from him than he's willing to give me, he lies down beside me. I turn and snuggle against him, and my hand starts to slide down towards his hardness. But I force myself to stop. I need to respect what he's asked of me. So I slide my hand back up again, and rest it on his T-shirt. I suppose it helps, us both being fully clothed, even if I was hoping to be in some state of undress by now.

I move my hand up and down his chest slowly, just reveling in the notion that I can do this; that he's allowing me to. We lie in silence, and it's nice.

"What did Callum tell you?" he asks after a while.

"You're still going on about him?" He has nothing to worry about, if he still mistakenly believes I have any interest in that guy.

"He said he was lucky he met you when he did, and that he knew you when Lou spotted you."

"He was lucky. We both were. We used to fight in some shady places with the fight club."

"I was wondering when you'd tell me about that."

"Fight clubs are vicious."

"And the boxing you do now isn't?"

"What I do now is professional, and it's much safer than what I used to do. I wasn't just fighting there, I was also fixing fights."

"Really?" I lift my head up slightly.

He dismisses it easily. "We needed rent money, or rather, Nina did, otherwise we wouldn't have had a roof over our heads. I threw some fights to get extra money in backhanders."

I don't understand, so I say nothing. I don't know what it's like not to have money. I've never been that stuck in my life that I couldn't make ends meet. And even if I were to ever find myself in that position, my father is always there, as is my mom. I have the security of my family to fall back on.

Because I don't know what to say, and because I want to empathize with him, I kiss his chest again. This is a pathetic response, and I'm fully aware of that.

"We've had completely different lives, you and I. We started off differently, and we're going to go our separate ways and have our own different endings."

I swallow because I don't like what he's saying. I don't know where this will end, and I can't see beyond this moment, but I am willing to take each moment as it comes.

Second by second.

With him.

I'll take this moment here, because with Eli, I never know if he's going to give me another. So I say nothing, even though he just pierced a hole in my heart by talking about me as if I'm expendable.

"I don't always understand you," I say, because it is safer

to say this than to tell him I want to be with him, even when I'm done with this assignment. I can't get up to anything now while I'm covering this story, Merv would accuse me of giving a biased account and he'd probably fire me, because all he needs is a reason to.

"You won't. You were born on a different side of the track." I can see in his eyes that he's wandered off again, gone somewhere else. I touch his chin gently. "Hey, you. We're not so different. Our past doesn't define us, it's who we are now that matters."

His jaw tenses, and right away I can see he doesn't like this. "Not all of us have had an easy life like you, Princess."

That name is like a slap to my cheek, I don't like it, and I hate that he doesn't see that. But this is new, him and I, the most unlikeliest of people getting together, and I'm not about to ruin this moment.

In a way he's right.

My life has been easy. I've never known the threat of being homeless. I never went through the foster care system. I've never stepped into the world of child protection.

My parents always told me they loved me. I have always been needed and wanted.

I kiss his chest, because I want him to know that he is needed, too. That I love him, even though love might not be the right word to describe what we have, I feel a lot of love for him right now.

"You're going to win, and then your life will be on a different path. And I believe in you. I don't care what anyone says, I know you can do this." I kiss his chest again. He looks at me as if he not sure what to make of me. It's not a flirtatious look, or a hard stare, it doesn't look as if he's torn and can't decide on whether he wants me to stay or leave. He's looking at me as if he wants me here. "Is this allowed?"

I ask, dropping another kiss on his chest. I'm unclear about our boundaries but a kiss on a T-shirt seems tame in comparison.

"It's allowed."

I drop another kiss on his chest.

"I could get used to you being around," he says. It's the closest he's come to saying he likes me, and my insides turn all gooey. I want to move up and kiss his mouth, but that would set up a domino effect that would get us aroused again, and if we couldn't hold back, it would ruin everything. I have to respect his wishes, before the fight, that is. After that? He's mine.

"Look how far you've come," I say, in an effort to lift his mood, because he seems somber again. The playfulness of yesterday is missing. "You fought for money, to help Nina with the rent, and now you're fighting Trent Garrison."

"I sometimes wonder if I could have had it sooner if I hadn't messed up."

"Messed up how?"

"I almost had a chance to try out for the Olympic team, but I took a bad beating after one of the fights, and I missed the tryout."

I am horrified and put my arm around him. But I don't understand. "You took a beating after a fight?"

"I could have won. I *would* have won, but the organizers wanted me to lose. So I threw the fight. Some guys found out and beat the crap out of me later that night. It was four of them against me. They broke my ribs, and beat me up real good. Nina almost fainted when she saw me."

My head goes to a dark place, and I see him in my mind's eye. "Eli," I say, and hug him.

"It wasn't so bad."

Shock hurtles through me and I lift my head. "Sounds pretty bad to me."

"I was used to it. I had my aunt's boyfriend to thank for that. He used to beat me black and blue because he hated that he had two mouths to feed and he and my aunt had two of their own. He hardened me up. A leather belt and a seven-year-old don't go so well together, but after his beatings, it didn't hurt so much."

My jaw is in danger of hitting the floor, and I try to curtail my horror. I want to cry, and instead I swallow to brace myself.

Eli seems removed from it, like it has no effect on him. I want to tell him that I love him, and that he won't ever have to go through that again, and that he's older now and has escaped that nightmare existence, and that stuff is in his past, and it's better left there, but I don't say that yet, because he seems to be somewhere else. His eyes look faraway. So I just listen, for now, but I understand him some more. I know the things that have shaped him. I even understand why he calls me Princess.

I had never expected such awful beginnings for him. I shift my body up a little and rest my head just under his chin. Then I squeeze his arm and listen, because that's all I can do. "But you went to Grampton House, after. That was nice, wasn't it?" I ask, wanting him to think of better times.

"Is that what you think, Princess?"

He doesn't like this. So I don't pry. I wait. But he remains silent. We stay like this for the longest time.

And then he speaks. "Grampton House wasn't so bad at first, but..." His mouth twists and a line forms between his brows.

"But what?"

"There was a man who worked there. He wasn't a good man."

I lift my head again but I'm too scared. "He wasn't a good man to who, Eli?"

He stares at me.

It's written all over his face. The pain is too great, and he doesn't speak.

"He did things ... to me. Things a child should never know about."

Bile forms in my stomach and threatens to run back up my throat. I open my mouth, but Eli shakes his head. He doesn't want to talk about it. "Lie back down," he orders, and I do, but this time, I hold onto him.

When I lift my head, Eli is asleep. I stare at him for a while, because he looks so peaceful, and as much as I would like to stay here all night, I can't risk falling asleep in case Lou finds us both in bed. It would be entirely innocent, but I don't think we'd convince Lou.

I slowly unwrap myself from him and get ready to leave.

ELI

I feel her get up and leave me, and I open my eyes. Harper's staring down at me. "I didn't mean to wake you."

"You didn't." I wasn't asleep. I just wanted to lie there and have her snuggled up close to me. "Stay a while," I tell her. Harper makes me feel the kind of peaceful I haven't felt for a long time. Which is strange, and I don't understand it, but some things just are. I told her something

I haven't told a soul. Not even Nina, and I don't know why I did that.

"I can't," she says. "I don't want to go, but I can't stay." I wonder if she's keeping her distance from me because she can't trust herself around me, or because she feels sorry for me, on account of what I just told her.

I like that she doesn't ask anything more, because I want to forget the things that should never have happened but did.

As it is, I don't trust myself around her. It's not lost on me, the irony of the situation, given how I felt when she first arrived, but now there are things I want to do to her, kiss her for longer, kiss her everywhere. Make her come with my mouth and my fingers.

But I can't.

She blows me a kiss as she gets ready to leave. "Are you going to be okay? I can stay for a little bit."

I shake my head, and I don't blow a kiss back. "I'm okay."

"Goodnight, then." She closes the door behind her and I pinch my eyebrows. Why did I tell her? She's like a pill I take, one which relaxes me and makes me open up.

But this doesn't feel as bad as I thought it would. I feel no shame, only relief.

She leaves tomorrow, and at least the temptation will be out of my sight. I seriously don't know if my balls can take another night like yesterday. I'm here for another few days, and then I have a week before the fight. I'm probably going to have a boner the entire week at this rate.

The fight is on the horizon, now. I can see it. I can feel it. I am already prepared for Garrison's face in my mind, his demonic look as we face off standing in front of one another for the pre-fight weigh in.

In a few weeks' time, there will be a new world heavyweight champion. I can almost feel the belt in my hands. It's not the adulation of the crowd I crave. I learned a long time ago how fickle people can be. How they change allegiance and loyalty in a heartbeat.

This belt is for *me*.

I grew up being told that I was a worthless piece of shit, and winning this title will prove that I'm not.

People look at me like I don't stand a chance against Garrison, but they don't know me. They don't know what made me who I am.

CHAPTER TWENTY-NINE

HARPER

I tiptoed back to my room. Miraculously, I remembered the way back, and then I lay in bed for hours unable to sleep. Eli's confession set up home inside my brain and refused to leave.

That poor, poor child.

That poor, poor man.

On the surface, he's a hard-as-nails fighting machine, but inside, he's as broken as the most fragile flower.

He's never struck me as someone who has suffered so much. I never understood the motivation that makes a man voluntarily step into a ring and want to physically hurt another man in the name of sport. There has to be an easier and safer way to earn money, but boxers—my research has shown me—often come from tough backgrounds. A lot come from broken homes, and many have suffered sexual, physical and emotional abuse.

Everything that previously confused me about Eli now

starts to make sense. It makes me want to protect him more than ever, even though I am not the protector. I want to make him smile, and forget, and move on, and I vow to myself that I will do all these things for as long as he and I are together.

In my mind, there is a future.

The next day we keep up our charade, barely talking to one another. Eli concentrates on his training, and I help Margrit prepare lunch. After that, I bid my farewells and leave. Eli and I never get a moment alone to say our goodbyes, and perhaps it's better that way.

Leaving the boxing camp is hard and on my drive home I think of Eli all the way home. I even text him a few times when I stop to take a break, but he doesn't reply back.

I understand, even if I am slightly deflated. After two intense nights, I'm not prepared for the sudden cutoff. It's Eli, and I should know better, but I tell myself that I'm out of sight and out of his mind. He's concentrating hard, and I have to let him. I also have a better understanding of who he is.

I get back home around midnight, and as I'm about to get into bed, he calls me.

"Hey," I say, a permanent smile already on my face.

"Hey."

My heart lifts at the sound of his voice. "I texted you."

"I didn't get a moment to myself."

We've gone from being almost mortal enemies when I got there to being so intimate with each other by the time I left. Now we're talking as if we've been seeing one another for weeks. I have a feeling this smile will be on my face forever. "Where are you?" An image of the hot tub and the sauna room pops into my head. I close my eyes and wish I was there.

"In the sauna room."

"No." I stand up and gasp. "What are you doing in there?"

"Reminiscing."

I exhale louder than I intended. "Which part?" Excitement snakes through me as I relive our last few nights.

"All of it."

My mouth falls open, and I'm transported there again. But I'm also skeptical. I know about his determination and his commitment. Even though it feels good for me to know that I snatched a few moments of his concentration, I know what it is that Eli wants the most. The title. The belt.

Everything else is secondary. "You're not in the sauna room," I say, lying on the bed with my arm splayed out, feeling the cool satin against my skin. I so badly wish he were here lying next to me. "I miss you." It comes out, just like that, like my next breath would, and there follows an awkward silence.

"You're right. I'm not in the sauna room. It would be too much of a distraction," he says, completely ignoring my 'I miss you.' "I'm in my room, getting ready to go bed. I saw your texts. Wanted to know why you called."

I don't know what to make of this about-face. I couldn't resist him before and now that I've had a taste of what it is like to be with him, I'm addicted. I miss him and I was excited when he called, but now my hopes start to sink like the Titanic and I feel the chill of his cold words.

"It was to see how you were," I said, hoping my pseudo-cheery voice hides my disappointment well.

"I'm about to hit the sack," he says. His tone and his words spear my heart into two. I wait for the punchline, or the comforting words, or for him to say he's joking, and that he missed me and wants to talk to me, but he doesn't say anything.

I am still filled with longing and yearning for this man, and I can sense that our relationship has changed yet again during my ride home. The dynamics are different now than they were before I went to the training camp, and despite what happened there, they are different still.

The speed of the change gives me whiplash. I should not be surprised, I tell myself, because I know that Eli does this. He changes in an instant.

I give a short laugh. "You're going to bed?" *And you don't want to talk to me?*

"Yeah."

I'm starting to wonder if he's regretting what he did.

"I might have to block you," he says, offering his own little laugh. "I need to focus on my training. You don't know what this means to me."

I feel the ground beneath me shift. "I *do* know what it means to you, but go ahead and block me if it makes you feel better." Has he forgotten the conversation we had last night? I toughen up. "You make it sound as if I'm a groupie who's stalking you."

I wonder if boxers have groupies, or if it's only pop stars who do. I'm nothing of the sort. I've been quite controlled, if anything. We both lost it in the sauna room. It definitely wasn't a one-sided encounter. "It takes two to tango," I reply, because I'm annoyed, and because he's not forthcoming.

"I know."

"I didn't come looking for you."

"I know."

"And I only went to the sauna because I thought you

guys were out." I wouldn't have gone anywhere near it had I known he was in the building.

"I know."

"Is that all you're going to say?" The conversation has flipped 180 degrees. I was getting ready for some hot phone sex and he's getting ready to block my calls. There is a huge disconnect between where he and I are.

"I'm tired. Lou had me up at four, and I need to hit the sack."

"Goodnight," I shoot back in anger.

"'Nite."

I'm left with the phone in my hand, trying to figure out what the hell just happened here.

I have no idea what I did wrong, and I lie on my bed, going over the conversation for the longest time.

The next day I make my way to the boxing gym even though I know Eli's not there. Despite last night's short conversation, I look forward to seeing it again, even though I'm only going to pick up a few of my notes and my coffee cup that I'd left there. I've decided to end my time at the gym. I had planned to stay until Eli returned, and maybe spend one or two more days while he was at the gym, but I can't wait to leave. I'll call and tell Lou later.

Ernesto is surprised to see me. "I wasn't expecting to see you this morning," he exclaims, looking happy.

"I forgot a few things behind," I tell him, and hand him the coffee I brought for him from the diner.

"For me?" he asks, his mouth spreading into the widest smile. "Aww, you didn't have to, Harper." And then he thanks me profusely.

Of all the people I wanted to see this morning, Ernesto is at the top of my list. He's easy to be around.

I bought a cup of coffee for myself as well, and take a sip. Nina wasn't at the diner this morning. I don't know why I went there because I don't usually get my coffee from places like that. I much prefer the frothy, overpriced non-skimmed stuff from Starbucks, but this morning I found myself veering towards Frankie's Kitchen.

"When did you get back from the camp?"

"Last night."

"Liked it?" he asks.

After thinking about it for a moment, I nod. "It was an interesting experience." Though he obviously has no idea in what capacity I mean that. "The house is an odd building, don't you think?"

"I don't know. I've never been."

This takes me by surprise. "Haven't you?"

"I'm just the handyman here. This place still has to run as usual even when our prize boxer isn't here."

My expression must have dampened because he says, "What did he go and do now?"

"Nothing." I smile brightly, and then tell him about the training camp because all of that, most of that, was fine.

It was more than fine. Things only fell apart last night on my return.

"Are you going to the fight?" Ernesto wants to know.

"I don't know." I haven't had time to think about it even though Gerry asked me about it a while back.

The question isn't whether I would like to go, it's whether Eli would want me there and it doesn't seem like he would.

I don't need to go. I can watch the fight from home and do the write-up there, plus Gerry said he'd edit my article and help with the fighting part of it since I wouldn't know about the boxing rules and regulations. I'm not writing about the boxing techniques, I'm writing about the human angle, about the man behind the gloves. But I'm not confident that I'll be able to write an unbiased account.

We drink our coffee and I ask Ernesto what I've missed since I've been away, and I also let him know that I'm leaving today and returning to the office.

Merv wants me back there for good now, and I decided last night that now was a good time to do it. I also need to write up everything I have and if I wait for Eli to come back, the ocean of emotions he will put me through won't help me to focus.

"You're leaving us?" Ernesto looks disappointed. "We were only just getting to know you."

"I'm not leaving the country," I tell him. "I still live in Chicago."

"You'll have to come over from time to time," he says. "And when Eli brings the belt back, you'll have more of a reason to come back."

I'm not so sure about that anymore.

"Why are you really going, Harper?" he asks. "Because I recall you saying to me that you'd be back for a few days after the camp."

"My boss wants me back," I reply. I even manage a smile as I say it. I even manage to stare at Ernesto defiantly.

"Is that so?"

I swallow. I bet he never misses anything regarding his granddaughters. I also bet he's the perfect grandfather. "That's true," I insist, because it is, to an extent. Merv does want me back, but even if he didn't, I would return.

Though I wouldn't be able to explain my way out of it to Ernesto.

"Elias is a troubled young man," he says softly. "This gym, and Lou, have done wonders for him."

I nod. I can't imagine Eli telling him his secret, but it doesn't take a genius to see that Eli wrestles with his demons. People don't need to know which demons they are. "I can see that."

"Whether you think so or not, I think you've had a slight effect on him too."

I roll my eyes, because there is no way Ernesto can know what happened at the camp.

Then he freaks me out with his next words. "I'm talking about here, what I've seen here, with my own eyes. There's something softer about him. You might need to dig deeper to find it, but he's a little changed, and for the better, I would say."

I'm trying to figure out why he's telling me this, and why it matters, because clearly, he seems to think it does. I'm over Eli, or I intend to be. I intend to wash him out of my system from now on, but I take note of Ernesto's words.

"I'll take your word for it," I say, taking another sip of my coffee. Because I've come back and I'm none the wiser about Eli at all.

CHAPTER THIRTY

ELI

I train harder than ever once Harper's gone.

The night she left, we all sat down and watched clips of Garrison talking to the press. He boasted about how easy this fight was going to be.

He's a celebrity as much as he is a boxer, and that's his weakness. But watching him big himself up and play to the camera tells me this could go the other way. To him, I'm a relative unknown, a nobody, and he wants to make a scapegoat out of me. He's going to use me to show everyone that he's still got it.

If I go down easily, and if he manages to hit me where it hurts, it could happen. No matter how much we prepare for it, on the night, lady luck plays a part. Just as it did for me getting the chance to fight him, he could knock me out in the first two rounds like he thinks he's going to. Or I could knock him out in the first ten, the way I'm hoping this will play out.

But if I'm out, I won't get another shot again. He will, and he'll get another shot even if I win because that's how these things go.

I had all this going through my head, and I only called Harper that first night after she'd gone because I saw her texts. Maybe I also called because I needed to hear her voice.

But the moment she spoke, it put me back in the sauna room again. I thought I could keep my distance mentally and still have her around but I can't.

Her voice brings back everything.

And that's the problem.

I can't have her in my head.

So I kept my distance when we spoke and I could sense the quiet shock in her voice, but I can't have her calling me during the day, and definitely not during the night. I know how my sleep got messed up those couple of nights we were together and I can't risk that. I need to be at my sharpest.

And that's why I told her I was going to block her.

I didn't, but she never called or texted me again after that.

Doesn't mean I don't think about her in my weaker moments.

After five grueling days of working till I drop, Lou weighs me, and nods his head.

"You're ready. And you're bigger, bulkier, and the right weight. You're in the best shape I've ever seen you, kid."

"Maybe." I don't want to big myself up, not even in my own head, the way Garrison does twenty-four seven.

Jake and Santos laugh.

"You're ready, man."

"You've never looked so good."

They're building me up again, my wingmen. Garrison's

going to have a whole entourage on the big night. All the media and the press will be on his side. He's got the razzmatazz that the audience loves.

Me? I don't even have a nickname. The press keep calling me Chicago's New Hope, but I don't want to walk into the ring against "The Tank" with *that* name. It sounds lame in comparison.

Garrison will be blasting out a rock tune, and he'll have an army of people following him in the ring at Madison Square Garden.

I have no name, no tune, and only Jake, Santos and Lou. Even Nina's not going to come to watch. She says she can't bear it. She won't even watch the fight on the TV.

"Nobody knows you yet, Eli, but they will." Lou gives me a stern look, as if he's about to jab me in the chest to drive his point home, but stops because he gets how much I want this.

He believes in me, just like these guys do, and Nina does. And Harper does.

"Garrison has been the reigning champ for so long, he's had his moment. Now you need to take over and claim your moment."

The weight of those words sinks through me, and I nod in understanding. "I will claim my moment."

He points a finger at me. "You're the outsider, but this is going to be *Rocky* all over again."

"He lost in the first movie," I remind him.

"Then *Rocky II*." He makes a face as if this is irrelevant. "You being here might be pure chance, but you winning that fight will be due to pure strength, pure skill, and agility. Don't forget that."

I know all about sheer chances. Just like an accident of

birth gave me a bad start, it's only by chance that I'm in the fight. I can't mess it up. I won't.

I've already decided that this won't go to a rematch. I have to make my one shot count. That's the one people remember the most.

I train real hard for my remaining days and then we return to Chicago. The day after, I'm at the gym first thing in the morning.

It's been days since I've spoken to Harper. I managed to block her out of my mind, and it was easier to do while she was out of sight, but now that I'm back here, I expect to see her. I'd be lying if I said otherwise.

But after an hour in the gym, I still don't see her. I spend all morning wondering where she is. Because even though I said all that stuff to her on the phone, I expect to see her at her desk. I *want* to see her. And when I don't, it makes me suspicious.

It's not until the afternoon that Ernesto casually mentions that Harper won't be returning.

"Didn't she tell you?" he asks.

"No."

She never said a thing to me, but then, I didn't really give her the chance.

"Did you know?" I ask Lou later.

"She left me a message," he says, preoccupied with some paperwork.

I suppress my reaction.

But, *fuck*.

I didn't know that.

I manage to get through the rest of the day by doing what I do best: blocking out the shit and focusing on how to move on.

It's late when I finish for the day. I pass by the diner, but Nina isn't around.

I go back to my apartment and try to relax. The problem is, I'm so wound up, I can't.

It's not only the fight, it's everything; my days at the training camp have been brutal, and this first day back at the gym hasn't been easy either.

Lou says he's going to ease up now because my body needs to recover fully in order to reach peak condition. We leave for New York next week.

Seeing Harper might have taken the edge off things. It's the not seeing her, knowing that I won't be seeing her, that's gotten me wound up like a tight, tight coil.

CHAPTER THIRTY-ONE

HARPER

Eli will be back today. Ernesto told me they were all returning late on Tuesday night, so I assume, in fact, I know he'll be at the gym today.

I try not to think about him, but my mind is all over the place. I keep thinking of the moments we spent, precious moments that meant something, and I'm disappointed in him, in the way he's resorted back to his usual self.

I don't even know if I've been ghosted, because that's what a douchebag does when you've been in a relationship and all of a sudden they cut off all contact. What we had might not have been a relationship, but we had something.

Gerry has looked over my article and he wants me to spruce it up some more. I spent most of today doing just that, then, as I'm about to go home, he suggests that we go for a drink at the end of the week, seeing that I'm back in the office now.

"Why don't we go out tonight?" I reply. It's midweek,

not ideal, but I'm not feeling so great and I suggest this so that I don't have to think about Eli being back in Chicago.

If I go home, it will just be me and my thoughts and I don't want to be languishing at home by myself. I need something to keep me busy, otherwise I might be tempted to pick up the phone and call Eli. And if I do that, it's a sure guarantee that I'll do something stupid.

"Drinks?" Gerry asks, surprised.

"Why not? Do something daring for once," I suggest.

He looks around the office. "Who else shall we ask?"

"No one else," I say, picking up my bag. I glance at the desks in the open-plan office, at the other people I barely know. "Unless you want to ask them," I say. "I don't know anyone that well."

Gerry makes a dismissive noise. "Forget the others," he says. "I can't stay late, so let's go now."

And that is how we end up at a bar a few blocks away from the office.

"You've lost your sparkle," he says, when we're both sitting across the table from one another.

He has a beer, and I have a vodka cocktail. It's extravagant, given that there's nothing special about today, and nothing worth celebrating, but I need a pick-me-up. "Me?"

"Yes, you. Are you missing the training camp?" he asks, hitting the nail on the head.

I shake my head. "It wasn't a vacation."

"Maybe not, but it got you out of the office. Did you go out, or were you stuck inside all the time?"

"Mostly inside. There are enough things in the house for entertainment, but we went out one evening. It's a pretty little town. It made a nice change from the city, so it was good to get out and see something different."

"A nice change from the city," he says with a sigh. "I should have moved away years ago. The city strangles me."

I frown. "Strangles you? That's a strong word. If you hate it that much, why don't you move?"

"The divorce was costly."

"Oh. I'm sorry."

"Don't be. She was a bitch, my wife. My *ex*-wife," he says, as if he's getting used to the new label.

I'm stumped because he sounds so bitter, and because he's never talked about her like that. He's only had one drink but he's never been more candid. He seems wound up, irritated almost. Except I've seen close-up Eli-style irritation, and I know this is mild compared to that. Because I remain silent, Gerry starts to talk. "She reconnected with an old boyfriend online." He closes his eyes as if it pains him.

"I'm sorry." Something like that would cut like a knife wound. I have nothing on him, on years of being married, but I can imagine his pain.

"Don't be. She's moved on and so must I. What about you?" he asks.

I don't like talking about my personal life, not to work people. Especially since I haven't been here long and don't know them well enough. "Nothing at the moment."

"That's surprising," he replies.

I don't want him to ask me any more questions, or make some cheesy comment on why a young woman like me is single. I pray he won't.

"Spill the secrets then. What else did you get on Cardoza? What drives the man?"

I'm grateful that we've moved onto something else, but talking about Eli is hard. I put on my professional hat, try to phase out the personal stuff.

"What drives Eli," I say, tapping my fingers on the table. There are many things that drive him. Eli is multi-faceted and complex, and I'm certain I haven't scratched the surface of this man. "He almost had a chance to try out for the Olympics."

"So he did," states Gerry, and his I-know-it-too attitude is starting to infuriate me.

"But did you know that he got beaten up by a group of guys because he threw the fight? He couldn't take part in the tryouts because he was so badly injured."

"Now *that* I didn't know."

I smile with glee.

"Broke his ribs, and tore up his face. He was trying to get extra money to help his sister make the rent."

Gerry raises an eyebrow. "Tough life."

"He hasn't had the best start in life," I tell him.

"He was in a children's home with his sister for a year."

I snap my head up in attention. Gerry's done his research too. "Yes, he was. I'll have the piece ready in time, and with everything documented," I tell him, in case he thinks I'm not capable of putting together an in-depth piece of work.

Gerry is quick to reassure me. "I know you will. I have every faith in you."

His words make me feel better. "He seems to have turned his life around," I say. "Let's face it, how many unknowns would get a chance to be in a fight this big?" I take a sip of my drink. It's just the thing I need to take away the edge of the Eli's rejection. That's what his silence—ever since I returned—feels like. A rejection.

"He was young when he went to the children's home," Gerry prompts. "I imagine he had a difficult start, a lot of boxers do. Who knows what he suffered as a child?"

I know. "Abuse leaves scars," I reply absentmindedly. "And they're not always visible ones." I wipe away the condensation on my glass.

"There have been lots of rumors about Grampton House," he tells me. "They shut the place down five years ago."

I'm astounded that he knows this. There were rumors of abuse, but nothing was ever proven. "Are you secretly working on this assignment and not telling me, Gerry?"

This makes him laugh. "No," he blinks, then says it again, "No." It's the second 'no' which makes me suspicious.

"You seem to know everything I know."

"Not everything. Stop thinking you don't know enough. You do. Cardoza was abused by who?"

"Someone at the care home," I say.

He looks at me as if he's waiting for me to say more.

"I'm not putting that in the article," I state. The vodka has loosened my tongue and I wish I hadn't said anything.

"Why not?"

"He told me in confidence."

"It would make for a good story."

"We're not printing it, Gerry." I push my glass away.

"Okay, fine. Then we won't."

"*I* won't," I correct him. "It's my piece, unless you're going to overrule me and suddenly use all of my research and claim it as yours."

He leans forward, his expression hard. "I said leave it, then. I'm only offering you advice. I've made my mark. I don't need to take your work and pass it off as mine. Frankly, I'm disgusted that you would say such a thing."

I make an apologetic face. "I didn't mean it like that. We... we discussed a few things. He let this slip, but I know he won't want it out."

"That's fine. I don't know what you take me for, Harper. I'm on your side. I was the one who pushed Merv to give you this instead of reporting on some minor cat-up-a-tree type stories. I remember in your interview you said you wanted to do some hard-hitting journalistic work, and while this might not be a story on organized crime, or something as meaty, it's better than what you've been working on so far. This kid will be forgotten after this fight. He's in the limelight only because of who he's fighting, so make your article count. It will have a limited shelf life. Cardoza will be forgotten within a week." He lifts his fist and motions like a boxer, only on him it looks pathetic even if he's trying to make a point. I'm embarrassed for him.

"He might win," I say, because I don't like the way he dismisses Eli so easily.

Gerry's laugh indicates the opposite. "If you say so. We won't have long to wait. Has Merv mentioned about you going to the fight?" he asks.

I shake my head. "He hasn't said a word. He probably thinks the training camp trip was enough."

"You should come. You've done the whole piece on Cardoza, and you've done your dues at the boxing gym, and the training camp. It would be silly to not be there for the fight."

"I'm not sure Merv will be happy."

I don't jump with enthusiasm, partly because I'm guessing that Gerry going will be sufficient, but I don't know what Eli's reaction will be if I went, and that's the main reason.

"I can put in a good word for you."

I don't want him to. Gerry observes my lack of excitement. "Is it because you don't want to see Cardoza knocked out?"

"He's going to win," I say defiantly, because even though Eli's gone all cold on me now, I still believe in him.

Gerry chokes back a laugh. "Have you seen how Garrison's shaped up for this fight?"

I haven't paid any attention to Garrison. "Shaped up? I hope he's trained well for it. According to Lou, he's spent most of his time boasting that Eli's going to be easy to beat."

"He is going to be easy to beat," Gerry insists.

"Eli's going to surprise you all."

As if to prove a point, Gerry whips out his phone, taps it a few times, then shoves it in my direction. I'm looking at a picture of a well-oiled Garrison flexing his muscles. The headline screams about Garrison's unbeaten record so far.

Garrison is huge. Eli is big, powerful, ripped, but this guy really does look like a tank in comparison. All of a sudden, I'm worried.

"He's in the best shape I've ever seen him. The Tank is a pro, undefeated through his last twenty-four fights. This fight with Cardoza is a walk in the park for him. Your man doesn't stand a chance."

I jolt. "He's not *my* man," I retort and hand back the phone. "He has plenty of women hanging around him."

"I'm sure he does." Gerry glances at his watch.

"I have a few more details to add to my article, and maybe you could look over it once it's done?"

"Shall we get another round of drinks?" he asks.

"Another round?"

"And maybe some food?"

I'm not hungry and make a face as if I'm not sold on the idea. "You said you couldn't stay late," I tell him.

"I had something lined up, but it's not important. I don't need to go. How about some finger food?" he suggests.

Why not? I don't want to get drunk, and two cocktails

aren't going to do any harm, finger food would be good. "Okay," I say, as he opens the table menu and shows it to me. "You choose," I tell him. I hear a beep from my phone and fish it out of my handbag. My heart trips. It's a message from Eli.

Hey.

That's it? A *'hey?'*

I'm annoyed, but I'm also excited. I put my phone back in my bag, and mull over what this means. Gerry orders our food, and we continue the conversation. I try to pay attention but my mind is in full-on Eli mode again.

We talk about work, and he tells me of some interesting assignments he's been on. I smile at Gerry and pretend I'm listening. And a few moments later, as if I'm addicted, I pull the phone out and text back:

Hey.

This time I place the phone face down on the table. I say something to Gerry, to show that I'm listening, and he continues talking. My phone beeps again, and I excuse myself, because it's so obvious now, and I snatch my phone again. This new message plants a huge grin on my face:

I missed seeing you at the gym.

"What's so funny?" Gerry asks.

"One of my friends texted me a silly joke," I say, lying with ease. And because Gerry looks peeved, I add, "Sorry." And then to really prove that I'm invested in his story, I put my phone away on the table this time, but face down—even though it kills me to do this. I actively force myself to join in the conversation, even though my ears are on alert for a telltale 'ping'. It's a good thing the phone is face down, otherwise I'd be glancing at it every second.

When there's been no beep for a while, I quickly check my phone for messages, in case I missed something, but there are no new messages. My happiness sinks as quickly as it soared.

Our food arrives as do our drinks, and we talk and laugh and soon I forget about Eli as I help myself to the food. Gerry regales me with more stories about his life at the paper and his tales about Merv. He's funny and engaging, and because I am determined not to be Eli's puppet, and because Gerry's tales are truly hilarious, I soon lose myself in them.

When Gerry excuses himself to go to the bathroom, I pick up my phone and discover that Eli's sent a few messages but I didn't hear the notification beeps:

BTW, I didn't block you.

Then there's a good five-minute gap before the next message because he was clearly waiting for me to reply:

I didn't mean to be rude the other day.

And when I still didn't reply, he texted:

I can be a jerk.

You know this.
Make it up to you?

The last message sets my body on fire.

It also proves to me the power of abstaining. If I had replied, I would have given in, instead, he's the one who feels he needs to make it up to me with his trio of messages. I feel as if I've won a year's supply of chocolate.

"You're still texting?" Gerry's voice snaps me out of my fantasy bubble.

"Sorry," I say to him, and quickly type out my reply to Eli:

How do you propose to do that?

I send the text, my nerves dancing for joy.

"Those devices are a curse to the art of conversation," Gerry states. He sounds like a middle-aged parent, irritated by a teenager's thumb-readiness. "Women seem to be the worst offenders, after youngsters."

I wince, because now he's really showing his age. "It was Eli, actually," I reply, indignantly. I'm itching to see his reply, and when my cellphone pings again, I can't help myself. "Sorry," I say, even though I'm not remotely sorry.

In fact I don't care what Gerry thinks, in spite of what he's just said. I am bubbling with joy because Eli is back in touch:

Come over and find out.

That's one hell of a sexy text. It intoxicates me in one hit. Another text follows, with his address.

My heart literally stops beating. I hold the phone in my

hand and try to dampen down the grin that threatens to slide across my face.

I see Eli's face in my mind's eye, I see him smile. It's a rare thing, but in this moment it flashes across my brain as if he touched my face this instant.

I miss him all over again and I've forgotten everything he did. I don't care how I felt about him up until this moment.

"You're not really present, are you, Harper?" I glance up at Gerry's face. He doesn't look happy.

I can't blame him because I know what it is to be the person who sits around waiting for the other person to finish their online correspondence. In effect, I'm giving him the middle finger being so consumed by my messages. I'm texting Eli because I can't resist the man who holds me captive by his texts.

"Sorry, no. This is rude of me. I'm sorry."

I slip the phone away, determined to end the evening as best as I can.

Gerry starts picking at the food again with a cocktail stick. I'm no longer hungry. Not for food. I'm hungry for Eli.

"Why aren't you eating?" he asks. "I've ordered all this food."

"I'm not that hungry." But it would be extremely rude of me to leave like this so I pick at some mushrooms.

The entire time, I'm thinking of Eli, and how much I miss him. It's not like him to be this expressive. He seems softer, maybe a little sad. He sounds as if he misses me. He bared so much more of himself than I expected, and I want to believe that the connection I felt for him is something he now feels for me.

"It's impossible to even go out for dinner and enjoy an evening out when so many people are addicted to their devices," Gerry continues. The conversation has lost its spark, and it pales in comparison to Eli's texts.

Instead of regaling me with funny stories, Gerry's now lecturing me as if I'm a child.

I don't need to be here, when I have a man I am desperate to see, and who seems just as eager to see me. "I should go," I say. "I didn't want to stay out too late." I can't sit here a moment longer. I stare at the mushroom skewered by my cocktail stick and decide I don't want it.

My mind isn't on food right now. It's consumed by Eli. I want to hold him and put my arms around him. I want to do the things I've been dreaming of ever since I last saw him.

"You're leaving?" Gerry looks really pissed off, but I can't take another moment of being here with him. I pull out my purse to split the bill.

"Leave it," he says, and calls the waiter.

"It's only fair," I say.

"Leave it." Gerry's tone turns nasty. I haven't seen him be like this before, and I don't understand why he's so angry. We've been here for a while now, I've shoved some of the finger food down me, and we've had a pleasant enough evening. I want to contribute half towards the bill, but if he won't take it, there's not much I can do.

"You don't have to leave on account of me," I say, when he seems to get ready to leave.

"And sit here all alone? No thanks. I had a date lined up this evening. One of those group restaurant meetup events," he says, surprising me.

I open my mouth in shock. "You should have said."

His face turns dark. "Don't worry about it."

"But—"

"Leave it, Harper."

"Thanks for this evening."

We leave at the same time, and I quickly say goodbye to him the moment we're outside. But as I hail a taxi, I feel as if I've escaped.

I know this seems rude and I must seem ungrateful, but I can't explain how much this means to me. Eli texted me first. I didn't do a thing, and now he's promised to make it up to me.

Eli wants me to come over.

Nothing else and nobody else could ever compare to that.

The taxi takes me straight to his place. It's in a neighborhood I'm not familiar with, but I see a small rundown apartment building and my insides leap for joy.

I can't believe I'm here.

CHAPTER THIRTY-TWO

ELI

I t was easy to push her out of my mind when I was away,
but the moment we returned to Chicago, Harper's in
my brain again.

Nina's not around, and Lou has ordered me to slow
down and start taking it easy. I'm home and have nothing
to do.

We fly to New York early next week so that I have time
to get used to the place. Then there's the weigh-in the day
before the fight.

Everything is coming to a head.

I'm not nervous, but I feel more anxious than I should.
Being around Harper has stirred some shit inside me and
the past starts to play on my mind again. I'd pushed that
stuff away but it's back in my head and I can't afford to let it
mess me up.

That's why I need Harper. She calms me down. Not
seeing her for over a week hasn't worked out so well for me,

even though I'm the one who cut her off so cruelly. Now I'm suffering for it.

The knock on my door heralds her arrival and I feel as if the sun just shone down on me and lifted my spirits. This is insane. It tells me she matters more than I want her to. I open the door, and attempt a calm welcome.

"Hey." Harper's standing outside my crummy apartment, in a crummy neighborhood, and looking happier than she should. I didn't treat her right, and she still looks happy. She still came.

"Come in," I say, and immediately fold my arms because I might be tempted to reach out and touch her.

She looks smart in her dark pantsuit and white shirt. "You look good."

"Thanks."

"Was it only for me you dressed down?"

"I had to fit in at the gym." I remember my impressions of Harper that first time. She was too polished, too made up, and she reminded me of a porcelain doll that could break easily if pushed. Despite what she says, she didn't look too dressed down to me during those days, not from what I remember.

But she's in high heels today, and she's wearing jewelry. She looks like a model from an upscale magazine.

"Well," I scratch my ear, "you look good enough to eat."

She bites her lip.

"I didn't mean it like that," I say, even though I think back often to our time in the sauna. It always sends me down a wrong place, though; I lie awake thinking about her pussy, her arousal, her being naked. I want that every night, and I can't have it, not yet.

It frustrates the fuck out of me.

She's still smiling, as if she can't stop herself, and she

clasps her hands in front of her, as if she's afraid she might also be tempted to reach out for me.

I missed that smile. I missed that face.

She looks me over, her gaze running over my chest, my shoulders, my face, and back to my chest and my arms again.

"Miss me?" I ask, as we both stand awkwardly appraising one another in my dingy little apartment. There's no hallway. The door opens onto my living room with a table, a sofa and a TV.

"Did you?" she asks.

I had a speech prepared, words I wanted to say to her, but we're both standing and kind of dancing around one another. If this was a boxing ring, it would be the part where we start figuring each other out, and nobody is ready to throw any serious punches yet. "Yes."

Her eyes widen, as if she's just missed a step and not managed to fall. My eyes take in her appearance once more. "Did you come straight from work?" Even though our conversation is stilted and polite, there are undercurrents of longing floating in the air.

"I was out with Gerry."

I wasn't expecting that fucking answer. "You spent the evening with him?" I'm not jealous. I know Harper doesn't give a shit about the guy. She's not that way inclined. I can't see her getting friendly with a guy in order to secure a better position at work. But I hate that he got to spend time with her and I didn't.

It's my fault entirely, and I intend to make it up to her. I'm so frustrated and wired up from not seeing her that my cock comes to life as we stand and make small talk.

She shrugs. "I needed a distraction. I needed to do something, otherwise I would have called you, or come over, or done something silly because I'm confused and annoyed with you."

She what? I like that she feels this, even though I didn't want her to feel those emotions—I'd rather that she was happy—but I know I'm to blame for being distant with her.

"You're not silly," I say, reaching out to stroke her face. "I'm the one who messed up. I didn't mean to say that stuff to you. It's just been so hard lately."

It is getting harder with each passing day. There is so much stuff floating around in my head the closer I get to the fight.

"Are you worried?" she asks. Her expression softens, and she inches towards me. I tense, knowing that if she reaches for my face, I won't be able to push her away. I missed her, but having her here facing me, staring at me like she wants me, is a whole other level of trouble. I feel so out of sorts right now that I don't know how to be around her.

I texted her because I was lonely, and because I needed her, but now that she's here, I see that I've just led temptation to my doorstep.

She takes a step towards me. "I understand. You don't have to explain, Elias. This fight means a lot to you, and I know I'm a distraction."

I reach out and place my hand against her face. She leans into it, her cheek resting against my palm.

It takes a second of us looking at one another and then she's in my arms, tiptoeing up to kiss me. Her soft little mouth slides over mine and I melt.

I said I'd make it up to her, but she's the one who made the move, and the speed of it startles me.

It also ignites my pent-up desire. We kiss feverishly, and in between kissing and touching, she tells me she missed me, and that she's glad I texted her. All the while she rains tiny kisses all over my mouth, and her soft hands steal around my shoulders.

"I'm better when you're around me," I tell her.

My cock turns rock hard and her moan tells me she knows. I wrap my arms around her waist. She's so tiny, I can wrap one arm around her easily.

I have plans to taste her again, and I'm already salivating at the idea of stripping her slowly. She sucks my lower lip, and her hand snakes down my body. My breath hitches when she feels me through my clothes, her fingers gripping and stroking me in turn.

I moan against her lips. "Harper..."

"I've missed you," she whispers, her voice hoarse with need.

"I can't..." I attempt to move her hand away but she's like a woman possessed. My resolve is weak, and weakens further when she starts to rub me harder.

Fuck. If this isn't the best feeling. I've been wanting to taste her pussy ever since I sent her that first text, but she's in control of me, and I can't stop her.

I don't want to.

"No, no," I begin to say. The fight is only next week. I should hold out, but she grabs the moment to kiss me hard, her tongue exploring my mouth as if it's lost its way.

I kiss her back, and we go at it like wild things. Her smell, her taste, her lips, her tongue. Everything from the sauna room night comes flooding back.

I pick her up and walk with her over to the sofa. I sit back, and she straddles me again and we kiss for the longest time. Her hands are all over me, over my T-shirt, then under, while our mouths are joined. My hands go for her arms, her face, her breasts as I try to get those stupid little buttons on her shirt open.

I'm so hard, I think I'm going to explode.

I want to stand by my promise. I want to make it up to her, and plant my face between her legs again, but she slides down the length of my body and throws off her jacket. I hold my breath, waiting for her to whip off her shirt, my mouth watering at the thought of my mouth on her breasts.

I try to get up, because the curtains are half drawn, but she has other plans.

She stares at me with hungry eyes, her lips moist. "Let me have a taste," she begs. "Just a tiny little taste."

My mouth falls open, just like the front of my jeans which she's managed to unzip. She frees my cock from the boxers.

"No," I say, but it takes a serious amount of willpower for me to move her hands away. I can't have her do anything. I need to stay pent-up.

But she's on it.

Her lips swallow me, and I fall back, my jaw spasming as I fight to keep it together. I haven't had sex, or this, for months.

Gratitude seeps through me as I sink deeper into the sofa, enjoying her soft, warm mouth on my cock. It's the most beautiful sensation I have ever experienced.

She takes her mouth away, and stares at me. "Do you want me to stop now?" she asks, her voice all innocent, despite her swollen red lips. I can't speak, or think, and I am close to coming. Or passing out.

I don't want her to stop.

She licks my length, then my tip, and I jerk as if she's thrown a hot rock at me. A grumble hitches in my throat. "Don't... stop," I stutter.

She moves her fingers up and down with an expertise

that surprises me. "Are you sure? Because I don't want Lou to blame me if you're not at your peak."

She's killing me.

I pant out a breath because speech eludes me.

"I'll take that as permission to carry on," she teases. Then she laps at me again before slowly sliding her lips around me. She takes all of me in her mouth and I practically moan in gratitude. I fist my hand in her hair and try to hold back for as long as I can. I'm engulfed in wet heat, blood races through my veins, heightening my senses. She keeps a rhythm going, her hot mouth and fingers worshipping my poor lonely cock for the longest time.

She has rendered me completely helpless, and I lose it. I don't even have time to warn her or pull away.

She drains every last drop, leaving me soft and boneless. My amped-up frustration seeps out of me slowly. I relax. I become weightless. I float.

She gets up and sinks against me on the couch.

After a while I manage to put myself back in my boxers but it's a little longer before I can speak. She turns to me, bringing her knees up on the couch, and nestles against me with her hands on my chest.

I feel like Samson after Delilah cut off all his hair, but I don't regret this.

In fact, I love her for it.

I shift my position so that I'm lying on the couch, and she snuggles in my arms. We stay like that for the longest time, and I suddenly think how I could get used to this.

I could get used to having Harper around. It's the softest thing, her touch, her softness, her need for me.

I reach down and brush her hair away, not because it's fallen over her face, I can't see if it has or not, but because I can do it. Because I can reach down and feel her soft skin, and her warm face. She takes my hand and kisses it, then clasps it within hers and brings it to her chest. I breathe out louder than I intended.

"What?" she whispers.

Don't leave.

But instead, I say, "Shh... let me get some rest."

She starts to lift her head. "I should go—"

But I gently press her head against my chest again. "Just for a while," I whisper.

"Just for a while then," she says, resting her head against me again. "I've already broken one of your rules—"

"Shhhhh," I murmur, then, "I gave you permission."

She lands another kiss on my chest. My lips curl up. I want to fuck her so badly. And make love to her, as gently. I want to worship every inch of her body and not leave the bedroom for days. I tell myself that day will come, after the fight. Right after the fight, if I have any energy left to spare. "You're going to be my post-fight prize," I tell her. This earns me another chest kiss and a grope of my cock. Holy shit. I wish I could give her free rein to do as she wants. Her fingers are dipped in magic and so is her mouth. "*Post*-fight," I say, with difficulty, because I'm starting to get another boner and moving her hand away from my balls takes all of my willpower.

"I look forward to it," she tells me, and places her hand on my bicep instead. It's a safe-ish area. Not entirely safe. Harper's fingers anywhere on my body aren't a good idea. Especially because I've had a taste of her and I want all of her. I force myself to forget the sex, and to enjoy just holding her.

I hit and I am hit all day long—not too hard, because I'm preserving myself—but this, a woman's touch, is a rarity for me. My weary body, pushed beyond all limits, isn't used to the softness that Harper offers me. Everything disappears when she's around. The punches, and pushups, the strain on my body, my aching muscles.

She is my most unlikely savior, and now I want to hold onto her for longer.

I feel my eyes grow heavy and I hope I fall asleep, because sometimes, even after all these years, I still see his face. I see him beckon me as I'm walking down the hallway. I always try to be with Nina, because he won't look at me when Nina's around, but a few times, he managed to get me on my own.

Growing up, I told myself he didn't invade my body; that he made me do things to him. But that's a lie I've told myself over the years. It makes me want to retch just thinking about it.

There was a reason I sought out the gym. There's a reason I hit so hard. When I'm in the ring, it's not Jake, or Santos or Garrison I see in front of me. It's Swain. He's the one I want to kill. It's his face I want to smash, his ribs I want to crack, his skin I want to tear. That's why my aim is laser-sharp and powerful enough to kill a man.

Because there is a man I want to kill, and his face is on the face of every opponent I've ever fought.

CHAPTER THIRTY-THREE

HARPER

He's snoring. It's a gentle sound, not so much a snore as heavy breathing.

I lift my head and look at Eli sleeping. I'm in love with this man and I realize this with a certainty only now, in this moment as I watch my sleeping giant. I bite back a smile, and restrain my hand from stroking his face, but then I run my fingers around his lips tenderly. He let me in again just when I thought we were done.

I want him. I want him in my bed. I want him inside me. My nights have been restless because of all the things I see us doing, naked and sweaty and all over each other.

I shift slightly, then prop my elbow on the armrest, and look down at him. But he starts to stir, as if he can sense I'm looking at him. His brow furrows, and he lets out an angry sigh. I move back a little.

"No," he hisses.

He's dreaming about the fight. I lower my head.

"Don't want to."

Don't want to what?

Maybe he's not dreaming about the fight. He starts to move his head, starts to move his body, and then he jerks violently, causing me to fall off the couch.

His eyes snap open, and he looks dazed. There's a look in his eyes I don't recognize, and he scares me, because he doesn't look like the Eli I know. I scoot back on my bottom and it seems to snap him out of whatever dream state he was in.

Then he seems to see me on the floor.

"Shit," he cries and is on the floor in an instant. "Did I push you?" He takes my hand and pulls me to him. We're both on the floor, both staring at one another as if we didn't have that intimate moment not so long ago.

"Bad dream?" I ask, but he doesn't answer. "Eli?"

He stands up, then helps me up. "I get them sometimes. Haven't had one in a while."

My concern for him wipes away my fear and I put my arms around him. "Were you dreaming of Garrison?"

He looks at me, puzzled, as if it's the furthest thing from his mind. His gaze drops to the floor. He looks defeated and it unnerves me because I've never seen this look on his face before. He looks broken.

"Eli," I whisper, feeling fearful now. He sits on the sofa, but this time it's as if he's been knocked down, as if the life has been sucked out of him.

I'm on the floor, kneeling between his legs, holding his hands, my face tilted up towards him. This powerhouse of a man looks so much smaller all of a sudden. I can't understand, can't believe the transformation that just occurred. "Where did you go?"

"Nowhere good." He looks as if he could curl up and die.

"Hey," I say, taking his hand, kissing it. I make a stab at it. "If you were thinking about the past, it's gone. It has no power." I wait for him to deny it, but he doesn't. His eyes are locked into mine and he's listening. I wish I could make him forget, I wish I could wipe my hand over his face and erase all those memories, but I imagine that these things don't disappear so easily. I lift up from my knees, so that we're nose to nose, and hold his face in my hands. "That man is a piece of worthless shit. He can't hurt you now. Nobody can."

"I know."

"Whatever he did, you've put yourself back together again."

He nods, then closes his eyes as if the pain is too much. I kiss his hand again because I want to kiss away all the hurt. "You overcame everything."

"Sometimes, I don't know if I did." He shakes his head as if he's trying to get out an image that's stuck in his head.

I touch his lips, then rest my forehead against his, as if it might transport the good thoughts from my head into his. He opens his eyes. "There were others. It wasn't just me. I can't forget their faces."

I don't know what to say to that. I don't know how to comfort him. But I try. "You're the bravest and strongest man I know, Eli." I've led a gilded life, and I've known a lot of douchebags but I've never known survivors, the people who graft, and have had such awful, miserable beginnings that getting through each day is survival, not living.

But Eli came into my life and now I am forced to share a sliver of his horror. And even that is too much for me to stomach. So I do what I can, I will take this beautiful, brave and broken man and I will try to make him whole again.

People think he's strong; most think he's an underdog getting into a fight he has no chance of winning.

They don't know the Eli I know. They don't know of the horrors he has already lived through. Fighting Garrison is tame compared to what this man has been through.

"I love you," I tell him, with our foreheads pressed together. I move my head away an inch because I want to look into his eyes, but his eyes are closed. "I love you, and I believe in you, and I feel lucky to have met you. I don't know of anyone who's walked your path and still come out fighting the way you have. You're already a champion in my eyes, Eli."

He opens his eyes, and they're shiny. I can't tell if it's because he's going to cry, or if it's because he's so happy.

CHAPTER THIRTY-FOUR

ELI

A load has been lifted.

Harper isn't just the woman I dream about, she's become my therapist, my analyst, my salvation.

I told her my deepest, darkest, dirtiest secret, and she didn't turn away from me. She told me she loved me, and she said the things my heart needed to hear.

It's a double-edged sword though. She comforts me and calms me. She gives, and cares, and I need that. I need it more now that I have a taste for it because I've never had that kind of loving. But it's also a distraction. Her softness is my Achilles heel. She's made me soft. Made me think and probe deeper, and a week before the big fight, this isn't where my head needs to be.

But with Harper, I feel as if I can finally start to trust again.

She left that evening, even though we both want to

spend the night together, it's a waiting game now. We will get that night one day soon.

She told me about Gerry behaving like a douche, and I told her that he likes her. She still refuses to believe it. He wants her to come to the fight. *I* want her to come to the fight, and she told me she will, even if she has to pay for it out of her own pocket.

Whether she's there with Gerry or not, I know she's going to end up in my bed once the fight is over.

I'm at Nina's place, a small apartment, probably smaller than mine, and a few blocks away from me. It means we're close enough to be there for one another in case either of us are ever in any trouble. We're also far enough to be out of each other's hair.

She's made dinner.

"Do you ever think of Grampton House?" I ask, as I fill the water jug up.

She lets out an exhale and stops ladling out the stew. "Why are you thinking of that now?"

I breathe out slowly. "I'm anxious about the fight."

We sit down to eat.

"Are you sure that's enough?" she asks, all motherly and concerned, and not wanting to discuss the other matter.

"It's enough." I'm inwardly debating on whether to persist. It's a miracle that we got out of Grampton House when we did. That we both did. But sometimes, I wonder what happened to the others. He used others too, but I'm glad he stayed away from Nina. I'm glad that Swain used me, and left her alone because that's what he promised me.

"You're worried about the fight, huh?" she asks, noticing that I haven't yet picked up my cutlery.

I nod. It's got nothing to do with the fight, but I gladly

take the excuse she's given me. "Garrison's the favorite, and sometimes it gets hard to stay positive."

"He can be the favorite. Let them see what you're made of when you step into the ring. Then we'll see who's the favorite." She picks up her cutlery and starts to eat.

I can't keep up the pretense. I stare back, and nod, but images of Grampton House flash through my head. Something in my expression changes enough for her to notice.

"What's wrong?" she asks, catching me staring at her. Now her face twists with anxiety. It's on the tip of my tongue to say something. I feel like I've choked up bile, as if telling Harper loosened some of that soot that had ground into the lining of my stomach weighing me down like a boulder. I feel the urge to clear the rest of it out. "It's not the fight."

Nina puts down her cutlery for the second time, and looks as if she's going to be sick. I've made her uneasy. I've broken an unspoken rule.

We *never* talk about that time.

It's selfish of me to want to bring it up just because I'm starting to feel whole again. Nina isn't where I am. I can't tell her. "It's Harper," I say, instead.

My sister's face lights up, and she smiles. "Yeah?"

I'm glad I have something else to switch my focus to. I can't tell this to Nina ever, no matter how cleansed I will feel, I can't ever tell her of the abuse. She will feel guilty, and hate herself, she's always prided herself on being my protector—crazy given that she's so small—but she will. My sister will blame herself for something that was never her fault.

I don't want to put that on her.

Harper is a good distraction. "She's going to come and see me fight."

"Brave woman."

"Why don't you come?"

"I can't, Elias. We've been through this before. I can't watch you get hurt."

"I won't get hurt."

She frowns at me. "You can't guarantee that."

I can't convince her. I want Nina to be there as much as I want Harper. Lou and the boys are my team, but Nina is my family, and Harper is the woman who's claimed my heart.

"Okay."

"I'll pray for you."

"Pray for Garrison," I shoot back. "He's going to need it."

HARPER

G erry is nowhere to be seen. I don't go actively looking for him, but from where I sit, I can see his office a few tables away. The upper half of the front-facing side is all window, I know he hasn't been in for two days.

On the third day, he comes in, but he's in his office with the door closed.

I've finished my piece on Eli, and I sent it to him a few days ago because I need him to look at it before it goes to print. I'm in a rush because my dad has summoned me to lunch. He's been calling and complaining that he hasn't seen enough of me and so I decide to get this over with, especially since I'll be gone this weekend, cheering Eli on from the ringside.

Gerry hadn't put in a word to Merv about me going to see the fight, like he said he would, but I've spoken to Merv and convinced him that I need to go.

I also want to pop into the diner at some point and see if I can persuade Nina to come along. I'm sure Eli would want her to be there. As I rush off towards the elevator, Gerry comes out after me. "I've read your article," he tells me. "Got a moment?" He's distant, and not his usual self, and I don't know what's up. This can't be anything to do with me leaving the other evening, can it? Gerry has more sense than to get upset about trivial things. His marriage breakup has definitely made him more irritable.

"Now?"

"It won't take long. We're on a deadline for this."

I follow him into his office. I know we're on a deadline but he's the one who's been away for two whole days and has hidden himself away in his office for the entire morning.

"It's a good piece," he tells me. "But I feel you can improve it a little."

I raise my eyebrow. I'm in a hurry as it is, because my dad's expecting me to have lunch, and then I have a million things to take care of before I leave for New York.

"You need to remain impartial at all times, Harper, but I don't feel you are. You speak almost in glowing terms about Cardoza."

"I talk about his work ethic, and his determination," I insist, "And his difficult childhood."

Gerry looks annoyed. "There's more. What about his past? His illegal fights?"

"I told you," I say, regretting every inch of that drink session with Gerry. "I'm keeping that to myself."

Gerry pushes his hands further into his pockets. "Our readers deserve the raw facts. They want the nitty-gritty story, not the rose-tinted glasses variety."

"I don't want to mention those things." My voice takes on a pleading tone, because I realize that in his position, Gerry can overrule me. "Please, Gerry."

"It needs to be factual, Harper. I can't cover for you."

I frown. I've written about his childhood, the things that are known, and embellished them a little without revealing his secret. I haven't painted him as an angel. I've written him as I found him, a raging bull, a man who could be so tightly wound up, you didn't know if he was going to hit you or just look at you with a deadly stare.

"I'll revisit it," I tell him, then glance at my watch. "Sorry, but I have to go, I have to meet my dad for lunch."

"Revisit it and let me have the final version."

CHAPTER THIRTY-FIVE

HARPER

I rush off, pissed with Gerry. He seems to want me to take the article in a different direction than the one I have planned.

I won't.

I'm late meeting my dad. I jump in a cab and rush to the golf club, my father's second home.

I go straight to the eating area, where I know he'll be, but to my dismay, he's standing around with a drink in his hand, and a bunch of his cronies; a couple of guys his age and their younger versions whom I presume are their sons. I'm annoyed because I didn't want to come here and make small talk with his friends.

I assumed it would be only the two of us. I stop, and briefly consider bailing out, but he sees me and beckons me over. His silver-tinged hair gives him an air of authority. He dresses well and gives off all the right signals; the expensive watch, the top-of-the-range Mercedes.

He has carved a beautiful life out for himself. He plays golf so often that I forget he works. He used to joke that he doesn't really work because he's on the board of so many companies and that going to the golf club was as good as working because he makes so many deals while he's on the golf course.

"Here she is, the daughter I hardly see," he announces, loud enough for his friends to all turn and look at me.

I smile at them all, and say "hi." I'm even more annoyed when he introduces me as his daughter who works for the Chicago Daily Herald.

He leans towards me and we kiss on the cheeks, and luckily his friends all resume their conversations again.

"You're always too busy to make time for me, honey," he complains. "I haven't seen you for weeks."

"I've been busy working, Dad," I tell him. "I was away at the training camp."

"What in the blazes were you doing there?"

"My story on the boxer, remember, I told you?"

His mouth twists. "They still have you doing that?"

"How have you been?" I ask, ignoring the displeasure in his tone.

"I'm having a swell time, as you can see."

I nod. I'm happy for him. He's worked hard, and deserves his rewards, but I wish he wouldn't turn his nose up at things he knows nothing about. "You know there's a Ladies Luncheon here every first Tuesday of the month. Why don't you come? Join the club. I'll pay for your membership if you can't afford it. You'll get to meet some good people. Make all the right connections."

I'm about to ask him what he means by 'good people' but I hold back. There is no point. "I was hoping we could grab a quick lunch, just you and me." I steal a look at his friends, my expression ice cold.

"I wasn't sure if you would show up today. They were free so I told them to join me. Join us, honey." He nods at the young guys while my insides inwardly combust.

One of the younger guys comes up to me. "Interesting, so you work for the Chicago Times?"

"The Chicago Daily Herald," I correct. "It's a smaller paper."

"Interesting."

I marvel at his range of vocabulary, and then at his hair which looks styled to perfection. I imagine him to be a banker or someone as shifty, and I wish he would go away but his friend joins us instead. He says nothing. He doesn't even smile. In fact, he looks a little intense.

"What are you working on?" Mr. Intense asks.

"She's working on the boxer," my dad replies, and they both look at him, then at me, as if they don't know whether my father is joking or not. "He's Chicago's New Hope, allegedly." I'm not comfortable with my father talking about my work since he doesn't sound too enamored of my career path.

"I didn't know Chicago had any hope," one of his older friends chimes in as he joins our group. The others laugh but I don't join in. He's only heard the tail end of the conversation and I doubt that he has any idea what we're talking about. It takes a huge effort on my part for me to remain quiet.

"Interesting," says Mr. Interesting. "Are you really doing a story on Cardoza?"

I'm surprised that he knows. "Yes."

"Who?" Mr. Intense asks.

"Elias Cardoza," I reply.

"The name rings a bell," one of the old guys says.

My dad shakes his head. "I don't have a clue who she is talking about but she seems to enjoy it, don't you, honey?" He points at me with his glass in his hand.

"He's the one fighting Garrison, Dad."

Mr. Intense turns to me with something bordering on interest. "Oh, *that* guy?"

"Yes, *that* guy." I grit my teeth.

"He doesn't stand a chance," Mr. Interesting states.

"That's your opinion and you're entitled to it," I shoot back.

"Yeah," Mr. Intense replies. "We're placing bets on him at work. He's not going to win."

"My bet's on Garrison, too," his friend agrees. "Nobody even knows about Cardoza. The guy's going to get his fifteen minutes of fame because the others messed up."

My father sniffs. "These things are a big spectacle, nothing more."

Mr. Interesting nods his head in agreement. "Boxers are stupid. The only people making any money are the promoters. Now, *they're* smart. Talk about leaving it to the idiots to knock each other's brains out in the ring."

They descend into a chorus of laughs.

"They have balls, though," I say, "Bigger balls than you probably do. It takes guts to step into a ring and fight."

The air prickles with my words.

"Harper," my dad says, the use of my name indicates that he's annoyed. "You're taking this too seriously."

"It is serious, Dad. It's someone's livelihood."

Mr. Interesting and Mr. Intense are still in shock. My dad's friend clears his throat, and I decide that I'm not hungry.

"Actually, Dad, I need to get back. I have some work to do before the fight."

My dad frowns, not understanding.

"I'm flying to New York to watch the fight from the ringside. I'm cheering Eli on."

It's like his jaw dropped and hit the ground.

"You're going to see the fight?" someone asks me.

"Yes," I snap back. "I'll call you when I return," I tell my father. I'm not in the mood to hear what he might have to say about that. "Nice meeting you all," I wave to the others as I leave.

I'm glad to get away. That was awkward. My father by himself would have been easier to handle. He still doesn't like the idea of me getting involved in the boxing world, and it worries me because as far as he's concerned, this is an assignment I'm working on, and nothing more. I don't even want to think about his reaction if he knew that Eli and I were involved.

As it is, I've never been to a fight before and I'm a little nervous about going to see Eli's fight. It's not the type of event I'd ever be interested in, but I'm doing this for Eli. He doesn't know I'm going to be there, and I want it to be a surprise. I lied and told him that Merv wouldn't pay for me to go, and that seemed to satisfy him.

Merv has let me go, and my plane ticket there, and the hotel and the ticket to the fight are all paid for by the company. Even if he hadn't agreed to it, I would still have gone and I would've paid for everything out of my pocket. I would have bought an expensive ticket to an event I have no interest in attending. But I'm doing this because I want to support the man I'm falling for. Eli has nobody going. No family, or friends as far as I can tell, only his team.

I'm still worked up after leaving the golf club, and I'm not ready to go into work and face grumpy Gerry.

Luckily, I'd already decided to pass by the diner because I'm going to try to convince Nina to come. Eli's told me that she never comes to any of his fights but I know it would make his day if she showed up.

She's not here by the looks of it, and when another waitress comes up to me to ask if I'd like to be seated, I remember that I still haven't had my lunch. So I sit down.

I'm tempted to go into the gym after, but I can't. I won't. Eli's busy preparing for New York. He leaves for the fight soon and we've promised not to see or contact one another until it's over.

I look at the menu and put away my cell phone because I expect my dad will call me at some point and ask what the hell happened. There was no way I could stand around listening to him and his friends spawning rubbish about things they know nothing about. Playing golf, for Christ's sake, and talking about Eli as if he's an idiot. It was making me choke listening to them. What do they know?

Eli probably wouldn't have picked the life of a boxer if he'd had an alternative.

I'm still slightly vexed as I read the menu, so when the waitress asks what I'd like, I look up a little too angrily. Then my face softens as I see Nina. "Oh, hey," I exclaim, my mood brightening in an instant. "I didn't think you were working today."

She smiles and I see a little of Eli in that smile and in her expression. "I was in the back, sorting out a complaint from a customer. Two times they complained about their fried egg, said it wasn't to their specification." She rolls her eyes. I widen mine in surprise.

"I didn't think there was much to get wrong in making a fried egg."

"I don't think there's a problem with the egg. A lot of the time people *are* just miserable about something else and they find it easier to *direct* their anger at something completely unrelated. Most times, *from* what I can see, the problem is internal."

"Wow. You must see all sorts of things here, huh?"

"It's eye-opening, for sure."

I'm sure it is. We chat a while and ask one another how we've been. I haven't seen her since that night at Waquito's, and she has no idea how much things have changed since then. I wonder if she knows about me and Eli, but neither of us talk about him.

I place my order and she disappears, only to return a short while later with my sandwich and bottle of water.

"Thanks," I tell her, then ask her if she's got a minute to talk. I'm always wary of getting her in trouble with her boss.

"Sure, what is it?" She doesn't sit down but leans closer.

"Eli says you don't watch his fights. He says you're scared to see him getting beat up."

Tension releases in her face, which makes me wonder what she thought I was going to tell her. "There's no way I would ever watch him fight. I can't even watch it on TV."

I know this. I know her reasons, yet I am compelled to ask her anyway. I feel as if I'm treading on toes, but I also feel bad for Eli.

"I'm going to the fight," I tell her, "but Eli doesn't know I'll be there. I want to surprise him."

She gives nothing away, not even a hint of surprise at why I might say this. "And I'm going with a guy from work who is..." I pause trying to think of what to say. If Gerry's weirdness earlier today is anything to go by, I'm dreading spending the weekend with him in New York watching the fight. I need Nina to be there as much for me as for Eli, as selfish as this might sound. "Who I'm not so eager to go with," I say, releasing a sigh.

"Why?" She looks as if she doesn't follow. As if she has no idea why I'm telling her this.

"Oh... long story." There is no story, because I'm sure it's just a phase with Gerry, but I'm hoping this two-pronged attack on Nina might convince her to at least consider my proposal. "I know you're scared to watch him, but I'd hate to think of Eli being there all alone with nobody but his team rooting for him. He's not the favorite. The crowd will mostly all be on Garrison's side. It would be such a big boost to Eli if he saw you in the crowd." I let my words sink in.

Nina chews her lip.

"Garrison is so convinced he's going to win. It's not just the physical fight that's going to matter on the night, Eli hasn't even fought at that venue and this match is huge. I'm afraid for him, afraid that the magnitude of the occasion might overwhelm him, and if he doesn't see anyone in the crowd on his side... " I sigh loudly this time. "I'd hate for him to lose hope and give up."

Nina gives me a hesitant look. "I *want* to support him, but... "

"But what?" I sense an opportunity since she appears to be thinking about it.

"I can't see him get hit."

"Me neither, Nina." I've pushed that thought away the entire time. I have this notion that I'll look away, or look at my phone, or cover my eyes like I do when I watch horror movies. Or I'll be so irritated by Gerry sitting next to me that I won't have the presence of mind to watch the match intently. "We can help keep each other distracted," I offer jokingly. "Gerry isn't always the best company and if you're there, you and I can support one another through it."

She opens her mouth, then hesitates. "I...I would like to be there for him."

"Then come!"

"But the tickets..." She looks worried.

"Don't worry about that. I'll have a word with Lou in secret. You're Eli's sister. There's no way you getting a ticket is going to be a problem."

"I don't... " She doesn't say it, but I have a feeling I know. "I don't get paid until the end of the month, and my boss isn't going to give me an advance."

"I'll advance you," I say brightly. "It's not a problem at all, and I already have a big hotel room. With two beds." I don't, yet. But I will soon.

She looks sheepish, and a little embarrassed, and I understand. I also know the salve to soothe this over with. "You would be helping me out, Nina, and we'd be there for Eli. That's what matters, doesn't it?"

CHAPTER THIRTY-SIX

ELI

Harper and I have agreed on a complete communication cutoff ever since I arrived in New York a few days ago.

It's the day before the fight and Garrison and I have had the pre-fight weigh-in where we've squared up to one another in front of the cameras. Garrison owns the room; he really does, and the press loves him. Everyone wants to talk to him. He is a one-man show and he loves it.

He loves the fame, and he shines like the million megawatt star that he is. I sit on the stage quietly biding my time and watching my tongue.

I had dinner again with Nina the night before we flew to New York. I told her I have a cool hotel room to stay in, and there's a ticket for her if she wants it.

She knows this fight is big and I could see the guilty look on her face. I tried to convince her, because even though I'm not scared of Garrison, I'm slightly nervous about walking into a place full of thousands of people and none of them being on my side.

It makes me feel abandoned and unwanted all over again. It makes me feel not good enough. But I couldn't convince my sister, so I left it. I wish Harper could come, but she says her boss won't let her, and that she's got to make a few changes to the piece she's done on me. I miss her. I miss her like crazy.

Tommy Cairns, the promoter, has put us up in a nice place not so far from Madison Square Garden. He's as shifty as a mob boss and I don't trust him one bit. Lou doesn't either, but if it wasn't for him thinking I'd be an easy opponent for Garrison, I wouldn't be here.

Either way, I stand to make money. Life-changing money, apparently, though I'm not entirely sure of the exact amount. Lou mentioned something about four million dollars. That's crazy. It's a leap into the unknown. It means freedom—for both of us.

I don't want to focus on the money too much. I want to focus on winning. Those are two separate things to me. But that kind of money is something that neither me nor Nina can imagine. I don't even know what a hundred-dollar bill looks like. In any case, it would mean we crawled out of the gutter and now we're on level ground.

It means Nina doesn't have to work stupid hours at the diner, and she can maybe pursue work related to those courses she keeps taking.

It doesn't mean I'll stop boxing. I have a taste for it and if I can make big money from it, I'll gladly do it.

The room is buzzing. Garrison's in a good mood as he answers questions about his training and his love life. The camera doesn't pan to me much. I don't get asked many questions, but I'm content to sit observing the show.

Then one of the reporters asks me how I feel about being called '*the kid with nothing*'.

Garrison butts in. "Damn right he's the kid with nothing, 'cos he's gonna walk into the ring with nothing, and he's gonna leave with nothing... no title, no belt." He guffaws loudly, causing a ripple of laughs among the press. "Nothing but punches and bruises and maybe a couple of broken bones," Garrison adds, still grinning like the big ugly oaf that he is. The reporters love this baiting. He rises to it. "Going out with nothing, and on a stretcher," he says, cutting me a mean look and flexing his muscles.

I can't figure out if he's a comedian or a boxer. I've fought meaner-looking guys at the fight club.

"What do you have to say to that, Elias?" someone asks me.

I sit forward and look around the room before replying. "He's right. I *have* nothing, and I also have nothing to lose. I took this fight on short notice after a handful of not-so-great potential opponents turned it down, and I saw my chance. I'm a 29/1 shot to win this. Not just this but multiple titles; WBO, WBA, IBF and IBO. That's what Garrison has to lose."

And I have everything to gain.

The room quiets briefly, Garrison looks slightly confused by my statement, as if he's expecting me to trash talk back, as if he's waiting for me to say more.

The reporter looks baffled, as if he too is waiting for me to say more. But I have nothing more to add.

Some boxers get into the ring to make money, to hit the bigtime. Those things are important to me, but they are secondary. I'm not supposed to step into the ring wanting to kill a man, but I can't help it. Boxing is my therapy, and my opponent is at a disadvantage before the fight has begun.

Garrison has no idea who Swain is or what he did to me, and he has no idea that he's wearing Swain's face.

See?

I told you.

Garrison's already at a disadvantage before we step into the ring.

The air in the room suddenly turns heavy, then Garrison starts talking trash again, and the tension pops like a balloon.

I sit back and let Garrison enjoy his celebrity for the few hours he's got it.

CHAPTER THIRTY-SEVEN

HARPER

"This is Gerry, one of the guys I work with." I introduce Nina to Gerry.

"And this is Nina, Elias's sister," I tell Gerry. "We met at the diner a few weeks ago."

"So we did. Nice to meet you." Gerry seems annoyed that Nina is with me, despite his attempt at friendliness.

Nina seems a little wary of him, probably because of all that I've told her about Gerry.

We're all staying at the same hotel, and Nina and I are sharing a room. It was easy to tweak my arrangements. I changed my flight so that I could fly here on the morning of the fight, instead of coming with Gerry the night before. It made sense to come with Nina, otherwise I was afraid she might bail at the last minute if I left her to come on her own.

We're all booked on the same flight back tomorrow night, though. With only hours to go before the fight, I'm anxious for Eli and I can't wait to see the look on his face when he sees us ringside.

New York is busy and noisy, as is the hotel where we're staying. It's around the block from where Eli is staying, so there's no chance of us bumping into him, but it's as if most of the people watching the fight have booked into all the hotels within a one-mile radius of the venue.

I feel like an ant in a colony and I don't suppose the fight will be any easier.

We're meeting to get something to eat before the fight. It doesn't start for a few hours, but we want to eat early and chill out.

I sense that Nina is as nervous as I am. I wish this fight was over and that I could just go to the changing room now and hug Eli.

'Garrison vs Cardoza' posters and fliers are everywhere, all over the billboards and in the newspapers. The air buzzes with electric anticipation. The fight is all everyone talks about. Or rather, Garrison is all everyone talks about.

My belief in Elias starts to waver a teeny bit. We are surrounded by an ocean of Garrison fans, and as hard as I grip onto my hope for Eli, it's impossible for my faith not to waver a little.

I am so happy that Nina is here. She's easygoing, if a little quiet, and we get along well. She doesn't know me, so I understand her desire to keep her distance. I've never shared a hotel room with a total stranger before, but her being Eli's sister doesn't make her a complete stranger. This weekend would have been a whole lot nicer if it was only me and her. With Gerry, our small group seems a little strained.

He is still mildly distant towards me, and I don't know if it's because he suspects that something's going on between me and Eli, or if he's put out about Nina being here. I soon find out, however, when Nina excuses herself and heads to the bathroom.

"How close are you to Cardoza?"

That primes me, the way he throws Eli's surname at me.

"You mean Eli?" I say, purposely wanting to piss him off. He can't know anything about us. We haven't engaged in any public displays of affection, and even at the training camp, our adventures were under the radar.

"What's that supposed to mean?" I ask, because his question is so vague.

"You're here with his sister."

I peer at him coldly. "She's his sister. I got to know her because she worked in the diner around the corner. We became friends."

"And you and Cardoza?"

"He's the subject of my article. I had to get to know him."

He nods and he's about to say something when Nina returns.

We revert to small talk again.

"Nervous?" I ask her, when Gerry disappears to make a phone call and to get away from the noisy restaurant.

"Your boss doesn't like me."

"He's not my boss," I clarify.

"You said he was the senior sports editor."

"He's still not my boss."

"I can tell he doesn't like me," she claims.

"He's a Garrison fan," I reply, as if that explains it. "And he doesn't like me much either."

We laugh.

"Can you see why I was so desperate for you to come with me?" I ask.

CHAPTER THIRTY-EIGHT

HARPER

My heart feels like it's going to pop, and the fight hasn't even begun.

Nina's knuckles are white, and she already looks as if she's going to throw up. We've been here for an hour, waiting. I can't bear to wait another moment, but I've said this for every minute since I sat down.

There have been other fights taking place before the main one. We arrived halfway through and started watching.

But now it's time for the main fight to start.

Garrison vs Cardoza.

Garrison struts in first as if he owns The Garden. His entrance is pure showbiz. Music blasts out into the arena, and the crowds scream their excitement. He is surrounded by a mini army of stern-faced men marching beside him. It's a show complete with lights and music and dramatic effect.

I would expect nothing less from him.

Eli's entrance could not be more of a contrast. It's simple. There is no tune, just him walking in with Lou and the boys behind him.

He looks focused. Hard and determined. There is no anxiety in his expression. No sign of weakness or of overwhelm.

I'm the one who feels anxious, and scared, and worried. I'm the one shifting on my seat, feeling completely overwhelmed. Actually, it's me and Nina who both feel this way. I can tell each time I glance at her.

The fight starts and my insides jolt. I clasp my hands together and coach myself to breathe.

I resist the urge to run out. Nina looks as if she's seen a ghost. Her hands still grip the armrest as if she too is ready to scramble.

They dance around, and then Garrison throws a jab, and it hits Eli straight in his ribs.

Already?

I sit up and stare without blinking. I forget to breathe. He recovers from it though, and his hands are up again, in ready-to-fight mode.

They dance around some more, and Garrison is smiling as he's moving. They're both quick-footed, moving around the ring with ease, oblivious to the thousands of pairs of eyes trained on them.

I forget to breathe every few minutes.

This is only the first round, and I can't see myself getting through to the twelfth.

I pray this will finish in three rounds.

Garrison swings out again, and this time Eli blocks it, until Garrison hooks him with a sharp uppercut that catches him at the side of his face.

The crowd screams in delight.

I sink back into my chair.

Now *my* hands are on the armrest, on top of Nina's. I move them away then rest them on my lap.

I want to close my eyes because Garrison takes another swing but this time, Eli blocks it and lands a powerful punch to his abs.

Garrison doubles over.

A low murmur ripples through the crowd.

It's tiny, but it's an upset.

And the bell rings.

After a quick rest, they're back up again for round two. Eli evens up. They dance around. It's a perfect match, punch for punch. Jab for jab. They look almost equal to me.

I tell myself this is good.

No, this is *great*.

Again, I forget to breathe.

I turn and glance at Nina from time to time.

And I force myself to witness the man I love fighting in the fight of his life.

I don't want to be here, but I also can't walk away.

I don't want to watch this, but I also can't look away.

I lose count of who's hit who the most. Sometimes Eli is in the lead, and sometimes Garrison comes out with a killer punch. The rounds roll by, and the whole time I forget to breathe. I forget to blink. Before we know it, we're into the fifth round. Eli is hit and he bounces against the ropes. He staggers as he comes off them. Garrison eyes him like a predatory lion, waiting, waiting, waiting to pounce again.

Eli shakes his head, and I see his eye is cut.

The ref stops the round, and Eli goes to his corner where Lou and the cut man tend to his wound.

I swallow, then realize I'm gripping Nina's hand on the

armrest again. I pull it away, and glance at her. She looks at me, and we both look worried.

We turn to Eli again. I can't see his face because Lou's crowding over him, probably telling him what he needs to hear.

I pray.

Then Eli gets up, and the angry red gash over his eye is clearly noticeable.

And then he sees me. It's a quick look. We're three rows from the front. Even from this distance, I can see Eli blink in disbelief.

I want to wave, but this isn't a pantomime. I can't make him lose concentration.

The round continues. It's hard to tell who's in the lead because it's such a tight match, but surely the crowd, and all the doubters, can see that Eli's more than holding his own?

We reach round six, but even though we're almost halfway through, I don't think I can make it to round twelve.

I squeeze my eyes shut and massage my temples. I'm doing nothing but sitting here and watching, and yet I feel drained. I find it hard to watch this. Eli has put his heart and soul into this fight. I recall the grueling training sessions at the gym and at the training camp. I remember our conversations and his hopes and dreams, and I remember his nightmares and horrors, too.

I desperately want him to win, and in my frustration I find myself wondering why he hasn't knocked Garrison out yet because I so want this fight over with. They're both so equally matched that it's hard to figure out who is ahead. Gerry would offer an opinion, but I have no intention on listening to anything he has to say.

The crowd roars, and I look up, but I missed it. I was so

absorbed in my selfishness, that I didn't see what Garrison did, but Eli's on the floor.

I'm at the edge of my seat again, but what I really want to do is run over to him. The ref starts to count as Eli lies on the floor.

Get up! Get up!

I strain to make out movement. He lifts his head, and I squint to see his expression. But he gets up quick as a flash, and this time he looks mad.

He dances around Garrison so fast that I'm not sure where he got this sudden burst of energy from. Garrison tries to land some punches but Eli doesn't let any of his blows touch him.

I don't know what happened, but Eli's suddenly sped up.

I sit forward even more because I sense a shift in something. Eli looks sharper. He looks like he did back in the gym when he was sparring with the boys.

Garrison senses the shift too. Or maybe he's tired.

He seems a little shaky to me this time, as if he's not as nimble as he was four rounds back.

It's a game of minds, of mental strength because, just when it seemed that Eli had the upper hand, Garrison's arm goes back as if he's about to land another killer left hook. I close my eyes, fearing the worst.

Only I don't hear it.

I don't hear the smack of fist on skin.

But I open my eyes in time to see the killer punch Eli delivers to Garrison's side.

Garrison falls to the floor with a thud. I gasp. Nina does too. The crowd goes quiet.

Garrison gets up and staggers around. He looks at his

corner, shakes his head. Looks at Eli, then pulls up his hands, readying himself again.

Only, he doesn't look as ready, or as sure as he did before.

When the bell rings, he staggers to his corner and slumps on the stool.

I stare at Eli. Aside from the cut above his eye, he looks untouched.

CHAPTER THIRTY-NINE

ELI

I believed I could do it.

And now Garrison's starting to see that maybe I can.

When the seventh round starts, I tear into him.

The unheard of is starting to become real.

The unthinkable is slowly taking form.

My punch sends Garrison staggering back against the ropes.

He eyes me warily, but he glances at his corner.

Indecision, that's what I sense.

I pounce towards him.

I see Swain.

I hook another uppercut on his jaw, his face reverberates.

He staggers some more.

I hear cheering.

I can sense the wind shift.

I dance around him, but I don't need to.

This guy isn't going anywhere.

Garrison doesn't look too good to me.

He glances at the ref who motions to continue.

I should end this.

I'm more than pumped.

Garrison comes at me again, but there is no aim, no mastery, no speed. I smell desperation, and easily counter the pathetic punch he throws.

He goes down again, and then scrambles to his feet once more. Psychologically, I'm at an advantage because I'm not the defending champion. I don't have a title on the line.

He does.

He has it all to lose and believe me, he's going to lose it.

We paw at one another, because it's getting tiring. Garrison took me by surprise when he hit me hard in the first round. I wasn't as fast-footed as I should have been, but it was mostly because I was overwhelmed from being here.

Still, I quickly got back into it. My survival tactics kicked in. I recovered.

Now I'm warming up.

I'm playing with him.

He's a fighter too. A survivor, as all fighters are.

But I want it more. I have more to prove, and nothing to lose. More to prove to myself, and to Nina.

My heart is full. Harper's here, so is Nina. Grampton House flashes before me.

I see Dennis Swain.

The moment slows down.

Freeze-frames.

Garrison tries to hook me, but I block it.

I see flashes of Swain.

I see Nina taking my hand as we walk down the hallway.

I see Swain wink at me.

My blood boils.

I go into attack mode, battering Garrison with my combinations.

He's on the floor again.

The guy staggers around as if he's downed eight whiskies.

Somebody save this fucker.

Why is the ref allowing this to go on?

I can hear the crowd cheering.

The booing has stopped

I've earned their respect.

We're into round nine. Three-quarters of the way through.

We've been pawing and punching for a while now. Too long.

I can make this end sooner.

I go from his body to his head, jab, jab, jab. I'm on the attack.

I can do this. I always knew I could.

Garrison winks at me.

Or is it Swain?

Adrenaline swells inside me.

I land a solid left, and Garrison is on the floor.

This time he stays there.

The ref counts.

I hold my breath. Try not to shake because blood races through my veins.

Garrison doesn't get up.

The bell rings.

It's over.

I freeze.

This is happening.

This has happened.

I've done it.

In the background, I hear the loud cheer of the crowd.

They're going nuts.

Garrison's on the floor with the doctor and his trainer standing over him.

In the next moment, he stands up, a little shakily, but he's on his feet, which is a relief to me.

He nods, as if acknowledging his defeat. I look over to the audience and locate Harper and Nina. They're both on their feet hugging each other and jumping for joy.

I demolished Garrison and gave the audience what they wanted; a worthy champion, not Garrison, but me.

The referee should have stopped the fight at the end of the sixth, but he didn't.

My gut tells me that everyone, the ref included, expected their golden boy to bounce back. They hoped that he would pull out his magic and deliver a blow that would finish me.

They kept hoping and hoping.

And I let them.

I let Garrison think he could do it.

I was biding my time.

Garrison started strong. I put it down to his experience, and having the crowd on his side, but I knew I could do it. Didn't bother me one bit that no one but my team were on my side.

I've been there before. Abandoned. Unwanted. Unloved.

That the audience didn't believe in me didn't get in my

way because I had this. When nobody believes in you, you have to summon that belief out of thin air, and you have to have faith in yourself.

Faith can move mountains.

But so can wrath.

CHAPTER FORTY

HARPER

We scream and jump for joy.

That's all I remember. Everything unfolds like a dream sequence. Nina is crying, and Eli doesn't look surprised. He looks valiant. It's the referees, and Garrison's corner, and the MCs who look dazed.

I remember Gerry is here. Next to me.

"Told you," I say to him, jubilant.

"What the hell happened?" Gerry's face is a picture of puzzlement, like that of most of the crowd.

Eli holds the belt, his smile stretches from ear to ear.

The roar of the crowd is deafening. It's the same roar, and the same crowd who did this for Garrison not so long ago.

The MC shoves the mic at Eli. He looks at us, at Nina and me, then says something about belief, and about being lucky to have such a great team behind him. He says that not many people believed in him but a few people did, and he names us, one by one; Nina, Lou, Santos, and Jake, then Ernesto and me. He names *me*. My heart is about to overflow with happiness.

Nina takes my hand, and I see the tears running down her face.

When I wipe my hand across my cheek, I see that I have tears, too.

ELI

When they hand me the belt, I freeze for one precious moment. And then I raise it above my head and walk around with it.

None of this seems real. Not the belt, or the crowd or the win. I know it is real because I've played this moment in my mind thousands of times before and it's this moment now that has the sound, colors and emotions that are nothing like those that I imagined.

This is real and at the same time it's surreal, and I go from one end of the ring to the other, as if in a trance.

I seek out Nina and Harper in the crowd, and that grounds me. That's real. Jake and Santos are by my side, and Lou can't stop from grinning at me.

The MC puts the mic to me, and I say something, I don't even know if it makes sense, but it's spoken from the heart. I want to thank the people who matter.

I name them, make sure I don't forget anyone. It's not as if the list of people I have to thank is big.

CHAPTER FORTY-ONE

HARPER

Lou manages to get us into Eli's changing room but there are so many people who are fighting to get their hands on Eli that it takes a while for him to get here where we are all waiting.

Cameras, and reporters are everywhere backstage. It seems that we left the huge roaring noise of the crowd in the arena, for a smaller version of it hovering outside the changing room.

It takes a while before we see Eli. "Best surprise ever!" he yells as Nina rushes to him and they hug.

"Harper forced me," she tells him. He mouths a silent 'Thank you' at me over her head.

I let them have their time. She's hugging him and congratulating him and all around us, Jake and Santos and Lou are trying to keep the reporters out. "Give him some privacy," Jake yells at them.

There is noise and chatter and the air is filled with electricity. It's 1:00 a.m., and he must be exhausted; it's only pure adrenaline that's keeping him going.

I keep my distance, respecting that this is an important moment for him to share with Nina. But he beckons me over when Nina leaves his side. Of course she suspects something, given the way Eli and I have been staring at each other.

He takes me in his arms and we hold one another. "Hey, champ," I murmur into his ear and hold him tight. I have no fancy words. I'm just thankful that he didn't get injured too badly, and that he's okay. "I knew you would win. I just knew it!"

He holds me tighter and his lips graze my ear. "Seeing you and Nina in the crowd... that was awesome," he croaks. He sounds tired and he looks beat.

We stare at each other and my gaze goes to the ugly red gash above his eye. I wince and raise my hand towards the wound but I don't touch it. "Does it hurt much?"

"It looks worse than it is. The doc's going to take a proper look at it."

Good. That's what he needs first and foremost, to be checked out by the doctor. "I look forward to our personal celebration," I whisper, because now we can think about stuff like that.

"That's what got me through the fight."

This makes me smile. "When you get back, I'm all yours."

He hugs me again, and he's nuzzling my ear. "I can't wait that long," he says. I'm amazed that he has the energy to stand up, let alone think about sex. My fingers trace lightly across his bruised chest.

"Eli," I murmur. A knot tightens in my throat at the

beating he took, and what it took out of him. He won, and Garrison is in a worse shape, but seeing Eli's bloody eye, and the state of him, I want to wrap him up in cotton balls and keep him close.

I trace a finger gently down his chest. "You're in no position to exert yourself, not for a good week."

He winces.

"What is it?" I say, worried as I try to spring away from him, but he won't let me. His hand is firm against my back, and I couldn't move away if I tried.

"The usual aches and pains. Nothing that will get in the way, so don't worry. I can still perform."

This brings a giggle to my lips. I want to kiss him so bad, but his face is covered in splotches of blood, and sweat. This man needs to rest, and I need to let him.

"Get some sleep," I tell him.

"Come on, you lovebirds. It's getting late. The champ needs to rest." Lou claps his hands together from the other side of the room where he and the boys and Nina have gathered, and are giving us some alone time.

This isn't as much of a secret as I thought.

Then I remember Gerry.

Oh, shit, Gerry.

Oh, well.

"Stay with me," Eli says suddenly.

"I'm staying around the corner from you," I tell him, "with Nina."

He leans in and gives me a peck on the nose. "Thanks for convincing her to come."

"I knew how much it would mean to you."

"You have no idea what it was like to see you both in the crowd. But you lied to me about you." We're nuzzling noses now, and I forget about everyone.

"I wanted to surprise you," I say, touching his cheek.

"I'll thank you for that later. Stay with me," he says suddenly. "Get Jake to give you my spare hotel keycard."

"Tonight?" I'm dubious because I can see that Eli's in no state to get up to anything tonight.

"You help me to sleep."

In that case, how can I refuse? Of course I'll stay with him. I would do anything for this man. I nod. "Okay."

I'll explain to Nina, not that I'll need to explain anything judging by the way she's grinning at me as we make our way out.

ELI

It becomes too much. The onslaught of people around me. They all want a piece of me.

Tommy Cairns is so hyper, I reckon he's taken something illegal and is still on a high.

"That's the biggest fucking upset in boxing history for three decades, Elias." He says this every four sentences.

I count, because he's spouting a lot of shit right now, and Lou's trying to tell him that I need to get some sleep.

I've just gone nine rounds with The Tank, and I outplayed him.

The TV stations are going mental, Tommy announces, euphoria lighting his face.

"He needs to sleep, Tommy," Lou tells him. My body is

starting to feel heavy, but my eyes are wide open. It's not blood rushing through my veins, but adrenaline shot through with dynamite.

I could stay up all night, but Lou wants me to get some rest.

Finally, I get back to my room around 4:00 a.m. Harper's in my bed.

She is completely zonked out.

I manage to shower, then climb into bed.

"You're back," she whispers, and snuggles her arms around me as if we do this every single night.

I hug her close and hold her.

A phone call the next morning wakes us both up. I reach for the phone on the bedside table, then drop the damn thing, then curse as I bend down from the bed to retrieve it.

It's Lou. He's asking me to come downstairs for a press interview.

Meanwhile, Harper is raining kisses down my back. The commotion must have woken her up.

"Now?"

"It's eleven o'clock," he replies.

For fuck's sake. I was in the ring not so many hours ago. Why can't they understand and let me sleep in?

"Can we make it later?"

"There's a room full of reporters," he tells me. "You can't keep them waiting. I'm sending security up to your door."

"What?"

Harper hugs me from behind. She must have stripped

off her PJ top because I can feel her naked breasts against my back.

And her hand on my cock.

Oh, sweet, sweet mercies.

It was easier to knock Garrison out than it is to stop her.

"I gotta shower and go," I tell her.

She strokes me, and I turn bone hard. "Let me take care of this," she says, sliding her hands inside my boxers.

Shit. Her fingers wrap around my cock and I hiss out a sharp breath. "Harper," I groan, hating that I have to move her hand away. She's kissing my neck, and nibbling my ear. "Lou wants me downstairs. The press is waiting."

"Oh. We could get this over with now," she offers. "Quickly."

It's tempting. Extremely tempting, but I don't want to rush things. "It stinks. I'm sorry." I get up, and walk away.

Only then, when there is distance between us, do I make myself turn and stare at her. She's lying on the bed, completely naked. I bite my lip because this is hard to do—to look and not touch.

"Oh, boy," I say, averting my eyes, and raking my hand through my hair. I hear my breath laboring and my mind ping-ponging as I decide what to do next. I tell myself that when I claim her, I want it to be for hours.

"Stay there," I say. "I've got a press conference, and I'll be back."

"I fly back tonight. I'm catching the four o'clock flight with your sister."

"Don't go. Please don't go."

She sits up, her breasts jiggling as she does. My mouth waters. I harden some more.

This is agony, standing here, staring at her.

"I can't send Nina back alone, just her and Gerry."

"Yes, you can." I don't trust that dude, but my sister can more than take care of herself.

My eyes take in Harper's body slowly. Not being able to walk over and have my way with her is beginning to take its toll. "I need you," I tell her.

"I'll see what I can do." She covers herself with the satin sheet. "You should go shower, Eli. Don't keep the press waiting. This is your chance to shine."

"I can think of something else I'd rather be doing."

"Post-fight prize," she reminds me, then lies back on the bed. She's killing me. "Maybe when you come back, you can give me an interview," she asks, "Just some thoughts about the fight, you know, an exclusive just for me, from the new heavyweight champion."

"I'll give you more than that," I promise, and she rewards me with the brightest smile.

A few hours later, because it wasn't just one press conference and I had interviews to do for several newspapers, I'm ready to leave the hotel conference room and have some alone time with Harper. But to my dismay, I find her and Nina waiting for me outside.

I frown at Harper and give her a what-the-heck-are-you-doing-here stare.

"Nina's hungry," she explains. "I'm staying another night, but it would be nice if we all had something to eat together."

I try hard to ignore the pointed look Nina's giving me because my sister can see right through me. She's like the all-seeing, all-knowing oracle and it's freaky how much she can sense. Not the dark stuff, but other things.

"Let's go eat, then."

The hotel has given us a small private room, and it's just us—my family, my team. Lou has been talking business, telling me about the rematch that Garrison is demanding.

"You made history, Eli. You've caused the biggest upset in boxing history. Nobody believed that this was even possible, and you made it happen."

"You're beginning to sound like Cairns," I tell him. "Please don't."

"Okay, kid. Calm down. We'll be home in a few days."

I get it. I know, but I want some distance from everyone now. Everyone keeps telling me I'm amazing and what I did was unthinkable, and they don't stop. I don't want to hear it. I know what I had to do, and I did it. Now I want to take some time off. I'm tired. The fight for me didn't just take up one night, it took months of rigorous training and dedication. I need to unwind now.

After a while, Lou leaves to take another phone call. His phone hasn't stopped ringing all day. Jake and Santos quickly eat, then move away. They're busy on their phones. Everyone's phones haven't stopped ringing since last night. I've left mine in the room, haven't even bothered to charge it up because all the people who matter to me are right here.

"Did something happen at the training camp?" Nina asks, when Harper walks away to take a call.

"Like what?"

"You know exactly what I'm talking about, Elias. Don't pretend you don't."

I give her my best clueless face.

"Don't worry. I like Harper," my sister gives me her blessing. "But what changed? Because you didn't like her much before."

"The training camp might have had something to do with it." I try to suppress my smile. Every time I think of those two nights, I get a fuzzy feeling inside. I want more nights like that, and I want all of Harper. The anticipation of what is yet to come sets my thoughts on fire. "Being in a confined space can be difficult."

"Athena still has high hopes... "

"She can kiss them goodbye," I say, just as Harper returns from the bathroom. She sits down. "Are we having dessert?" She peers at the menu.

"Billionaire's cheesecake sounds good," Nina says. They both make approving noises.

"Do we have time?" Harper asks, "I don't want you to miss your flight."

"I can make time for dessert," Nina replies.

"Speaking of flights, what happened to ginger dude?" I ask.

"Gerry isn't happy with me. He's been weird ever since we came here."

"That's because he likes you," I tell her for the hundredth time.

Nina places the order for the cheesecakes, then leans in to the conversation. "Who likes her?"

"Gerry," I state as calmly as I can.

"He does not," Harper insists, with a shake of her head.

"I don't see it," my sister informs me. "I wasn't getting that vibe off him."

"Maybe he likes you, then," I say. Come to think of it, my sister keeps her private life private. I have no idea who she's dating and whether she currently has a boyfriend or not. It's another thing we don't talk about.

"Are you okay about going with Gerry?" Harper asks my sister.

"I will survive. I have my headphones, my phone, and a book. Even if we end up sitting together, don't worry, I can handle him. I've had stranger people for breakfast."

Harper and I blink at one another, not sure how to take that. "He's lonely, and divorced, and until recently he was still in love with his ex-wife, but she's now hooked up with an old school friend. Don't say I didn't warn you."

"I'll be fine," Nina insists.

CHAPTER FORTY-TWO

ELI

It's been a crazy day.

I am surrounded by people wherever I go. I couldn't even get into the cab to see Nina off at the airport because crowds mobbed the vehicle.

Tommy and Lou tell me I'm famous now that I've hit the big leagues, and I've made millions from this fight, apparently. This in itself is huge except that my brain is so fogged up at the moment, I can't process it.

In the space of twenty-four hours I've gone from being no one to being this 'overnight sensation'—Tommy's words, not mine.

Nothing about my success was overnight. Every step from the moment I was born led up to this.

Harper decides to see Nina off alone. I guess she feels bad because she asked Nina to come here, and she hasn't spent much time with her. And she's kind of left Gerry and Nina together.

My sister understands, and doesn't consider this a big deal, but Harper still feels bad. She has a big heart. I was so wrong when I think about my first impressions of her. She likely had the same wrong impressions about me.

It's a miracle that we ever got together in the first place.

I spend the rest of the day doing as Lou asks, doing interviews, and posing for photos. I am the heavyweight champion of the world, and I got the other titles too. Garrison must be feeling like life just kicked his ass. I've had that feeling most of my life, so I enjoy this new one, feeling like I'm the king of the world.

Harper has already told me that she has some work to do when she gets back from the airport; a write-up about the fight which she needs to send over to Merv and Gerry.

We're both busy, and I tell Lou that once I'm done with the press stuff, I want to go to my room and not be disturbed.

HARPER

I saw Nina off at the airport. That girl is so sweet, and she kept saying I didn't need to go with her, and that Eli needed me more, but I feel responsible, and I wouldn't dream of just ditching her when I was the one who got her to come here in the first place.

It all worked out like a charm in the end. I knew Eli would appreciate it, and I'm thrilled that Nina got to see the fight live. I have a feeling that in years to come, these memories will be priceless.

Eli's been busy all day. I wish they'd leave him alone,

because he seems so stone tired after the fight. Everyone wants him. He's like the new golden boy of boxing.

I told you, I want to scream to the world. I knew he would do it. Now the world is his, and my heart turns soft and gooey knowing that everything he worked for has paid off. I'm hoping this will go some way towards helping put the past to bed, as much as is possible.

When he returns to the hotel room, I'm on the bed, sitting up with the laptop on my legs.

He throws something at me. I laugh out loud when I see that it's a pack of condoms.

"Are you sure one pack is enough?" I ask, bending down to put my laptop on the floor.

He grins that cheeky, sexy, heart-melting grin, and throws another pack at me.

My eyes widen in supreme happiness. "Now we're talking."

He opens the hotel door again and puts out the 'Do Not Disturb' sign.

I've been waiting for this moment ever since the training camp. He's had the fight to preoccupy him, but I've had only him to preoccupy me.

"I don't plan on talking much," he says, his eyes and face full of promise as he walks towards me, discarding his clothes casually.

"No foreplay?" I ask, raising my body as I kneel on the bed. I start to unbutton my shirt slowly. The jeans I'd already taken off.

Completely naked, he joins me on the bed and takes over unbuttoning my buttons while I've barely had a chance to recover from seeing his hardness.

"I'm going to fuck you for hours," he promises.

"I'm counting on it." His body makes mine dance for

joy. I try to regulate my breathing as he undoes my bra, then kisses me. Blood rushes through my veins, my belly flip-flops as our mouths say a long, lingering hello. I wriggle out of my panties, which is tricky given that his fingers are playing with my breasts and his tongue is dancing with mine, and I'm about to lose my balance on the bed, but I want to be completely naked. I don't want to waste any more time. I've waited long enough.

We kiss and stroke one another, eager hands exploring each other as we tumble onto the bed, a tangle of hungry mouths, and entwined limbs. My fingers trace and linger all over him; he denied me this for so long, and now that I have him in the palm of my hand, I take my time to examine every inch, roll my fingers over every crevice.

The moment stretches out blissfully, and I am more than ready as he finally moves away and rolls a condom over himself. A throb of adrenaline shoots through me at the size of him, at the anticipation of what is to come. I can hardly breathe, hardly dare to blink as I savor the sight of him poised above me.

His eyes, once so hard and cold, now look down at me with a softness that makes me go limp. He leans down, pressing his hard cock against me, and I moan softly. His face is inches from mine but his fingers are below, stroking my clit, drawing out my pleasure. I touch him, and he growls. We feel one another up, as if we're playing with something new and precious for the first time.

He kisses me again, this time its deeper, a more intimate kiss that turns me to liquid.

My sigh rolls out. The pleasure is intense, building slowly, slowly, slowly, rippling from deep in my core, and spreading out to my belly.

"Harper," he moans, burying his fingers inside me,

making my back arch off the bed. My nerve endings dance, blood swirls, my senses heighten.

He spears me hard, and my body jerks from the contact. Sweet Jesus. Eli consumes all of me. My heart suddenly swells with so much love for this man, I think I'm going to pass out. I've never felt like this before. I'm used to the weight of his stare, but not like this, not with so much softness. He strokes my face and his mouth latches to mine and we suck and kiss greedily, swallowing one another. He is my heart and my soul. He is so deep inside me that I don't know where he ends and I begin because it feels as if we are one.

Then he pulls out, and I moan in disappointment. I feel like he ripped my heart and guts out and my face crumples in protest, but he slams into me again, and I cry out, gratitude pouring out of me. "Oh, yes," I gasp, low and breathless.

Yes, yes, yes.

And then he slams into me, over and over and over. This isn't lovemaking, this is pure fucking, and I love it.

I bring my knees up to hug his hips, and his eyes roll back for a sweet, sweet second. He gets a rhythm going, and I claw his buttocks. They're as hard as steel; there is no softness in his body. No place, no inch where the muscle is soft, or where the skin sags.

His all-over hardness makes being with him so unique. A pleasure, a privilege, something rare. I feel lucky to have him. Everything I touch—his biceps, his forearms, his back —is rock solid. It's a sensation that's new to me. I've never had a man who was so perfectly made, and now I have him. And he's inside me, pounding me mercilessly, and I am liquid and fire. Heat glides all over me.

"Oh, god, yes," I scream, as waves of my orgasm roll

over me. He doesn't let up, and my entire body jolts each time he rams into me. I don't want it to stop, and he doesn't look like he's about to. It's like we have a connection that goes beyond words. He is doing everything to my body I could wish for. Pleasure moves through every cell in my body. I think I'm going to die because it feels so good.

I love him inside me. I love the heat, and the sweat, and the messiness of him and me being together. There is nothing I wouldn't do for this man.

I think I love him.

That's my last thought as I descend into the abyss. My pleasure peaks and I shudder as I go to pieces, moaning and squirming beneath him. Right now I'd do anything he asked me do.

I arch my back almost off the bed, and he watches, sweat streaking down the sides of his face. His lips are parted, and his eyes are dark. It's intense, and intimate, this moment, and I'm in his grip. He rewards me with a kiss. His tongue pistons into my mouth with the same rough abandon that his cock drove into me.

He pulls away, letting me breathe. "Is this what you like, Harper?" he asks, between pants. He hasn't come yet, he's holding on for as long as he can. I marvel at his strength, but it shouldn't surprise me. "Yes," I beg. I'm suddenly on a precipice again, as if I'm ready for the next fall.

"You're so soft, so tight," he murmurs, burying his face into my neck. "I could go on all night."

"Please do." I am overcome by a feeling of connection, more deep, more honest, more pure, than any I have ever known. He drops his head lower and sucks my breast. I loosen my leg-hold on him as excitement shoots from my breast to my pussy, and I feel the beginnings of a wave. I have never come this many times before. After this, sex with anyone else is never going to compare.

But, after this, I won't want anyone else.

I come again, or maybe it's the same shockwaves still rolling over me. Another tide of pleasure rocks through me. I have no control over my body. It shakes and shudders, but I still have him in a hold. My legs are still crossed over his back. Even though I've had sex before, this feels like a first, for I have never been this closely entwined, or in tune, with anyone before.

"I love you inside me," I tell him, between pants.

I raise my finger to his lips, wiping some of the wetness from them, them plop my finger into his mouth. His hand moves over to my other breast, and he kneads it, pulling the nipple and circling it. I feel soaked and sweaty, as if we've been doing this for a while, but my body isn't done, and I want more.

"I dream of fucking you every single night," he tells me, his voice raspy and brimming with want.

I smile at the compliment. Elias dreaming of me every night is a compliment. He sucks my breast, as if he's never ever sucked one before, and I start to moan again because the pulsations between my legs become stronger.

He flips me over, and just as I start to make sense of what's happened, just as I start to raise myself up on my forearms, he shoves himself into me. The exquisite sensation sucks the air from my lungs. The push sends my face into the bed, and I savor this new position. My body tingles all over, and my breasts are pushed into the cotton sheets.

I push back slowly, his rough hands are all over my buttocks, kneading and feeling my flesh. He pounds me with a rhythm, then reaches over and strokes my clit. My senses are ready to explode. The mounting pleasure has peaked once more, and I want to cry out. I come again, clutching hard at the bedsheets as he slams into me over and over again. My pathetic moans become the orchestra to my release, and in the next second, he lets himself come, grunting once, twice, before impaling himself deep inside me.

It's a wonder I can breathe, for I have no energy, not even to move. I could happily stay like this.

He finally moves away, and we collapse onto the bed. He lies down with his forearm over his forehead, as if he's done a full day's work. I'm exhausted, but I'm not done. I don't think I'll ever be done. I think I'll want this feeling every single day. I don't want to move. I want to lie by his side and stay here forever.

CHAPTER FORTY-THREE

HARPER

We didn't sleep much that night, in between making love and talking, but mostly making love.

So, early next morning, we unwillingly let go of one another, and I stole out of Eli's room. It killed me to leave him, but I had a gut feeling that I was already in Gerry's bad books, and I needed to haul my butt back to work as soon as possible.

I caught the early morning flight back to Chicago and was showered, dressed and at work only forty-five minutes later than usual.

As I barrel through the doors of the building, I don't have time to wonder why my dad has left multiple voicemails on my cell phone.

Merv's terse voice when he summons me to his office causes me to curse under my breath.

It's when I walk in and see his red face that I begin to suspect something serious is up. The air is prickling with so much tension that I dare not sit down. I'm not even an hour late, I conducted 'some' sort of interview with Eli—Merv doesn't need to know I did it while straddling him in the bathtub—so I'm unclear as to why he's looking daggers at me.

Without saying a word, he hands me a large brown envelope.

"Take a look inside," he barks, when I stare at it without moving. This is most peculiar. I grab the envelope and flip it open. There's something inside that look like photos.

"Pull them out," Merv orders. I do as he says, then freeze. It's as if someone's thrown a bucket of ice at me.

The photos are of me on my knees, pleasuring Eli. They're grainy, and a little dark, but it's obvious what's going on. These were taken that night I went to his apartment, and I couldn't help myself. Eli's face registers pure ecstasy.

I close my eyes, then shove the photos back as if they're burning my fingers. My teeth clench, and I am too angry, too humiliated, too puzzled to worry about what Merv thinks.

"When I told you to get to know him, well, I didn't mean *that* well."

I try to think. We were in Eli's apartment, and who the hell would have even known I was there? Who would have gone to these lengths to humiliate Eli and why? I'm suddenly fearful for him.

Lou said there's a huge welcome home parade planned for Eli in a few days' time when he returns to Chicago. Will these photos damage his newfound fame and eclipse his win? I'm more worried about him than I am of what Merv thinks of me, and what he will do next.

Of course I'm embarrassed, but it's not easy to make out

that it's me and I have my back to the camera. Plus, I am not famous. It's Eli I worry about.

"Well?" Merv asks, his voice tight as if he's trying to rein in his fury.

I stare at him defiantly. "What do you want me to say, Merv? This was a private moment."

"Your piece on Cardoza was supposed to be objective. You and him and *that*," he jerks his head at the photos in my hand, "*that* doesn't help your case."

Shock hits me. "Are these... are these in circulation?" That would be disastrous.

The thought of these photos getting out suddenly slams into me like a juggernaut.

My body tenses. I would hate for my friends and my parents to see this. They would be able to tell it's me.

It would also ruin Eli's homecoming. I can't see it having too much of a negative impact on his reputation though; from experience, these things tend to work out better for men than women. The public will see it as him being caught in the act... the boxer who had to go without sex for months. It would be acceptable.

I'm the one who will be judged. It's bad enough that Merv is judging me now.

"Who else has seen this?" I ask, trying to figure out what possible motive the person behind this would have. Was it to embarrass Eli, or threaten him for money? I can't see that happening. The only person who would be embarrassed is me, and I'm not important or famous enough that this would matter if these photos got published online. I won't be able to look Merv in the face for a few weeks, but I'll get over it.

"Gerry's seen them."

I exhale loudly. Oddly, in this moment, it bugs me more that Gerry has seen these.

"They could surface online for all we know," Merv growls. "Other newspapers might have these in their possession. Eli is a huge story now. He's big news, and this? A member of my staff? You were supposed to write a journalistic piece on Cardoza's rise to fame and victory, instead of making a soft-porn movie with him."

I lower my head and stare at the table. "What do we do?"

"There is nothing to do. This isn't a blackmail attempt. It looks bad on you. Cardoza's win will help him. He's the current golden boy, and things like this won't matter much to him."

"Were they addressed to you?" I ask, as if a light has suddenly gone off in my head.

Merv nods. He looks so uptight, so uncomfortable. I don't need to worry about not being able to face him again, because he's having as much trouble for his part.

I need to listen to my dad's messages.

"Get out of here, Lindstrom," he tells me.

I look at him, expecting him to tell me I'm fired or suspended, but he seems to want me out of his sight more than anything.

I rush back to my desk and listen to my dad's messages, and when I do, he asks me to call him back. He doesn't sound too happy either.

I think I already know.

He answers his cell phone on the first ring.

"Are you trying to give me a heart attack?" he bellows. His tone gives me a heart attack.

"What's wrong, Dad?" I'm praying that it will be something to do with his girlfriend. I'd even be happy if he told me he'd proposed to her. It's news I'd hate to hear, but I'd prefer that over what I fear it really is.

"I didn't raise you to be a slut."

His words send me reeling into my seat. He has the same photos.

This isn't about Eli.

This is about me.

Somebody is out to get me, and cause me the most amount of humiliation.

"The photos," I say, rubbing my forehead as I close my eyes, wondering how it is that my world has imploded so suddenly.

"Yes, the damned photos," my father spits back. "Have you no shame?"

"Someone is out to get me, Dad."

"Is that the boxer?" he seems to struggle to say it.

"Yes."

"And that's your idea of working on him?"

He's so angry he's not even making sense. This is a double shot of shock for him. It would be for any father to see a photo of their daughter like this, and for my father, seeing Eli, 'that boxer,' with me, must be like dousing fuel over fire.

I have no words.

I have nothing to say that will explain any of it. Nothing that will make either of us feel better.

As far as I can see, there is no feeling better, not now, not after this.

That was a private moment between me and Eli, but some nosy, douchebag, vengeful, slimy piece of shit decided to teach me a lesson.

I know who it is. At least, I think I have a clue.

Only someone like Gerry would be that vengeful.

I storm into his office, but he's not at his desk. I grind down on my teeth because I want to have it out with this bitter and deceitful excuse of a man, and he's not here.

I don't have concrete evidence, but it's not too difficult to piece it all together, after all, he left the bar with me that day. He was angry that I was going to meet with Eli. It's not inconceivable that he would follow me. But I have no idea how he managed to take those pictures.

For the next hour, I'm in the bathroom, pacing around, trying to keep it together. I can't face being in the office around people, because I have no idea who will have seen those photos, but if Merv's been sent them, and also my dad, then who else?

I'll have to tell Eli at some point. There is no reason to tell him now when he's probably busy signing new deals and getting endorsements.

I need to check out the articles I wrote which would have been printed in today's paper, and also on the day of the fight and the day before.

I venture out of the bathroom a little later, but as I return to my desk, I can already hear my cell phone going off.

"Turn that goddamn thing off," Merv spits out as he walks past me. Turns out that he can't sit still either.

I rush to get my phone just as it stops ringing, but I catch sight of Eli's name flashing on the screen.

I call back, dreading the worst.

"What the fuck did you write?" he snarls.

I blink in confusion. What's he talking about. "I... uh ... " His question stumps me.

"You lying little—" he stops himself but I catch the hiss as he exhales.

Something is wrong. What the hell is wrong?

"You lied. You lied and snaked your way into my bed to get your fucking story."

My heart splinters, not just at his words which slice through me, or the tone, but at the accusation he makes. I don't understand what he's talking about. He's not talking about the photos. He's on about the articles.

"I wrote..." I try to remember what exactly I wrote. I know what Gerry wanted me to write, but I held back.

"You spilled my secrets; the things I never wanted anyone to ever know about."

My breath catches and stifles my surprise. "It was all about the story, wasn't it, you stupid little bit—" He doesn't finish the sentence. He doesn't need to. I can hear the hate in his voice crystal clear.

I rush over to the desk where the week's worth of papers are, and I pull out all the ones which contain the articles I wrote.

My stomach knots and twists with a sickening feeling. I'm almost too afraid to open the papers, afraid of what I might find.

CHAPTER FORTY-FOUR

ELI

"Is this true?" Nina asks me.

My heart is breaking. It's nothing to do with that love bullshit. I don't give a fuck about Harper. But my heart, the thing that keeps beating only because Nina and I made it in this world, feels like it wants to give up. I kept this dirty filthy secret from my sister because I knew it would crucify her if she ever found out. But Harper took my secrets, took my demons and exposed them for the world to see.

She used me to get her story.

The princess was good. She was very, very good. Even I fell for that shit.

"Is it?" Nina asks.

I want to lie. I really do, but she already knows the truth. She can see it on my face. I don't know I'm crying until I feel a tear roll down my cheek, and that one thing gives Nina her answer.

She puts her hand to her face and crumples to a heap on

the floor. I'm not prepared for this. I knew it would hurt her, but I am not prepared for this. She really has been like a mother to me. She really did think she had shielded me from the worst of humanity.

"It's okay," I say, rushing to her. I'm on the floor with my arms around her, holding her body as she cries. I don't understand this level of despair. "It's not your fault," I tell her.

She looks up. "I had no idea. I had no idea, Elias," she wails, and then, maybe because she catches my astonished look, she tries to calm herself down. It's noticeable, though.

"We were only children," I tell her. "Nobody would have believed me, and I couldn't tell you. I just couldn't."

I shake my head, because those memories are starting to lodge back into my brain like a cancer I thought I had finally cut out. "You couldn't have stopped it."

"Who?" she wants to know.

I frown then look away. I don't want to talk about it. I don't want to say his name out loud. I don't want to go back into that time or place.

"Who, Elias?"

"Does it matter?" Harper doesn't realize what she's done, but she has opened up so many festering, bleeding, pus-infected wounds. She's interfered in my life and fucked things up.

My hands have been permanently fisted ever since I found out. I can't relax. I can't sit still. I have an uncontrollable urge to hit something.

I despise Harper with every cell in my body. She keeps calling me and Nina, and leaving messages. She claims that she didn't know the articles had been switched. She blames Gerry for the changes, for mentioning the abuse, and the fight club, and the stuff about me throwing the fights.

I don't care so much about people knowing about that, but it was something I wanted to put behind me, like most of my early life. What I hate is that she broke my trust.

We shared little of ourselves with others—Nina and I. It was almost as if by not talking about it, we could pretend it didn't happen.

I guess I should never have trusted her. I blame Lou as well. He should never have allowed this to happen. I didn't need this type of fucking PR. He tells me that Tommy is on the case, that I'm going to get a person to take care of my publicity.

He wasn't too happy when I told him I needed to get back to Chicago tonight. I caught a late flight out, didn't want to wait a day or so.

"There's a welcome home parade for you," he insisted. "We'll go back on Wednesday. The city is putting on a hero's welcome."

I ignored him and came back, because Nina sounded so distraught on the phone after she's read the shit Harper had written.

"His name, Elias." She won't let go of it.

My jaw tightens and I don't answer right away. I hate to say his name out loud. "Swain."

Her face turns ghostly white and she rushes out of the room. Then I hear her throwing up.

Now I'm the one who's concerned.

I bang on the bathroom door. "Nina!" I bang again. "Nina!"

"Just... just give me a moment."

If I saw Harper now, I couldn't hurt her, not physically, but I would put a hole through the wall because I couldn't look at her face and not erupt. My hate for her is a million times more than when I first saw her.

She will go back to her rich-Daddy world, to her workplace with Merv the Perv and the slimebag that is Gerry, meanwhile, we're the ones who will have to put this behind us.

Lou told me this would blow over, that people would forget, that my win has made boxing history and people won't care.

But I care.

I never wanted the world to know.

I never wanted my sister to know.

The world loves a broken hero, but Lou has no fucking clue. This isn't about how the world sees me. It's about my deep dark past being revealed and made real all over again. It's about the trust that has been shot to pieces, leaving shrapnel in my daily life.

When Nina comes back, her face is ashen, her eyes bloodshot. I never expected her to take it this bad. "You were so little," she says, as if she needs to explain.

"You weren't much older yourself."

"Nothing happened to me," she throws back. "I'm sorry I couldn't protect you."

"Hey." I move towards her, but she's closed off. She has one arm around her stomach, and one fiddling around with the chain on her neck. She needs time. "None of this was your fault," I insist.

"I failed you."

"You were eight," I remind her. "We were children."

"He's dead. He died four years ago."

My eyes widen. "How do you know? *Why* do you know?"

She shrugs. "I read about it in one of the papers. It was a hit and run."

I pray it was someone seeking revenge, and I'm glad they got it. "That's good news."

There is a silence as the words sink in, and we both have our own memories of that hell.

"Why did she do that?" Nina asks. "Harper?"

"I don't know, but I'm going to fucking find out." I scrub my face with my hand. What a shitshow this has turned into. My last few days have been beyond unreal.

"She keeps calling me," Nina says, "but I don't answer." She takes a deep breath. "I really liked her."

I liked her too, and I trusted her, and in the end she fucked me over for a story.

CHAPTER FORTY-FIVE

HARPER

I couldn't find Gerry yesterday, and I went home early anyway. My evening was spent speculating on the nightmare that has swept into my life from out of nowhere.

I've called Nina and Eli multiple times but neither of them ever pick up the phone.

This morning I'm back at the office, and the moment I see Gerry come in, I charge into his office. I don't have conclusive proof about the leaked photos, but the more I think about it, the more I am convinced that Gerry is involved. But trying to get information out of that slippery snake is impossible.

"You're mistaken," he tells me when I accuse him of having some involvement.

"Mistaken?" I'm doing my best to keep my voice calm. Hard to do when I have this urge to put my hands around his neck and throttle him. "You had something to do with those photos, Gerry. Why don't you man up and confess?" I can't prove outright that he did, and I'm doing my damndest to rein in my anger.

"I don't know what you're talking about."

The lying little creep. Eli was right to be concerned about him. He never liked Gerry.

"You *do* know what I'm talking about." And though I can't prove outright that he had a hand in those photos of me and Eli, I do know that he changed my article and put in those things I was adamant stayed out; Eli's secrets—the things he had confided in me.

Gerry's deceit is coming to the surface slowly. I considered him to be my friend and mentor, and he took Eli's secrets and published them for the world to read. It's my fault for telling him in the first place, but at the time I still believed that he was a good friend, and not the soulless shitbag I now see him for.

"What about the articles?" I ask, when he refuses to say anything about the photos.

"What about them?"

"You changed things," I say, accusingly.

"I tightened them up."

Every time I close my eyes, I see Eli's face before me, only now he is cold again, and his eyes as hard as stone. He will never forgive me for this, and he has no idea about the photos, I assume, otherwise he would have mentioned them.

"You deliberately put in the things I told you I wasn't going to put in!"

He huffs out loudly. "You don't owe Cardoza a thing. There's no loyalty, there isn't supposed to be. He was supposed to be the *subject* of your piece, nothing more."

"My article was fine as it was. You didn't need to expose his secrets."

"You shouldn't have told me, then."

"We were friends having a drink, we were talking. I confided in you." Eli giving me a cold shoulder after the training camp might have made me susceptible to feeling I could trust Gerry. I wonder if that's how Gerry saw it. Then I think back to all the times I've confided in him and he's looked out for me.

Maybe Eli was right. Maybe Gerry did have a soft spot for me that I couldn't see.

My suspicion grows. I know he had something to do with the photos. It's too much of a coincidence with everything else going on. "I might not be able to prove it but I know you had a hand in the photos," I say. After all, he left the hotel with me that day. He could have easily followed my taxi, and given all the research he'd done on Eli, I wouldn't be surprised if he already knew where Eli lived. "At least have the balls to own up," I say, my anger simmering to boiling point. Any minute now I'm going to explode.

"I'm shocked and hurt that you would accuse me of such a thing, Harper."

"You gutless piece of shit." I don't hold back. He must think I'm stupid. "You changed the article to hurt Eli, and to make me look bad in Eli's eyes, and as well as that, you took the photos. I don't know how you did it, I have no idea how you got the angle and the height, and the camera to take those shots… " And then I realize. "You probably didn't take them, because you have contacts. You could easily get someone to do your dirty work for you."

He shifts uneasily in his chair and attempts a surprised look. I know it's fake because I've come to know Gerry well. He's been odd lately, as if he's been avoiding me. I equate avoidance to guilt.

I don't even care anymore whether he will admit to it or

not, because the damage is done. Eli won't want anything to do with me. The fact that neither he nor Nina answer my calls clues me in.

I will go see him and Nina, I will try to explain, but I don't see them letting me anywhere near them.

One thing at a time, though. First I have to sort this mess out. "It's too much of a coincidence that you added in the things I didn't want in the article, at the same time as Merv and my father received photos of me and Eli." I suddenly remember Eli's hunch. "You're jealous that I chose to see Eli that evening."

Damn.

That's it. That is exactly it.

He made Eli look like a dodgy dirty guy desperate for a quick release. And he's done his best to cause me the maximum amount of humiliation. My cheeks turn red each time I think of my father looking at those photos.

Rage seeps out of my pores, and I want to poke Gerry's eyes out, especially now as he stares at me with contempt. But he doesn't deny anything.

Initially, I had assumed that a freelance photographer might have looked for dirt on Eli, something that might sell for more if he won the belt.

I never dreamt that Gerry would be behind this.

He rests back in his seat, staring at me blankly, as I try to unravel what happened and he's amused by it. I imagine situations in his private life where he drove his ex-wife bonkers just the same way he's driving me bonkers, and I no longer feel as sorry for him.

"I amended the article slightly," he offers, after a lengthy pause. "But the other thing?" He shakes his head in disgust. "Surely you're not implying that I have nothing better to do than to follow you and watch you with your lover."

I jolt when he phrases it like that. It's exactly the type of twisted thing he would do.

"Did you get a kick out of it?" I ask. "Watching us like that?" I don't want to have this conversation, but his red face is the sign of guilt or something else. Eli always insisted that the guy liked me, and his gut instinct is probably much better than mine. Gerry swallows, and his face turns even redder.

"There's being lonely, and there's being a perv," I state.

"I'm not lonely. I had a blind date event I should have gone to, but I felt sorry for you. You're the one who suggested we go out for a drink."

"That's because I made the mistake of thinking you were a nice guy." The shock in my voice is real, because I finally see that Gerry isn't nice. That the guy I thought was safe, and sensible, and looking out for me is in fact a sick and twisted guy who mistook my social encounters with him for something else, and who believed that I snubbed him that evening.

"I had the wrong idea about you, Gerry. And the truth is I don't understand who you really are." Then I turn the knife in more. "I'm not surprised that your wife left you."

"Ouch," he mocks, full of exaggeration. "Was that supposed to hurt?"

"No," I reply wearily. "It was merely an observation. Why did you follow me?"

He stares at me silently. I wish the bastard would say something. I think back to our conversations and the dinners and lunches and how much I confided in him.

Was it possible that I gave him the wrong idea? Was that why, despite being relatively new here, he decided to let me have this assignment, showing a preference for me and not the others who'd been here longer than I had, and who now seem to hate me because he favors me?

"Women like you are calculating, manipulative little leeches," he says slowly, his words make my breath catch in my throat. I have no idea where he's going with this because I don't understand his warped and twisted way of thinking. "You led me on until you found someone else."

"Led you on?" I shriek, almost jumping out of my seat in extreme shock. My mind races over our every past interaction, and I nitpick every conversation and look for clues as to why he would think this.

This man is deluded.

"When you got your nails into the boxer... you went for him. Even if he'd lost, you would have basked in his short-lived fame for a while, except that you've hit the jackpot now. Haven't you, or have you upset him?"

The deceitful little shit smiles at me because he knows he's ruined everything for me.

"The least I can do is to let him know you were behind the photos," I threaten, "and you can be sure that Eli will know."

But after betraying his trust the way I have, I can't tell him about the photos yet. They're an added headache he doesn't need to know about.

I have to accept it. I've let Eli down, and nothing can change that. My mistake was to confide in Gerry. Now I fear that I will never find my way back to Eli again.

"As if he'd believe you," Gerry hisses. "You waltzed into this job because of your connections, and then you clung to Cardoza like a leech. You're no better than the hussy you claim your father's girlfriend to be."

I am stunned into silence. I remember telling him once,

complaining, more like, about my father's choice of partners. I was trying to make Gerry feel better when he was upset that his ex-wife had found someone.

"You're a sick and twisted psycho," I say, thinking of all the words I can hurl at him and only coming up with a few.

"Did I hit a sore spot, Harper?" I see fire flash behind his eyes. "I find it amusing that even when your privileged upbringing gets you a job that many would die for—many with better qualifications and experience than you—you still manage to mess things up by sleeping with the guy you're supposed to be interviewing. You're no better than a tramp."

I grit my teeth, searching the periphery of the room for something to hurl at him. I wouldn't do that, but I feel the urge to. He doesn't let up. "To think I convinced Merv that this would be good for you when he couldn't find something decent to give you. He didn't want your father complaining."

I'm so shocked that I start to shake. "Merv will hear of this, and Eli will too. Don't be surprised if he sues you for invading his privacy and taking photos without his knowledge or consent. He's got the money now to sue your sorry ass, and you can be sure that I'll help him to find the best lawyers in Chicago."

I've had enough of staring at his pathetic face, and there is nothing more to say. I storm out of his office and slam the door so hard that everyone looks up.

There are other people, people who I care about and have let down, and I need to make it up to them.

CHAPTER FORTY-SIX

HARPER

I haven't spoken to my dad since that day, and I need to get in touch and 'fix things', but I can't think of anything beyond fixing things with Eli first.

Nina and Eli still don't answer my calls. In my misery, I make a detour to the diner hoping to speak with Nina. I am desperate to tell her my side of the story.

Frankie's Kitchen is packed and a line runs all the way around the outside of the diner. Either it's become common knowledge that Eli hangs out here a lot, or he's in there right now.

I can't get a peek in through the windows because people are blocking my view by standing in line. There's no point waiting with them because even if Eli is inside, I won't be able to talk to him privately, so I walk away.

I need to talk to him alone and I need him to listen to me. It will mean asking a lot of him, given what's happened, but that's what I need to do if I'm to have any chance of putting things right again.

But I doubt that things will ever be the same between us again.

I doubt there will ever be an *us* again.

There is a huge welcome home parade and reception planned for him tomorrow. This puts a time limit on me because I want to sort things out as soon as possible.

Later, on my way home after leaving the office, I take a detour to his apartment. When he opens the door, he looks slightly taken aback. I attempt a smile, but he doesn't. Instead, he asks me what I want.

"Can we talk?" I ask, silently pleased that he opened the door to me at all. "I've called you and Nina so many times—"

"Stay away from Nina," he growls. "You've caused enough damage."

"It wasn't me, Eli. You have to believe me. I would never do anything like that."

"Yeah?" he cries, his voice rising in anger. "Then who the hell let that information out in the first place? My sister never knew."

It's as if he's aimed an arrow at me and hit the bullseye.

"She never knew, and I never intended for her to find out, but you and your fucking big mouth, you had to go and tell the whole world. It was supposed to be private. I *trusted* you."

My heart is thumping in my chest. Eli's eyes blaze with rage and his voice is hard and sharp like a knife edge. It hurts to be on the receiving end of it. "Gerry changed my article at the last minute. He added that stuff in."

"He added it in? Tell me, Princess, how the hell did he know what to put back in?"

His choice of endearment—dipped in poison—stings.

I hang my head in shame. "I told him not to. I told him that was personal stuff you didn't want to reveal," I begin to say.

"But you're the one who leaked it to him in the first place, aren't you? I trusted you, and I also told you I didn't like that guy. Why the fuck would you go and tell him of all people?"

Because I was stupid.

Because I didn't think.

Because I thought Gerry was a good guy. These kamikaze thoughts crash through my mind, but I say nothing. 'Sorry' seems inadequate. I wonder if I'll ever be able to make it up to him.

I've hurt Eli in the worst possible way, and because I hurt Nina, he will never forgive me. They are right to hate me so much, but I didn't set out to do this on purpose. If only I could make him see this.

"I never wanted to hurt you or Nina. I argued with Gerry about what to print."

"The thing I have a problem with, Princess," he spits the word out with so much venom that I edge back, "is that you told him at all. I'll never trust you again, *ever*." His brow wrinkles, as if he's thinking of something. "But I'll never see you again, so I won't ever make that mistake again."

My body slumps as if he's physically punched me. He sees me as guilty and I can't blame him. "I'm sorry, Eli. I'm so, so sorry. You were right all along about him."

"Don't go blaming the ginger dude. You wanted your story, and now you have it. You used me."

I shake my head. "No! None of this was for the story. I would never, ever betray your trust for a story."

"You *did* betray it. You don't even know how much

damage you've caused. You should *never* have said a word to Gerry, and I'm fucking shocked that you did."

I scratch the back of my neck. He's right. I should never have said a word. Ever. No matter how shitty I was feeling. "I'm sorry. I swear, Eli, I never meant to hurt you or Nina. It was my fault for letting that slip, and I'll regret it until the day I die, but you have to know it wasn't for the story. I was never going to expose any of that stuff. This is Gerry's doing. I accept that I was the one who made the mistake of telling him. But please believe one thing, I never did it for the story, none of it. You and me, that was all real. I care about you, Eli. I love you." I sound desperate, and it's because I am.

"Too fucking late. You've done the damage, now get lost. I don't want to see you ever again."

He's about to shut the door in my face. This can't be it. I shove my foot in the way. He's going to have to squish it if he wants to get rid of me.

"Fuck off, Harper."

His words smack into my stomach and hold there, winding me so that I struggle to breathe.

His anger and hatred is justified. I messed up, but none of this was on purpose. My mistake was to confide in Gerry. I try again. "I didn't know he was that twisted. You have to believe me, Eli."

"I don't believe you. I'll never believe you. I should have trusted my gut from the first time I saw you. I knew you were trouble then, and you've proved it. How I let you worm your way into my bed, I don't know." He peers at me. "Actually, I do know. You came to my apartment that night and had your way with me, and as for the night after the fight. I would have fucked anyone. You were there, and it was convenient."

I almost choke at that, because that's not how it was at all. He knows that.

And then I realize that he still doesn't know about the photos.

"You were desperate for me," he continues, his words coming at me like bullets. "At least you were good for something." His words slam into me like an uppercut and I almost stumble back in shock. In his rage, he's not seeing it the way it happened. He doesn't remember that he was the one who begged me to spend that first night with him after the fight, and he was the one who wanted me to stay an extra night. *He* begged *me,* it wasn't the other way around—yet now doesn't seem the right time to say this because he's hurting badly.

I decide to tell him about the photos, if only so he will see that Gerry did a dirty on me too, but just as I'm about to tell him, I hear footsteps behind me. When I turn around, I'm staring into Athena's beautiful face.

"What took you so long?" Eli asks her. She flashes him a smile that shreds my heart. "I came as soon as you called." She's got an overnight bag with her and Eli moves to let her in. My face falls, just like my heart bottoms out of my stomach. He doesn't even say 'bye'.

Instead, he slams the door in my face.

I made it back home without breaking apart. And I made it through the next day, and the day after that.

It's as if a numbness has swept over me.

I gave up.

The only person I wanted to hear me out doesn't want me anywhere near him.

He's replaced me in a heartbeat.

Nothing else matters.

And so, I am numb.

The rest of the week passes. I watch the news and see the huge welcome home party that the city officials have put on for Eli. I see him with Athena, always that wretched woman by his side. I watch her accompany him to the various parties and dinners that follow.

He's the toast of the town.

Frankie's Kitchen is done up with lights for a few weeks following the fight. I know this because I get the cab to the gym sometimes, and I think about getting out and having a word with Eli.

Then I chicken out and walk past the diner instead.

I blew it. The one thing he never gave anyone—his trust —he gave to me, and I blew it.

I am as much to blame for this as Gerry.

The weeks crawl by.

Life at work continues.

The world carries on.

My father and I don't speak, or call, or text. I can't bring myself to pick up the phone, and it seems that neither can he. I'm at a loss, both personally and professionally.

I continue to see Athena with Eli in the papers and in a few news clips. It's still in the early weeks after his amazing win, and he's on the news so often these days that it's almost impossible to miss him. I have to confess, it's become my favorite pastime, flicking the channels and hoping to get a glimpse of Eli.

Another week passes, and I see the lights around Frankie's Kitchen come down. The lines aren't so big anymore, and I decide it's time for me to confront Nina face to face since she still hasn't responded to any of my texts or voicemails.

My sadness for what I've lost with Eli is buried deep inside my heart. It's too fragile and raw for me to examine and dwell on just yet, but I feel compelled to confront Nina and tell her my side of the story.

She seems so eager not to give me a chance, but I am just as determined for her to hear me out.

I've been going to the diner very early all week, hoping to catch her on her early shift one day. It takes four days before I see her.

Her brown eyes widen the moment she sees me, and because it's so early, there's no one else for her to tend to, and there's no other waitress around. It's been almost a month since the fight, since I last saw her.

She begrudgingly comes over to take my order. "What can I get you?" she asks in a voice that has lost all the warmth I remember it for. It's hard to believe that she and I traveled to New York together, shared a room together, and watched Eli fight together.

"A few moments of your time," I say, and her face hardens in an instant.

"Your order. What will it be?"

"Please, Nina," I beg. "You've heard Eli's side of the story, please hear mine."

"There is no side," she informs me coldly. "There's the truth, and there's trust, and there's betrayal. You're guilty of the last one. I despise you for what you did to my brother."

She walks away, and my heart drops. This is my chance, and she's not letting me have it. But then she returns with a coffee pot and a cup, and pours me some coffee. "In case my boss sees me doing nothing," she explains.

I relax a little. She's willing to hear me out. "I love your brother," I tell her, because I'm desperate for her to hear me, and because it's the truth, and it's all I have. "I never wanted to hurt him. Gerry did this. Eli said he was jealous, and I see that now."

She's set down the coffee pot, and sits down opposite me. She's listening. This is more than I could hope for. She's giving me her ear.

"It wasn't just that he added things to my article, he also did other things." I lower my voice even though there's no need to because we're the only two in here.

"What other things?" Nina asks, suspiciously.

I don't know how to tell her. It's a delicate matter, but then, my father's seen those pictures. Telling Nina is easier in comparison.

"What other things?" Nina asks, obviously getting riled up.

"Sit down," I plead. "Will you at least sit down so that I can explain?" Her hovering over me like that is making me more nervous than I need to be.

"There were pictures." I lower my head, because I can't look directly at her. "Of me and Eli, in compromising positions."

"What do you mean?"

My jaw tightens and flexes. "Just... a private moment at his place. We were... doing stuff. Normal adult stuff," I tell her, because I can see that she looks visibly worried. "It's normal stuff," I reiterate. "But we were being watched, and someone took pictures."

She puts her hand to her mouth. "You mean for the newspapers?"

I angle my head. "Thankfully, no," I tell her. "That's the strange thing about it. You'd think some twisted guy would want to blackmail Eli, but no... it was to get back at me, I think, because those photos were sent to my boss at work and to my dad."

Nina gasps. It's low, and not a high-drama gasp, but it tells me she feels my pain. "Your dad?"

I nod.

"And your boss?"

"Yes."

"When?"

"Around the time that the article was printed, a day or two after the fight."

She sits backs, obviously more relaxed now, because she puts the pencil on the table as well as her notebook. "What did your boss say?"

"He's not happy with me. He says my article was flawed since it was biased, because of my relationship with Eli. I told him Gerry tampered with the article and that he added things I didn't want in there, but he said that's what good journalism is about, and that maybe I ought to consider a different career. He said a lot of things, but I won't bore you with them."

"Do you know who did it?"

I nod. "I have an idea. I'm pretty sure it was Gerry."

She doesn't sound surprised at this, and simply nods. "I never did like him."

"Neither did Eli."

"Does Eli know?" she asks.

I shake my head.

"You didn't tell him?"

"I haven't had the chance to. I went to see him, a few days after the story broke, after his win, but he didn't want me around. He hates me, and I understand his anger. He told me to get lost. Actually, he told me to fuck off."

I try to read Nina's face to see if I can glean any

information from her, but she gives me nothing. "Athena showed up, and he slammed the door in my face," I tell her. And still she gives me nothing. "I guess they got back together again?"

Because she says nothing, I take her silence for confirmation that they did. I take a sip of my coffee but it tastes really bitter.

"I didn't know you had all this going on."

"There's no reason why you would know."

"It can't be easy, working with that man."

"I'm thinking of leaving. Looking for a job somewhere else. I can't stand him, and we stay out of one another's way, but I feel out of place there. I never felt as if I belonged anyway. It's complicated, but that's the gist of it." No need to tell her that Merv hates me more than ever, and that the rest of my work colleagues, even though they know nothing about the intimate photos, hate that Eli and I were together.

I'm not liked at all.

She stares back at me. It's almost as if she feels sorry for me. "Did your boss punish Gerry?"

"Who, Merv?" I wish. "No. As far as he's concerned, Gerry did the right thing."

"But what about the photos?"

"I'm not sure Merv believes it was Gerry. Or maybe he does and he wants to pretend it wasn't. I don't think Gerry actually took the pictures, I think he got someone to take them for him because he'd have the right contacts to do that kind of dirty work, but what does it matter now? I'm the new girl, and they despise me because my dad pulled some strings and got me the job. There's nothing I can do."

"What about your dad?"

I run my fingers around the rim of the coffee cup, taking some comfort in the warmth. "We haven't spoken since then. I've left him messages, but he's not ready to talk, I guess." I exhale loudly, because this is helping me. I've had nobody to talk to or confide in about any of this. Nina is the first. Saying it out loud gets that stuff off my chest. "I'm going to give him some time."

"Sounds like you've had a rough time of it as well."

I look up and attempt a smile, but it doesn't quite form, because I'm suddenly not feeling so great. "I'm sorry for all the hurt I caused you and Eli. I never meant to hurt you. I never meant to hurt him. I didn't write those things in that article. Gerry did. He put them in behind my back. My mistake was to tell Gerry. I don't even know why I did, but I did and the damage has been done. If I hadn't told Gerry those things, he wouldn't have known to print them."

"Whichever way it happened, you abused Elias's trust, Harper. He's never opened up to anyone like that before."

Every precious moment Eli and I spent together magnifies and comes alive in my head. Everything he told me, every kiss he gave, every touch he excited me with. Everything.

I had hoped time would lessen the impact of having had him in my life, so that it would be easier to forget about him, but it hasn't. And I haven't forgotten anything about him.

Eli captivated me from the first time I set eyes on him, and he continues to do that even now.

"I'm sorry. I can't ever tell you how much I regret doing what I did."

Nina looks around because a couple of new customers have arrived. "Did you want to order something, or do you need more time?"

"I'll just sit here a while, if that's okay with you?"

"It's perfectly fine." She peers at my coffee cup. "A refill? Or something else?"

"I'm fine for now. Thanks."

Maybe I'm desperate for her to forgive me, but her voice seems softer, and she's not as cold as she has been. Hopefully she sees my side of things. "I didn't get a chance to thank you for convincing me to go to the fight, but, thanks. I'm glad I went," she says, getting up from her seat. "I'll never forget that night."

I swallow. I'll never forget that night either. "I knew how much it would mean to Eli to have you there."

"I should be able to pay you back soon."

I shrug. "There's no hurry. You can pay a little at a time, if it makes things easier." The tension in her face eases some more.

"That's really kind of you. Thanks." She turns to walk away, then stops and turns around. "Don't be a stranger."

I nod and wonder what that means. I like Nina. I can see us being friends. I *could* have seen us being friends, but that's as unlikely as me and Gerry ever going out for a drink again.

Work is beyond dismal. Thankfully, Merv hasn't mentioned the photos again, but he barely acknowledges me. He has me researching a local story about a woman who's house is overrun with cats. It's a far cry from what I'd been working on with Eli.

Even though I've told Merv about my suspicions about Gerry and the photos, he's done nothing. I'm not too surprised, but I am disappointed. Merv and Gerry go back a long way. They will stick together no matter what, and it's only Eli and me who got hurt in all this.

The photos are in the past and nobody cares about the consequences. Merv and Gerry won't care that I lost Eli and my father.

I still call and leave messages on my father's phone. I've

told him numerous times that I'm sorry he had to see those photos, and I've told him that I want to meet him and explain, but he never calls back. I'm not sure what I'm going to explain. I was madly in lust with Eli when those photos were taken. I was even falling in love with him, and I would have done anything for him.

I still would.

I have no regrets.

If I met my father, I probably won't mention Eli, unless my father brings the subject up, but it doesn't seem as if I'll get a chance to do that anytime soon. I want to meet with him because, as interfering and as protective as he can be, and as much as his girlfriend irritates me, he's still my father and I still love him.

My mom doesn't know any of this, and I'd rather keep her out of the loop. But my dad is the one I have more regular contact with, and with all my relationships in such a mess, I feel lonely. I have my usual circle of friends, but I've been out of touch with them ever since I started my assignment with Eli. I don't feel up to explaining what's been going on since I last saw them, and so, I've kept a low profile as far as they're concerned.

So here I am. I no longer have my family, work colleagues, friends or lover in my life.

It sucks.

This is what life has been for Eli and Nina, and why they are so close. I can see now how I waded in and messed things up for them.

As I sit here and remember Eli, a knot of guilt sticks in my throat.

I still think of him every single day.

I still miss him.

Most days now it feels as if New York didn't happen.

The fight at The Garden was a dream. He and I being together in his hotel room was something that happened in an alternate universe.

I was at the highest of highs with him that weekend, and I fell to the lowest of lows not long after.

Each day I pick myself up and carry on because there's nothing more I can do. I can't get Eli back, and he now has Athena to keep him company.

I have no hopes about salvaging anything, because I've lost him forever.

ELI

Fame is a bitch. Having had a taste of it, I'd gladly go back to my old life where no one knew me. But it has its advantages, and I'm trying to focus on those. Garrison has a taste for it though, and he's missing it. He wants a rematch.

Lou and Tommy have been tossing around some dates, but my head isn't in that space at the moment.

Things have come out—it doesn't affect anyone else, but it affects me. I start to wake up again at night. Start to remember those days. I'm on edge, and restless, and I don't feel like a champion so much even though I'm in all the papers, and magazines, and on TV.

Tommy talks about crazy sums of money. I have an insane sum of money to my name now. I'm on TV. Lou tells me to take it easy for a few weeks. I've proved myself. We're in no hurry for the rematch. McNeilly's Gym is doing well. Membership is going through the roof. He and Ernesto have had to turn people away. I don't want to train in a gym that's packed full of people.

Santos laughs and says I can afford a kickass house now, with its own gym and pool, and I won't have to come here anymore.

But I want to come here. I want the gym to be like it was before. I don't like the fame. I hate being recognized when I'm at the diner. I hate being mobbed.

I want things to be like they were just before the fight. I had everything then. Hope, and a dream, and the motivation to fight for my dream. It was also a time when Nina didn't know about Swain, and I would give anything to have that be the case again.

I also had Harper in my life, back then when I could trust her.

At least things are returning to some degree of normality again. The welcome home parade the city threw for me was insane.

Athena would like to think she's won her way back to me, but I keep her at bay. It confuses the heck out of her, especially after I let her come with me to all the events, and everyone thinks we're together. I thought the belt would make me feel worthy, and it did, for a couple of days, but I found out that it's all temporary. It doesn't last. That feeling —the glory, the rapture, the adulation—they don't make you happy forever. It's fleeting.

The new publicist Lou hired for me—at Tommy's suggestion—said that the quickest and best way to have people forget the stuff they read about me was to be seen with a girlfriend. I had to show everyone that I was just a regular guy, with a regular girlfriend and happy as anything, and that's why Athena was back in my life.

It sucked that she showed up on my doorstep when

Harper came to see me, because Harper will think we're together. At first, I liked that it hurt her. I could see the anguish on her face when Athena came over with her overnight bag, as if she was going to spend a few days with me. She wasn't. She came over to show me and Nina some of her outfits because she was worried she wouldn't look the part of a heavyweight champion's girlfriend.

The fuck she is my girlfriend. That girl gives herself so many ideas, her head will explode if she's not careful.

It's a charade I'm happy to put on for now. Athena does it because she thinks it's a way back into my life.

It's not.

After Harper's betrayal, I'm not ready to let anyone into my life for a long time.

Nina tells me to listen and do as I'm told. She wants me to ride the success train for as long as I can. I'm getting so many requests for endorsements and deals that the money is just flooding in. Lou's talking about a rematch in the next six to nine months.

I don't know how much longer I can keep the Athena-girlfriend charade up for, but the publicist is adamant that I do, at least until the next rematch. I don't understand why I still need to pretend I have a girlfriend.

"Nobody wants to know you're still carrying that baggage around," Lou tells me. By 'that baggage,' I assume he means all the things that make up my past.

I can't shift them. They'll always be a part of me, but I feel as if a weight has been lifted with it all coming out into the open.

I never expected that to be the case, but the decision was made for me—by Harper and Gerry. I've found though, that not having to hide it has freed me.

The only thing I regret is Nina knowing, because I never wanted her to hurt the way I've been hurting.

I've told her she can give up working at the diner and pursue every single course in the A-Z of night school courses, but she is adamant she doesn't want to change a thing.

Things will change though.

I can afford nice apartments for both of us. I quite like the look of where Harper lives. Maybe something like that. Maybe not near her though. I'm trying to put her behind me, but it hasn't been easy.

I've done my morning run, and I head over to the diner for some breakfast. It's still early enough for it to not to be packed full of people, and I much prefer it like that. I also like that they've taken the lights off. Frankie, the owner, said he wanted to give the place some 'pizzazz', knowing that people would come because they knew my sister works here and that I'm often here.

It has been a crazy month.

I pull the door wide open, and find myself staring directly into Harper's face.

That, right there, is like a defibrillator to my heart.

Shit.

We stare at one another in total shock. Her lips part slightly, and I can't tell if it's because she's surprised, or if it's because she's about to say something.

I don't want to hear it, so I step aside and look away, hoping that she'll get the hint and move on.

She does.

I should feel okay, because, I tell myself, I'm over her. But I don't feel so great. I feel as if I slapped her just now, and I would never, ever do that to a woman. But that's what this feels like.

It's going to take some time, I tell myself as I find a place at my usual booth. Nina's tending to a few customers, so I sit back and try to get over the shock of seeing Harper.

"Good morning," my sister says, coming over with her pot of coffee. She pours me a steaming hot cup. The bitter coffee aroma sails into my nose, zinging my nerves wide awake.

"Hey."

She tilts her head. "Did you... did you see Harper? She just left."

I nod. "The usual, please." I tell her. Scrambled eggs on toast without the yolks.

"You did see her," Nina concludes, given my reply.

"What was she doing here?" I ask, purely out of curiosity, and not because I care. Honestly, she knows I hang out here, and if she understood what I told her, she would stay away. She has stayed away up until now, and we haven't seen each other for a while, so I'm curious to know what the hell she was doing here now. She doesn't even work around here. Ernesto was good to her, so maybe she's still in touch with him, who knows?

"I owe her some money."

I bite my lower lip. "For what?"

"For the ticket to New York. To see you fight."

"You never said you needed money." We've discussed the fight and that weekend numerous times, so why is this the first time Nina's mentioned that she owes Harper money? It never occurred to me to ask Nina if she was okay with money. Things have been nuts for me ever since the win, but I really need to take time out and sort out my finances, and make sure Nina is okay financially, too.

"It was a surprise. Harper insisted I go. She said it

would mean the world to you. I would've told you this, but we've avoided discussing her lately, haven't we?"

She walks over to the serving hatch and passes my order to the kitchen, then comes back.

"You need to buy a place," I tell her. "And I'm going to help you out with money."

"Don't you want to know how she is?" my sister asks, bringing the conversation back to Harper again.

I stare back at her. "No. She's dead to me."

Nina sits down and clasps her hands in front of her. "So you don't want to know about the photos Gerry took?"

I shake my head. But I'm curious. Because I don't put anything past that ginger dude.

We sit in silence for a while. She's testing me, but I can sit through this and say nothing.

"Intimate photos of you and Harper together."

I sit up. "Say what?" Now my brain is rushing into overdrive. We only had a few times like that. And that fucker wasn't at the training camp. "What photos?"

She shrugs. "I don't know. She didn't tell me."

I frown. "Where are they?"

"The photos?"

"Yes, the photos," I reply with irritation.

Infuriatingly, Nina gets up and walks over to the other customers, and pours them some more coffee. Then she stands around doing her waitressing thing—chatting and smiling and being friendly. Meanwhile, I'm sitting here with my anger simmering.

What photos? It was either at the hotel in New York, or at my apartment. But other than the articles Harper wrote about me, there have been no intimate photos printed anywhere. I'm perplexed.

While I'm still trying to figure it out, Nina comes over

with my breakfast, only I've lost my appetite, even though I need to eat. Lou's warned me that Garrison wants revenge. He needs to save face because my win has been a huge upset for him.

My glory was his downfall. People are saying that he's past his prime, that he doesn't have his golden touch, that he's all mouth and no punch.

The Tank is going to come back on me hard, and I intend to do the same. I'm not a one-hit wonder, and I intend to be here for the long-term.

I push my plate away because I can't face food right now. I need to know what goddamn photos Nina's talking about.

"Where are the photos?" I repeat when Nina sits down again.

"You said she's dead to you."

"She is. But if they're intimate photos, I need to know where they were taken and who took them."

"She thinks it was Gerry."

I almost grunt with surprise. "Gerry?"

"Yes. That asshole."

Fuck that. "Gerry?" I shake my head. "How the hell was that dude able to take photos of us?"

"She doesn't think he took them. She thinks he got someone to take them. At your place, apparently."

My neck tenses. And then my face. I close my eyes and picture Gerry, the fucking king of douchebags, watching us. I know exactly what photos now. I warned Harper that he liked her.

I warned her. The guy strikes me as a total pervert though, if he went to those lengths and, for the first time, I allow myself to feel sorry for Harper.

"You know which photos?" My sister asks, reading my expression.

I nod.

"How bad were they?" It's awkward being reminded of that event by my sister, even though she has no idea exactly what happened.

"Bad for others to see." I think of us sometimes. It's impossible to completely shut away those moments in life which make us feel alive. I had those moments with Harper. With her, it wasn't only the way in which she and I connected—sexually and physically—she made me *feel* good. With her, I no longer felt dirty. I've tried to push those times out of my mind, because she lost my trust, but now I'm forced to remember them again.

She made me feel happy, and loved, and wanted. She made me feel the very things I've never felt in my entire life. I trusted her, I loved her, and she stabbed me in the back.

"Eli?" Nina taps my hand. I stare up at her. "You okay?"

"Yeah."

"You can't hate her. She's going through a tough time of her own. I'm not sticking up for her," she says quickly, "but she's a victim too. And she said she didn't write that stuff. Gerry did."

"I know."

"She said she'd told you."

"She did."

"She thinks you and Athena are together."

I grunt.

"I let her think that," my sister says.

Good. But I'm not sure now that I want her to believe the lie. I can't quite erase the look on Harper's face the day she saw Athena outside my place. It was kind of how she looked just now when we saw each other and I ignored her.

Damn it, she's crawling back under my skin, and I swore I wouldn't let her.

The betrayal, I remind myself. I can't forgive her betrayal of my trust.

"She's thinking of leaving her job," Nina says, as the diner starts to get busy. Another waitress appears, and Nina is content to let her run around after the customers.

I raise an eyebrow. "She'll find another job easily. Or her father will get her something. Women like her don't need to work. She'll be fine whatever happens."

"Her dad isn't talking to her. He's annoyed."

I take notice this time.

Nina picks up her notepad and pencil, seeing that people are waiting at the tables. "I forgot to tell you, those photos? They were sent to her boss and to her dad. They're both disgusted with her. She said she hasn't seen or heard from her father since then and he won't return her calls." And with that bombshell, she moves to the table next to me to take their order.

I flex my knuckles and wish I could take a swing at that loser Gerry. He really did have it out for Harper. He fucked us both over.

I still blame Harper, but now I start to feel a little sorry for her. She was silly to trust the ginger dude. I have a gut instinct for people and situations, and I knew from the moment I saw Harper with him that he liked her. She never believed me, and that says a lot about her naiveté.

I have a lot to think about.

CHAPTER FORTY-EIGHT

HARPER

I decided to look for work, and I spent the past week sending out my resume to different places. I won't tell Merv yet, but I made the decision the day I saw Nina at the diner. It was as I left and bumped into Eli; the way he cold-shouldered me cemented my decision.

I decided to look for work out of state. As far from Chicago as I can get it, and I've been looking at jobs in New York or Boston.

A new start will be good for me. There are too many memories of Eli in Chicago and I need to escape them. Eli has gone from being Chicago's New Hope to Chicago's Hero and his face is everywhere.

How can I live in this city with his face plastered everywhere? How can I exist here knowing that he hates me so much?

The following week, Nina calls and tells me that she

has some of the money she owes me. She says I can come in and collect it when I'm next over that way.

I decide to meet Ernesto for lunch there one day so that I can do both things at once.

"Moving so soon?" Ernesto asks, when I tell him about my new plans. "You haven't even been in this new job for a year. What are you running away from?"

"I'm not running away."

He eyes me as if he can see straight through my lies.

"Time for a fresh start." I play around with the salad on my plate.

"A fresh start from who?"

Smart man, that he knows it's a 'who' and not a 'what'.

"I love New York," I answer, not wanting to get into the exact details of why I'm running away.

"You young people all seem to. Can't see the appeal myself, but what do I know? But why the rush? Did you get fired?"

I laugh. "I'm not that bad at my job." He obviously must know about the article that Eli detests, but he's kind enough and wise enough not to bring it up.

"What does your father think of your move?"

I grit my teeth together. Ernesto doesn't know, and I'd rather not talk about the situation with my father right now. Ernesto would understand, but the subject is still so sore that I can't bear to mention it. "He understands."

Ernesto makes a 'Hmmm' sound in his throat, and before I can think of what to say next, Eli appears at our table.

"Chicago's Hero honors us with his presence," says Ernesto with a grin. He's being overly jokey, overly smiley, and the sudden change in his mood tells me he knows exactly why I'm leaving and who I'm running away from.

"Mind if I interrupt?" Eli sounds almost polite. I try not to stare at his face, at the way he looks in his white T-shirt and sweatpants. I try not to think about the sexy tattoos on his body.

"Too late, you already have," says Ernesto and stands up before I can protest.

"You don't have to go," I say. He's finished his lunch, even though mine is mostly uneaten.

"Lou's probably found me something to fix while I've been at lunch," he says, rolling his eyes. "And you need to finish your lunch, young lady. We'll meet again, maybe next week?"

"Next week it is," I tell him.

I suggested we eat here because Nina was giving me the money, and maybe because I like hanging around the diner knowing that Eli could appear at any time, but now that he's actually at our table, I'm suddenly nervous.

He slides into the booth and the shock of him sitting across from me again makes the breath stop in my throat.

"Nina says she owes you some money."

This isn't what I was expecting. And it's definitely not what my heart was expecting.

"She's paid me."

"She's paying you in installments?"

I don't see what this has to do with him, and I can't imagine Nina being too pleased that he's getting involved in her financial matters.

"This is between me and Nina."

He frowns. "I offered to pay up, but she won't have it."

"That sounds about right for your sister."

"Yeah."

I quit playing around with my fork altogether and fold

my arms. I sense that Eli might be trying to make conversation.

I feel hopeful.

"I heard about the photos,"

Ah. So that's what he wants to talk about. "Nina told you."

He nods. "I warned you about Gerry."

"So you did."

"It's not Merv who's the Perv. It's Gerry."

I agree with his statement. "He's weird. Frustrated, I'd say."

"What he did was sick."

"And twisted," I add.

"I hear you're looking to leave the paper."

"I'm looking elsewhere." If I'm being deliberately cagey with my replies, it's because I don't know how I'm supposed to react. As always is the case with Eli, I never seem to know where I stand.

He stares at me and it's a little like how it was before; there is interest and curiosity behind that expression.

"I heard about your dad. I'm sorry."

"I hate to think what went through his mind when he saw the photos. I'm giving him some space."

"I'm sorry the ginger dude did that to you."

"Me, too," I reply. Why are we letting Gerry win? Why are we letting him ruin what we had? I don't say it out loud, but it's there, staring me right in the face. I wonder if Eli sees it, too.

But if I had any hopes that he's going to forgive me, they're soon dashed. "Nina said Swain's dead."

A breath escapes my mouth. "He is," I say slowly. I found out a few things about him during my research into Grampton House.

"She said it was a hit and run."

"Yes, on a quiet street, but also..." I found something out from digging deeper, because it wasn't mentioned in the papers.

"But also what?"

I was going to tell Eli a few weeks after the fight, after the celebrations were over because I didn't want to taint his victory with news of Swain, but we never got to have our 'after'.

"Tell me, Harper."

"His body was mutilated."

Eli blinks and his shoulders sag at my words. "Mutilated?"

"Somebody shoved the broken ends of glass bottles into his face and genitals."

He slumps back in his seat, then closes his eyes. It seems he needs a moment to process this.

I wish I could put my arms around him and help him through this, but I can't. He won't let me even if I tried, so I don't.

"I'm not sad," he says when he opens his eyes. "The fucker deserved it."

I nod.

"Did they ever find out who it was?"

"No."

We sit in silence, and I wait and watch for what Eli will say next. I hadn't foreseen any of this; that I'd be sitting across the table from him today, or that we'd be talking about Swain of all people.

But we're talking, and that counts for something.

"I'm going to miss this place," I say, in an effort to pull him out of whatever dark hole he's slipped into. I don't want him to dwell in memories of the past.

"You can still come to the diner," he says. "I won't bite your head off."

I'm not sure if that's his attempt at humor, and I dare not smile or laugh because I can't gauge what territory we're in; the friend zone or mere acquaintance territory. "Frankie's Kitchen isn't a chain, is it?" I ask.

"You're not staying in Chicago?"

"I'm looking at New York or Boston."

He says nothing, and that fact alone tells me that he doesn't like what I've just said.

ELI

I only meant to let her know that I knew about the photos, and to remind her that I warned her about Gerry. I didn't expect to come away feeling like shit.

Any mention of Swain always makes me feel like shit. It takes me back to when I was a seven-year-old. And no matter how hard I try, I simply can't forget. I'm the heavyweight champion of the world, and still that S-word turns me into a helpless child.

I don't sleep that night. I toss and turn for hours.

Sometime around five in the morning, I consider calling Harper since she's the one who told me the news about him. It's also because I haven't slept as well as I did when she was in my arms.

I manage to resist the urge to call her, and then spend the next few hours thinking about her instead.

I don't like the idea of Harper leaving Chicago. I don't like the idea of Gerry being such a big dick and doing stuff to split us up. I especially don't like that his actions have dumped a whole heap of crap into Harper's life.

She's ended up with nothing. And I've ended up with everything.

This isn't how it's supposed to be.

I don't like injustice, and it seems to me that Harper has been dealt an unfair blow.

I want to believe I can trust her again, and now that enough time has passed, and I've calmed down, I consider the possibility that I might be able to. She's apologized to me, and to Nina, and it really does seem that she's genuinely sorry.

I toss and turn some more.

I go to the gym later than usual, and Lou tells me that I look like shit. "What the hell happened to you?"

"Rough night."

"I don't want to know," Lou says, throwing his hands up in the air.

"Not that kind of night," I reply.

"Go for your run," he tells me. "And do an extra two miles. That'll help you sleep," he chuckles.

I'm back to the same old grind, the same hard workouts at the gym, pushing my body to the limit. Only now there's nothing to look forward to at the end of my day. No Harper. No nice moments. No falling asleep peacefully.

I take a detour on my run and end up at the offices of the paper she works at.

I call her, and I hear the surprise in her voice when she answers. It's magnified when I tell her I'm downstairs, and that I need to talk to her.

She comes outside to meet me moments later.

Damn, if she doesn't look good in her work clothes. A charcoal gray business suit and a white silk shirt.

"What are you doing here?" Her hand goes to her neck again, and she scratches gently.

I want to ask her what she's doing looking so damn good, but I don't. "You hurt me," is what I say.

She looked so perfectly put together just a moment ago, but my words seem to make her crumple. I wipe the sweat from my brow.

"I know, and I feel awful for it, every single day. If there was a way to make you see how bad I feel, I'd show you. If I could turn back time, I would, Eli. I'm sorry."

I nod and put my hand up. I didn't come here to have her apologize to me again. She's already done that many times. I simply haven't chosen to listen.

But I hear her now.

"You hurt me, but you also made me happy." I swallow and try not to look at her, because her eyes turn glassy. She folds her arms and presses her lips together, as if she's trying to hold herself in. "I was happy when I was with you," I tell her.

Her eyes open a little, and then she schools herself not to look so surprised. "I was happy, too," she says a few seconds later.

I stare at her. "I know you made a mistake, and I know Gerry had something to do with this whole mess. I don't see why we should let him win."

She blinks, and then waits. I was hoping I wouldn't have to spell it out to her, especially when I'm not sure what it is exactly that I want to say to her.

I want her back. That's what I want.

I want us to have another chance.

I don't want Gerry to be the cause of all our pain. Hers and mine.

"What are you saying?" she asks me.

I want to tell her that the belts and titles don't make you. They pump you up for a sweet, short moment, but they don't last, and they're not solid. The people in your life are what make you.

Instead I say, "I miss you," because it's that simple. "I want you back in my life. I want to be able to fall asleep and stay asleep."

She opens her mouth, then says nothing at first. "You miss me?"

I tap a finger to my head. "I've been doing a lot of thinking these past few days. I don't want you to leave Chicago because of me."

"Who said I was leaving because of you?"

"Weren't you?"

Her silence tells me all I need to know.

"What about Athena?"

"She was for show," I tell her.

The line in the middle of her brow creases even deeper. She doesn't understand. I will have to spell it out. "I didn't do anything with her."

She tilts her head slightly, as if weighing up my words. She's still unsure what to believe. "I didn't even kiss her," I say.

"But she was always with you."

"The publicist said it would help."

"It gave me sleepless nights," she confesses. That brings a smile to my lips, because it reminds me of the sleepless nights she and I had the last time we were together.

I want another night like that with Harper again. I want more of them, and I know afterwards I'll fall asleep because Harper has that effect on me.

"She was just a decoy?" she asks, and I can tell she's

questioning everything she saw and heard about us being together.

"That's all she was." That's the truth, and I'm willing to wait until she believes it. "Do you want us to try again?" I ask.

"Yes," she answers, nodding her head. "There's nothing I want more."

EPILOGUE
ONE MONTH LATER...

ELI

Our clothes are lying all over the floor. Her floor. Her apartment.

I'm still having my new place refurbished. It's two blocks away from Harper's apartment. I can't see either of us living alone. We'll probably be in each other's places all the time; maybe we'll even end up living together. She's the first woman I've ever thought I could do that with.

Her dad called first thing in the morning. He interrupted us; morning sex is one of the best things about having Harper around.

I could name twenty good things about having her in my life, but morning sex would make it into the top five.

She's taken the phone in the other room, while I catch my breath. I don't plan on getting out of bed until the afternoon.

I lie back, taking a little break, catching a breath while

she's on the phone. A little while later, she comes back, her face glowing, her smile wide.

I prop myself up on my elbows, I'm completely naked, and I make sure there's no comforter covering me so that we can continue from where we left off.

She straddles me.

Looks like we're definitely continuing from where we were. This must be good news, and I'm relieved for her sake.

"What did he say?" I ask. My head rests on the pillow, and I get a great view of her naked body, especially with her sitting the way she does.

"He's invited us to dinner. I said I'd check with you first."

"He's invited me too?" I ask, to clarify. From everything I've heard about the man, I have a gut feeling he's not too keen on me. Or that he wasn't.

Maybe seeing pictures of me and Harper in the papers this morning, at an awards ceremony last night, might have helped him form a better impression of me.

Athena is no longer needed.

Harper is my real girlfriend and ever since we got back together a couple of weeks ago, we've been inseparable.

Lou's given me a few weeks to 'make up for lost time', he says. But I'm back onto a strict training schedule soon enough.

"He's invited both of us," she says, leaning over and planting a kiss on my lips.

Something stirs between my legs. Something big. Any moment now she's going to feel it.

I plant my hands on her buttocks and squeeze.

"Will I need elocution lessons?" I ask.

She frowns at me. "He's not that judgmental."

"Are you sure? Because with the picture you've painted

of him, I don't know." No man, no father is ever going to see his daughter the same way after seeing those pictures. "I think it would be better for the two of you to meet alone first," I suggest.

She moves her face away an inch. "Are you scared of my dad?"

"No." Maybe a little. I want him to like me but that's more for Harper's sake than mine.

"I think it would be better, for this first time, if we both go. That way there won't be any talk about the ..." She clears her throat, "About the *photos*." She whispers the last word.

"Only if you're sure," I reply, giving her a chance to change her mind. This makes me happy that her dad has made a move and called her. The guy behaved like a jerk, if you ask me, ignoring her for as long as he did. It tells me that he's got some issues. Money and status, and all that bullshit.

My gut tells me I wouldn't get an invite to dinner had I not beaten Garrison. I don't care what he thinks of me, in all honesty. I just want him to like me for Harper's sake. She wants him to like me, and I wish the dude would do what makes her happy.

She's happy as far as work is concerned. She got a job working for a tech magazine, and did this without her father pulling any strings. It's something different, she says, but more importantly, it gets her away from Merv and Gerry.

She finishes next week at the paper, and I have a surprise vacation for her. It wasn't four million dollars I made from the fight, but more like eight million. If I win the rematch, we're talking about even crazier numbers—numbers I can't imagine. I can afford to take her away somewhere far, somewhere exotic, and stay in the most expensive places, and eat the most expensive food, except that I'm not that kind of guy, and I don't think Harper would want that either. So, we're spending a week in a log cabin in the Blue Ridge Mountains. There's a hot tub and a sauna, and that's all we need; me and her together for a week uninterrupted.

We have some memories to rekindle.

I used to think boxing was my salvation, and it was, before I met Harper, but now she is. Even though our getting together didn't start from a date, or a movie or a dinner, there is hope for us for a future together. I can already see it in my mind's eye.

You could say we met in the boxing ring. We danced around for more than a few rounds, judging one another, appraising, hating, and fighting. But that's where the analogy ends.

In the end, we succumbed.

I got my title, and she got her story. It may not have turned out exactly as we imagined it, but it gave us each other.

And for that, I have no regrets.

Thank you for reading THE WRATH OF ELI! I hope you enjoyed Eli and Harper's story as much as I loved writing it.

THE PROBLEM WITH LUST is the next book, and this is Max and Trinity's story:

She tries to resist, he tries to hold back...
Sex-Mad Max rushes home for a hookup but an unexpected collision with a schoolteacher ruins his plans.
Trinity Weldon is on her way to the Vet's to pick up her cat before going to her weekly crochet class.
Discover what happens next in this opposites attract virgin-meets-bad-boy romance.

Get THE PROBLEM WITH LUST NOW!

If you want to find out what happens to Nina (Elias's sister), and you want more of Elias and Harper, you might like THE LIES OF PRIDE.

SIGN UP FOR MY NEWSLETTER to find out when new books release!
http://www.lilyzante.com/news

I appreciate your help in spreading the word, including telling a friend, and I would be grateful if you could leave a review on your favorite book site.

An excerpt from THE PROBLEM WITH LUST follows.

Thank you and happy reading!

Lily

EXCERPT: THE PROBLEM WITH LUST

MAX

"Hot Gina's in town?" Al asks. There's a hint of jealousy in his voice.

I wipe the grease off my hands with a cloth and nod, a huge smile spreads across my lips. "She sure is."

"You let me know if she—"

"Yeah, yeah, I know." He wants to hook up with her friend, *any* friend of hers, Al says, but he's joking. He's been with Sammy for years and has eyes for no one but her. Sometimes, like on a Hot Gina weekend, a sliver of excitement passes over his expression, but I know it's only fleeting. He would never risk losing what he has with Sammy to have what I have.

Besides, I don't know about Gina's friends. We don't waste time talking about insignificant stuff. Come to think of it, we don't talk much at all, not immediately when we see one another. Gina is unique. She has the sexual appetite of a man. She's a bona fide nymphomaniac, and I've known a fair share of them to be able to confirm this. She's coming home for the weekend, on leave from the military, and that means forty-eight hours of sex.

She calls, and I answer on the first ring.

"Haven't you left yet?" she cries. I hear the anger in her voice, and it adds to my frustration. I'm already mad at Enzo because a customer walked in at the last minute and needed something looked at and Enzo told me to deal with it.

Forget about going home to freshen up. "I'm coming," I tell her, as I walk over to my locker.

"I should be coming," she grumbles, clearly not amused.

"You will be, over and over again," I promise her as I pull out a clean shirt. Absence makes the heart grow fonder, some people say, but I can tell you that absence makes the dick grow harder.

"How long are you going to be?" she asks. "I have pizza slices all over me."

"All over you?"

"On me, like I'm a plate. I'm not wearing anything either."

I hiss out a breath, and in the same instant my cock hardens.

"Gimme ten minutes," I tell her, as I unbutton my shirt and quickly take it off.

"Hurry up! I feel like an idiot lying here like this."

I can see I'm going to have to make it up to her big time when I get there. I quickly whip out a clean T-shirt from my locker. "I'm going to have to take a shower at your place—"

"I have to wait for you to take a shower too?"

"No, no. Just lie back and spread your legs. I'll take good care of you first, and that's a promise."

"That's more like it." I can imagine the huge grin on her face as she says this.

"Don't move a muscle," I order. "See you on Monday," I say to Al.

"Come over to Waquito's. Rumors are Cardoza's going to be there."

I scowl at him.

"The boxer. The heavyweight champion of the world. Chicago's New Ho—"

I raise my arm in a dismissive gesture. Al is a huge fan of Elias Cardoza—the local underdog who surprised many by winning the belt. "Gonna be busy, dude. Probably not going to get out of bed."

"Goddamn lucky son of a bitch," he mutters good-naturedly and loud enough for me to hear.

I rush out of the door and over to my bike.

Weekends like this are few and far between. With my regular friends-with-benefits setups—and I have one or two lucky women here in Chicago—it's just an instant gratification, before I return to my place after. Or she leaves to go to hers. We never spend the night together. It's an unspoken rule.

With Gina it's different, because she only gets leave once in a while and it's usually only for the weekend. With her, we spend the whole weekend together.

We fuck like rabbits.

It's beautiful.

TRINITY

"You're doing amazing, Dylan. Absolutely amazing. I love this drawing." School only started a few weeks ago, and this scrawny, skinny little boy has already stolen my heart.

Each morning he comes to my classroom looking a little rougher, dirtier, hungrier, and sad, but by the end of the school day, his eyes are all lit up, and there's a smile on his face. But also, by the end of the day, he's in no hurry to go home, unlike most of the others. He drags his feet as if he doesn't want to leave.

I shouldn't have favorites, and I try not to, but as I'm slowly getting to know my new class of seven-year-olds, something about this child makes it impossible for me not to reach out. This isn't about having a favorite, it's about me adding something to this kid's life to make him smile.

"Oh, look," I say, pulling a banana out of my bag. "I forgot to eat this at lunchtime. I'd hate to waste it. Would you like it?"

He eyes the banana without blinking "You could have it tomorrow, miss."

Smart kid. "I could, but I'm worried I might squash it by the time I get home." I hold it out to him. "It would be a shame to let it go to waste." This is the third time I've done this in the past few weeks, and it's getting to a point now where I deliberately don't eat my fruit and save it for him.

"Can I eat it here?"

It's the first time he's asked this. I don't want him to stay too late because I know his mother will be waiting for him. "Here? Won't your mom be waiting for you?"

He shrugs, and seems reluctant to take it. "Well, sure, you can eat it here," I say.

No sooner has he peeled the banana than he wolfs it down greedily. It disappears in about three seconds. I hold my hand out for the banana skin.

His mouth is still full, but he nods, a sort of 'thank you.'

"Off you go, and don't forget your reading."

He rushes off, and I stare after him long after he's

disappeared from sight. I worry about him, but I'm also not sure if I'm reading too much into things.

"Are you still here?" Ed, my colleague from the classroom next to mine, walks in.

"I'm killing time before I pick Benji up from the vet. What's your excuse?"

"Prepping my lessons for next week." He walks up to my desk with a smug smile, obviously pleased at himself. "How is your soulmate?"

I grin at the term of endearment he uses for my cat. Though, he's not far wrong. My furry friend and I have shared many a cozy night in front of the TV. "Benji is well, but he doesn't like going to the vet."

"Is he ill?"

"No. He's getting up there, though, and it's his usual yearly check-up, all the blood work, etcetera. He's going to be in a stinker of a mood when he comes home," I state, and am glad that I have my crochet class later to escape to.

"You give that cat too much importance."

"He rules the roost. What can I do? He's the best company."

I'm no better when it comes to leading an exciting life. Ed is staying behind on Friday to prepare next week's lessons, and I have a crochet class.

Sex, drugs, and rock 'n' roll is an alien concept for both of us. We're both similar in some respects. It's probably why we get along so well, aside from the fact that he usually passes by my classroom for a quick chat on most days.

"Any plans for the weekend?" he asks, straightening his tie.

"We have a trip to the Nature Sanctuary over by North Pond."

"We?" There's a spark of uneasiness in his tone.

I relax and sit back, trying hard not to smile. "My adult art class."

His expression smooths to a smile. "I can't believe how you give up your weekends for these things, Trinity. Your life is already hectic enough."

"Best way to be." I volunteer on Monday evenings to teach art to adults with minor learning difficulties. This weekend the other teacher and I have organized a picnic at a local nature reserve. We never work weekends, but this has become a yearly thing. I don't mind giving up most of my Saturday for this. It's something different for the students and they're all excited about it.

Ed looks at me the way he usually looks at me, with curiosity, as if he can't quite figure me out. But there's something else behind those irises today. He looks especially nice this evening in a dark shirt. He's almost always in a white shirt and the contrast of him in something dark makes him look slightly sexy, at least, to my eyes.

He and I are on the same page. He's not overly pushy, and I'm not overly flirty. In fact, I'm *never* flirty, though I do take a few seconds longer to gaze at him today.

"Isn't teaching seven-year-olds enough?"

"I love my job, but you know me, Ed—"

"Do I?" he asks. His comment stops me momentarily, and suddenly I'm not so sure what he means.

"What do you mean?"

"Do I know you, Trinity? I don't think I do. We've been friends for what, two years now? And I still don't think I know you that well."

This naturally begs the question of how well does he need to know me?

"Maybe..." He clears his throat and then seems to hesitate.

"Maybe what?" I ask. Does he have a point to make, or is he still making small talk?

"Maybe you're just too nice for your own good."

"Meaning what exactly, Ed?"

"Spending a weekend going on a picnic with your art class?"

"It's only for a few hours and on one day, not the entire weekend," I correct him. "You teach Sunday school and you do that every weekend. I only teach art classes on a Monday night. I'm not as selfless as you, when it comes to these things."

"It's just a few hours on a Sunday," he clarifies.

I'm still not sure where he's going with this, but Ed has a way of going around and around in circles and can take forever to get to the point. But I'm used to it now.

"How about you? What are your plans?" I ask him.

"I'm looking for a new bed."

I widen my eyes a little to show interest. "A new bed?"

He nods. "I'm not sleeping well and my back's starting to hurt. The foam in the mattress is worn out and I can feel the springs more."

"I highly recommend a memory foam mattress."

"A memory foam mattress?" he asks, with interest. "Is that what you sleep on?"

I nod vigorously. "I swear by it."

"I'll take your advice."

We fall silent. Us both talking about a bed is, and isn't, weird. A bed is an intimate part of the household furniture, or it's a place to sleep. Nobody has ever shared my bed, and I know, through our conversations, that Ed is like me, saving himself for marriage. One life partner forever.

Our gazes lock for a moment so fleeting that I'm not

sure if I imagined it. Even though all we've ever done is talk, I sense that Ed likes me.

I like him, too.

He's sweet.

This is nice enough, and pleasant enough, and it is *enough*; talking, and getting to know one another. He makes me smile whenever he walks into my classroom for an end-of-day chat.

Maybe we'll talk for another year or two before he makes a move. That suits me just fine. He's good-looking, well, *pleasant* looking, I'd say. He's no Chris Hemsworth. He's skinny and angular, with thinning hair, but more importantly, his eyes don't drop to my chest during our conversations. I am aware that most men can't shift their eyes away from my ample bosom, because I see this with the dads at parents evening.

Ed is nothing like that.

He's the type of man I can see myself with. The type of man I am saving myself for. He plays it safe, as do I. Life isn't exactly riveting, but it is smooth sailing which is fine by me.

I hear some of the sob stories from a few of my teacher friends—broken hearts, a trail of cheating boyfriends, jealousy and heartbreak. If that's what love is all about, I don't want it. I don't want to risk wading through a load of boyfriends before I find 'the one'.

No, thank you.

I'm saving myself.

"Well, if you ever have a weekend free, maybe...maybe we could ...uh...go for a pizza or something," he offers, looking at the floor as he shuffles from one foot to the other.

"A pizza?"

"Or something. Just you and me."

"Oh." My heart sinks a little, and I'm not sure why. It's definitely not a heartbeat skip, more like a feeling of it sinking slowly to the pit of my stomach.

"Like, maybe next weekend or the weekend after that," Ed continues, his face looking slightly shinier now.

"Sure." I say, feeling confused as to what he's asking.

"Have a good time at the picnic," he says quickly, then leaves.

"Enjoy your mattress hunting."

So, that was it. That was the thing he'd been wanting to say all along; it just took him longer to say it.

I'm still not sure if that was a date, or a maybe-date, or pizza with friends. He and I don't really get together outside of work, though he did come to the Christmas get-together with the crochet class last year, and he met Christina, my best friend. It turned out to be a good night now that I remember it.

Ed surprised me, and it reminds me that he can be good fun socially.

One day, who knows? Maybe Ed and I will end up sharing a memory foam mattress together.

The Problem with Lust is now available in paperback

BOOKLIST

Honeymoon Series: Take a roller-coaster journey of emotional highs and lows in this story of love and loss, family and relationships. When Ava is dumped six weeks before her Valentine's Day wedding, she has no idea of the life that awaits her in Italy.

Honeymoon for One
Honeymoon for Three
Honeymoon Blues
Honeymoon Bliss
Baby Steps
Honeymoon Series (Books 1-3)

Italian Summer Series: This is a spin-off from the Honeymoon Series. These books tell the stories of the secondary characters who first appeared in the Honeymoon Series. Nico and Ava also appear in these books.

It Takes Two
All That Glitters

Fool's Gold
Roman Encounter
November Sun
New Beginnings
Italian Summer Series (Books 1-3)

The Billionaire's Love Story: This is a Cinderella story with a touch of Jerry Maguire. What happens when the billionaire with too much money meets the single mom with too much heart?

The Promise
The Gift, Book 1
The Gift, Book 2
The Gift, Book 3
The Gift, Boxed Set (Books 1, 2 & 3)
The Offer, Book 1
The Offer, Book 2
The Offer, Book 3
The Offer, Boxed Set (Books 1, 2 & 3)
The Vow, Book 1
The Vow, Book 2
The Vow, Book 3
The Vow, Boxed Set (Books 1, 2 & 3)

Indecent Intentions: This is a spin-off from The Billionaire's Love story. This 2-book set consists of 2 standalone stories about the billionaire's playboy brother. The 2nd story is about a wealthy nightclub owner who shuns relationships.

The Bet
The Hookup

Indecent Intentions 2-Book Set

The Seven Sins: A series of seven standalone romances based on the seven sins. Emotional, and angsty romances which are loosely connected.

Underdog (prequel)
The Wrath of Eli
The Problem with Lust
The Lies of Pride
The Price of Inertia
The Other Side of Greed
The Seven Sins Books 1-3

A Perfect Match Series: This is a seven book series in which the first four books feature the same couple. High-flying corporate executive Nadine has no time for romance but her life takes a turn for the better when she meets Ethan, a sexy and struggling metal sculptor five years younger. He works as an escort in order to make the rent. Books 4-6 are standalone romances based on characters from the earlier books. The main couple, Ethan and Nadine, appear in all books:

Lost in Solo (prequel)
The Proposal
Heart Sync
A Leap of Faith
A Perfect Match Series Books 1-3
Misplaced Love
Reclaiming Love
Embracing Love
A Perfect Match Series (Books 4-6)

Standalone Books:

Tomorrow Belongs to Us
Love Among the Ruins
Love Inc
An Unexpected Gift

ACKNOWLEDGMENTS

I would like to thank my wonderful group of proofreaders who check my manuscript for the errors, typos and weird words and phrases which sometimes find their way into my story. These ladies give me the confidence to release each book and I am eternally grateful for their help and support:

Sherrie Brown
Marcia Chamberlain
Nancy Dormanski
April Lowe
Dena Pugh
Charlotte Rebelein
Carole Tunstall

I would also like to thank Tatiana Vila for creating my awesome covers:
www.viladesign.net

ABOUT THE AUTHOR

Lily Zante lives with her husband and three children somewhere near London, UK.

Connect with Me

I love hearing from you – so please don't be shy! Email me, message me on Facebook or connect with me on Instagram or TikTok

Shop | TikTok |Instagram | Website | Facebook | Email

Newsletter sign-up
Follow me on Bookbub
Follow me on Goodreads

www.ingramcontent.com/pod-product-compliance
Lightning Source LLC
Chambersburg PA
CBHW061620210726
48287CB00001B/221